George Melville Baker

The Mimic Stage

A Series of Dramas, Comedies, Burlesques, and Farces...

George Melville Baker

The Mimic Stage
A Series of Dramas, Comedies, Burlesques, and Farces...

ISBN/EAN: 9783744771405

Printed in Europe, USA, Canada, Australia, Japan

Cover: Foto ©Andreas Hilbeck / pixelio.de

More available books at **www.hansebooks.com**

THE

MIMIC STAGE.

A SERIES OF

DRAMAS, COMEDIES, BURLESQUES, AND FARCES,

FOR

PUBLIC EXHIBITIONS AND PRIVATE THEATRICALS.

BY

GEORGE M. BAKER,

Author of "Amateur Dramas," "An Old Man's Prayer," &c.

BOSTON:

LEE AND SHEPARD.

1869.

Geo. C. Rand & Avery,
Stereotypers and Printers,
3 Cornhill, Boston.

To

MATT. A. MAYHEW, ESQ.,

PROPRIETOR OF

THE "HANDS" AND "LAUGH"

WHICH HAVE SO OFTEN

GIVEN ASSURANCE OF SUCCESS.

PREFACE.

THE gratifying success of a previous volume of "AMATEUR DRAMAS," and the increasing demand for pieces of a light character suitable for representation without the usual costly theatrical accessories, has induced the writer to prepare a second volume for publication. Like the first, it contains pieces which have been specially prepared for occasional exhibitions, society benefits, and parlor theatricals, and which have only been admitted to "the mimic stage" after having stood the test of public approval. For their production, no scenery is required. A moderate-sized room, having folding-doors or hanging curtains to separate the audience from the actors; costumes such as the modern wardrobe will easily supply, with now and then a foray on some good old grandmother's trunks; a wig or two; a few pieces of chalk; red paint; and India-ink, — is all the "extraordinary preparations" and "great expense" necessary. For benefits, fairs, and temperance gatherings, many of the pieces will be found particularly appropriate. To give variety, three dialogues, originally published in "Oliver Optic's Magazine," have, by the kind permission of its popular editor, been added to the collection. Amateur theatricals have now become a part of the regular winter-evening amusements of young and old; and, with proper management, no more rational, pleasant, and innocent diversion can be devised. Endeavoring to avoid bluster and rant, relying more on touches of nature, hits at follies and absurdities, for success, the writer trusts his little book may contain nothing which can detract from the good name those amusements now enjoy.

STAGE-DIRECTIONS.

R means Right; L, Left; C, Centre.
The performer is supposed to be upon the stage, facing the audience.

All the pieces in this book have been published separately, and can be obtained by addressing the publishers.

CONTENTS.

DOWN BY THE SEA.

A DRAMA, IN TWO ACTS.

CHARACTERS.

ABNER RAYMOND, (a city merchant.)
CAPT. DANDELION, (a city flower.)
JOHN GALE, (a fisherman.)
SEPTEMBER GALE, } (Protégés of John Gale.)
MARCH GALE,
JEAN GRAPEAU, (an old French peddler.)
KATE RAYMOND, (a city belle.)
MRS. GALE, (John Gale's wife.)
KITTY GALE, (John Gale's daughter.)

ACT 1.—JOHN GALE'S *house down by the sea. Fire-place,* R. *Doors,* R., L., *and* C. *Table right of* C., *at which* MRS. GALE *is ironing.* MARCH *seated on a stool,* L., *arranging fishing-lines.*

March, (sings.)

" Oh, my name was Captain Kyd
As I sailed, as I sailed.
Oh, my name was Captain Kyd
As I sailed ! "

Mrs. G. Do, March, stop that confounded racket !
March. Racket ! well that's a good one. Mother Gale, you've got no ear for music.

7

Mrs. G. More ear than you have voice. Do you call that singing?

March. To be sure I do. (*Sings.*)

"Oh, my name was Captain —"

Mrs. G. March Gale, if you don't stop that catawauling, I'll fling this flat-iron right straight at your head.

March. Now, don't, Mother Gale. Don't you do it. The iron would enter my soul. (*Sings.*)

"As I sailed, as I sailed."

Mrs. G. Dear, dear! what does ail that boy? March Gale, you'll distract our fine city boarders.

March. Not a bit of it. Don't they come from the great city where there's lots of grand uproars, organ-grinders, and fiddlers. I tell you, Mother Gale, they are pining for the delights of the city; and I'm a public benefactor, when, by the sound of my musical voice, I wake in their hearts tender recollections of "Home, sweet Home." (*Sings.*)

"As I sailed, as I sailed."

Mrs. G. I do wish you were sailing. Now, do stop, that's a good boy. You make my head ache awfully.

March. Do I? why didn't you say that before: I'm done. But, Mother Gale, what do you suppose sent these rich people to this desolate spot?

Mrs. G. It's their whims, I s'pose: rich people are terrible whimsical. Mr. Raymond told your father he wanted a quiet place down by the sea.

March. Blest if he hasn't got it! It's almost as desolate here as poor old Robinson Crusoe's Island.

Mrs. G. Well, well! p'raps he had a hankering for

this spot, for he was born down here. Ah, me! how times do change. I remember the time when Abner Raymond was a poor fisherman's boy. Law sakes, boy, when I was a gal, he used to come sparking me; and he and John Gale have had many a fight, all along of me. Well, he went off to the city, got edicated, and finally turned out a rich man.

March. You don't say so. Why, Mother Gale, you might have been a rich lady.

Mrs. G. P'raps I might, March; p'raps I might: but I chose John Gale; and I never regretted it, never.

March. Bully for you, Mother Gale, and bully for Daddy Gale, too. He's a trump. But I say, Mother Gale, isn't Miss Kate a beauty? My eyes! Keep a sharp lookout, Mother Gale, a sharp eye on our Sept.; for, if I'm not much mistaken, he's over head and ears in love with her.

Mrs. G. Goodness, gracious! what an awful idea!

March. Awful! perhaps it is; but she likes it. I've seen them on the rocks as chipper as a pair of black-birds; her eyes glistening and her cheeks rosy, while Sept. was pouring all sorts of soft speeches into her ears.

Mrs. G. Heavens and airth! this won't do! I'll tell your father of this the minit he comes home.

March. No you won't, Mother Gale. Hush, here's the young lady now.

Enter KATE, R.

Kate. May I come in?

Mrs. G. To be sure you may, and welcome (*places a chair,* R., *and dusts it with her apron*). It's awful dirty here.

Kate (sits). Dirt? I have not yet been able to discover a particle in the house. It's a miracle of cleanu-
liness. Well, March, what are you doing?

March. Oh! fixin' up the lines a little.

Kate. Who was singing? While I was sewing I'm
sure I heard a musical voice.

March. No: did you though? Do you hear that,
Mother Gale. Miss Kate heard a musical voice. I am
the owner of that voice, and I'm mighty proud of it;
for there's precious little I do own in this world.

Kate. You should cultivate it.

Mrs. G. Fiddlesticks! there's no more music in that
boy than there is in a nor'easter.

March. Now, Mother Gale, don't show your ignorance of music. Yes, Miss Kate, I should cultivate it;
but then, you see, I'm an orphan.

Kate. An orphan?

March. Yes, an orphan, — a poor, miserable, red-
headed orphan. The only nurse I ever had was the sea,
and a precious wet one she was.

Kate. Do you mean to say you are not the son of
John Gale?

March. That's the melancholy fact: I'm nobody's
son. I was found upon the sands, after a fearful storm
and a shipwreck, very wet and very hungry, by Daddy
Gale. This little occurrence was in the month of
March. Fearing, from my youth and inexperience, I
should be likely to forget the circumstances of my birth,
Daddy Gale christened me March, and it's been march
ever since. You march here, and you march there.

Kate. And September?

March. Oh! Sept. came in the same way, by water, a little sooner, the September before. Daddy Gale evidently expected to complete the calendar, and have a whole almanac of shipwrecked babbies.

Kate. He is not Mr. Gale's son?

March. No, he's a nobody, too: we're a pair of innocent but unfortunate babbies.

Kate. Strange I have not heard this before. I have been here nearly a month.

Mrs. G. Bless your dear soul, John Gale doesn't like to talk about it. He's precious fond of these boys; and I tell him he's afeard somebody will come and claim 'um. But he's done his duty by them. No matter how poor the haul, how bad the luck, he always manages to lay by something for their winter's schooling; and, if ever anybody should claim them, they can't complain that they have'nt had an edication.

March. That's so, Mother Gale, all but my singing; but I have strong hopes of somebody coming to claim me. I feel I was born to be something great, — a great singer, or something else.

Mrs. G. Something else, most likely.

March. Yes. I expect to see my rightful owner appearing in a coach and four to bear me to his ancestrial castle.

Mrs. G. Fiddlesticks!

March. Mother Gale, your ejaculations are perfectly distressing. I don't open my mouth to indulge in a few fond hopes, but you ram your everlasting " fiddlesticks " down my throat to choke all my soaring fancies.

Mrs. G. Well, I should think your throat *would* be sore, with all those big words.

March. Yes, Miss Kate: I have strong hopes of being rewarded for my blighted youth with one or more parents of some standing in the world.

Kate. I trust your hopes will be realized. This is a strange story, and will interest my father, startle him; for years ago he lost a child by shipwreck.

March. A child, — a boy?

Kate. Yes, a boy, the child of his first wife, who left France with her infant in a ship that never reached her port.

March. Good gracious! when was this?

Kate. Oh! a long, long time ago, before I was born, for I am the daughter of his second wife: it must have been twenty, — yes, more than twenty years ago.

March. A boy, shipwrecked twenty years ago. Good gracious, it almost takes away my breath.

Kitty (*outside*, c.). Much obliged, I'm sure. You'd better come in.

March. Hallo! there's Kitty. (*Enter* KITTY, c.) Hallo, Kitty! who's that you are talking to?

Kitty (*tossing her head*). Wouldn't you like to know, Mister Gale?

March. To be sure I should.

Kitty. Well, you can't: a pretty idea, that I can't have a beau without being obliged to tell you who it is!

March. A beau! It's that Bige Parker: I know it is.

Kitty. Well, suppose it is, Mr. March Gale.

March. I'll just give him the biggest licking ever he had: you see if I don't.

Kitty. What for, pray?

March. What right has he to be tagging after you, I'd like to know?

Kitty. Suppose I choose to let him, Mr. Gale; and suppose I like to have him, Mr. Gale. What do you say to that?

March. That I'll punch him all the harder when I get at him.

Kitty. Will you? You're a pretty brother, ain't you? Won't let your sister have a beau without making a fuss!

March. I ain't your brother: you know I ain't. I'm a shipwrecked innocent.

Kitty (*laughing*). Oh, ho, ho! you're a pretty innocent, you are!

Mrs. Gale. Kitty Gale, stop your laughing and behave yourself. Don't you see Miss Kate? Where have you been?

Kitty. Oh! I've been over to Mrs. Parker's.

March. Bige Parker's. Darn him.

Kitty. Mrs. Parker was not at home (*looking slyly at March*): nobody but Bige.

March. I'd like to get hold of him: I'd send him *home*, and keep him there.

Kitty. Oh, dear! I am so hungry!

March. I am glad of it.

Kitty. Bige Parker wanted to give me a great thick slice of bread and butter; but I knew there was somebody at home (*looking at March*) who could spread bread and butter better than he.

March. No: did you, Kitty? you just keep still, and I'll bring you a slice. (*Exit,* L.)

Kate. O Kitty, Kitty! I suspect you are a little coquette.

Kitty. Me! why I never thought of such a thing.

Mrs. Gale (going to door, C.). It's about time for John to be back. (*Enter MARCH, L., with slice of bread and butter.*)

March. There, Kitty, there you are!

Kitty. Oh! ain't that nice, now if I only had a seat.

March. Here's one: here's a high old seat (*attempts to lift her upon the table, burns his hand with the flat-iron, yells, drops Kitty, and runs, L.*).

Mrs. Gale. I told you you'd catch it (*takes iron from table, and places it in the fire-place*).

March. You didn't tell me any such thing: I found it out myself. Look at that (*shows his hand*). There's a blister.

Kate. Dear me! I forgot I had a message to deliver. Father would like to see you in his room a moment.

Mrs. Gale. I'll go right up.

Kate. Where's Sept., March: I haven't seen him this morning?

March. I saw him off the point about an hour ago: it's about time he was in.

Kate. Come up to my room when you have finished your luncheon. I've something to show you. (*Exit, R.*)

Kitty. Yes, I'll come right up.

Mrs. Gale. Now, March, be careful of that musical voice of yours while I'm gone: don't strain it. (*Exit, R.*)

Kitty. March Gale! you ain't a bit perlite: why don't you give me a seat?

March. Well, I'll give you a seat, now the flat-iron's out of the way (*lifts her to table, where she sits swinging her feet and eating bread and butter*).

Kitty. Isn't she pretty ?

March. Mother Gale?

Kitty. Mother Gale ! No : Miss Kate.

March. Yes, indeed.

Kitty. And she's so rich, and dresses so fine. I suppose she lives in a big house with a buffalo on top, and a pizzaro, and a miranda, and all that.

March. Yes, indeed, she's very rich; but then you just wait till my mysterious parent turns up. I know he's a rich man : you never heard of a shipwrecked baby but what had a rich father, — never. Sometimes I think he's a rich English lord, or a French marquis, or a Turkish bashaw. I do hope he's a Turk : I am very fond of Turkey.

Kitty. So am I, with cranberry sauce.

March. Oh, pshaw ! what's the use poking fun !

Kitty. Do you know what I would do if I was rich?

March. No : what is it?

Kitty. I'd have some molasses on my bread.

March. You won't have to wait for that (*runs off, L.*).

Kitty. Now, ain't he obliging. I do like to be waited upon : and there's plenty to wait upon me ; for, between March and Bige Parker, I'm very comfortably settled. (*March runs in, L.*)

March. Here you are Kitty (*pours molasses on her bread*).

Kitty. Oh, ain't that sweet !

March. Yes, Kitty, I've been thinking that it's about time I should make an effort to find my father.

Kitty. But what can you do? there is nothing by which you can be identified.

March. No, but instinct will guide me. I know, if I once set eyes on the man who is truly my father, there will be a come-all-overishness that will cause me to rush into his arms, crying, " Father, behold your son!" In the mean time I must wait.

Kitty. While you are waiting, suppose you take me down from this table.

March. All right (*lifts her from table*), down you come. I say, Kitty, what did Bige Parker say to you?

Kitty. Oh! lots of sweet things.

March. Darn him!

Kitty. Let me see, — what did he say? He said that the sand seemed like shining gold when I walked upon it.

March. I'd like to stuff his throat with it: perhaps it would change the color.

Kitty. He said the sky seemed filled with beautiful rainbows.

March. I'd like to paint a rainbow round his eyes. He might see stars too.

Kitty. And the water —

March. Oh, confound the water! you set me on fire. I'll punch that Bige Parker, you see if I don't.

Kitty. Why, March, you're jealous.

March. Jealous! well, perhaps I am. But I won't have that Bige Parker sneaking after you: mind that, now. And the next time I see him grinning at you, he'll catch it: mind that, too. He's a confounded sneak, darn him. (*Exit*, c.)

Kitty. Well, I declare, March is really jealous. Now, that's too bad. (*Enter* JOHN GALE, L.)

John. What's too bad, Kitty? Where's all the folks? where's your marm? where's Sept.? Where's anybody?

Kitty. Where's anybody? why, don't you see me?

John. Yes, I see you, you chatterbox. Where's your mother?

Kitty. Up-stairs.

John. Up-stairs: now, *what* is she doing up-stairs?

Kitty. I'm sure I don't know.

John. Then run and find out.

Kitty. Well, I suppose —

John. You suppose! Now, *what* right have you to suppose? Run and find out, quick!

Kitty. Gracious, the fish don't bite. (*Exit*, R.)

John. Pretty time of day, this is. Cold, wet, and hungry; and nobody at home. Wonder where my rich boarder is? Having what he calls a *siesta*, I s'pose. Well, every one to his taste; but the idea of a live man snoozing in the house when there's salt water, a bright sun, and a roaring breeze outside. Bah! (*Enter* MRS. GALE, R.)

Mrs. Gale. Well, John, back again?

John. Back, of course I'm back. You don't s'pose I'd stay out after four hours' fishing, without a bite, do you? Hey!

Mrs. Gale. Well, you needn't bite me. You've had bad luck.

John. Now, what's the use of telling me that? Don't

2

I know it?   I tell you what, old lady, if we ain't mighty careful, we shall have nothing to eat one of these days.

Mrs. Gale. When that time comes, we'll begin to complain. But with two sich boys as our Sept. and our March —

John. Now, what's the use of talking about them boys? What are they good for? Where's Sept.?

Mrs. Gale. Off in his boat, I s'pose.

John. His boat! a pretty boat he's got. If he's not kerful, he'll see the bottom afore he knows it.

Mrs. Gale. Our Sept.! Why, he's the best boatman along shore. You needn't be scared about him.

John. Not when he's a stout plank under him. But that skiff of his is as frail as a shingle. Where's March?

Mrs. Gale. I left him here a minnit ago.

John. There's another beauty. I tell you what, Mother Gale, I'm going to turn over a new leaf with these boys. I won't have so much of this shirking work. Sept. shall sell that boat; and March —

Mrs. Gale. Why, you ugly old bear! what's the matter with you? Turn over a new leaf indeed! Well, that's a good one. Only this morning you were blessing your stars you had two such boys, — the best and smartest —

John. Humbug! you don't know what you are talking about. I tell you they're a good-for-nothing, lazy pair of — Hallo! here's Raymond. (*Enter* Mr. R., R.)

Ray. Halloo, Gale! back already? what luck?

John. Hem! hmk. Precious poor.

Raymond. I'm sorry for that. But, Gale, my

daughter has been telling me a strange story about these boys. They're not yours.

John. Who says they ain't? I'd like to know who's a better right to 'em.

Ray. Well, well, I'm not going to dispute it. But I *would* like to hear the story from your lips.

John. It'll be a precious short one, I can tell you. Well, they *ain't* my boys. They were shipwrecked on the coast twenty-three years ago.

Ray. Twenty-three years ago?

John. Yes, exactly twenty-three years ago, in the month of September, we were awakened one night by the booming of guns off shore. 'Twas a black night, I tell you, — a roaring gale, the sea dashed over the rocks almost to our door, and the rain poured in torrents. We hastened to the beach. Half a mile off, stuck fast in the sands, was a ship, blue-lights burning and cannons firing. It was no use: mortal man could not reach her in such a sea. In the morning, scattered pieces of the wreck, a few dead bodies, and a live baby, was all there was left of her.

Ray. A living child?

John. Yes, our Sept. A precious tough time he had of it, I can tell you: we thought he'd die; but mother's care and a healthy constitution brought him through, and there is not a smarter boatmen or a better lad on all the coast than our Sept., if I do say it.

Mrs. Gale. Why, John, you said just now —

John. What's the use of talking about what I said just now? You never did take kindly to him; but I say he's the best lad —

Mrs. Gale. John Gale, you're stark, staring mad! Don't I idolize 'em both?

Ray. But the other, Gale?

John. Well, he came in the same way. 'Twas very queer; but the very next March, in a blinding storm, we were again turned out at night by the booming of guns. Another ship in the sands: more blue lights; in the morning, more wreck, more dead bodies, and another live baby.

Ray. March? (*Enter,* MARCH, C.)

John. Yes, March; and he was a roarer, I tell you. We haven't had a shipwreck since: the squalls of that brat, night after night, was enough to scare off all the ships in creation. He weathered it; and though I do say he's a smart clever — (*sees March,* L.) You confounded scoundrel! where have you been?

March (*Aside*). My! touching biography. (*Aloud.*) Where have I been? been looking for you.

Ray. But, Gale, was no inquiries ever made for these lads?

John. No; and I didn't take particular care to hunt up their owners. If they don't care enough for 'em to hunt 'em up, I'm content. They've been well brought up: they're a credit to anybody. There's a good home for 'em here; there's the broad ocean for their labor; and there are honest hearts here that love 'em as their own; and, if they're not content, 'twill not be the fault of John Gale.

March. Hurrah for John Gale!

John. Now, what do you mean by yelling in that way, you good-for-nothing —

Mrs. Gale. Smart, clever, — Hey, John?

John. Now what's the use of talking —

Ray. But these lads, Gale : was nothing found about them by which they could be identified?

John. No ; Sept. was well bundled up in nice soft flannels, while March was tied up in an old pea-jacket : but no name or marks about them.

Ray. This is very strange — very strange. (*Enter* KITTY, R. *hurriedly.*)

Kitty. Oh, dear ! — run, quick ! — run, quick !

March. Run quick ! where, what's the matter?

Kitty. Oh, dear ! I'm so frightened !

John. What is it?

All. Speak, speak !

Kitty. Oh ! do wait till I get my breath ! No, no ! run quick !

Mrs. Gale. Lord sakes, Kitty ! what is the matter?

Kitty. I was up in Miss Raymond's room, looking out of the window —

All. Well, well !   [happen.

Kitty. Oh ! if you don't run quick something will

March. Well, well, where shall we run?

Kitty. I saw Miss Kate walking on the rocks —

All. Well, well !

Kitty. When suddenly she slipped —

All. Well, well —

Kitty. And fell into the sea.

Ray. My daughter.

Mrs. Gale. . Goodness ! Gracious !

John Gale. Overboard !

March. Man overboard !

\} (*together.*)

All rush for door, C.   *Enter* SEPT., C., *with* KATE *in his
arms*.

Sept.   Very wet, but safe and sound.

Mrs. Gale.   Thank Heaven!

Ray.   My daughter! (*Takes her from* SEPT.   MRS.
GALE *places a chair*, C., *in which they seat her.*)

March.   Hurrah for Sept.!

Mrs. Gale.   Here, Kitty, March, run for my cam-
phire. (*March takes a flat-iron from the fireplace. Kitty
runs off*, L., *and brings in a bucket of water.   They rush
around the stage two or three times.   March, finding the iron
hot plunges it into the bucket of water*, L.   *Have iron hot so it
will sizzle in water.*)   Land sakes, what are you doing?
ye'll set the house afire.

March.   Darn your old irons: there's another blister.

Kate.   Don't be alarmed, there's nothing the matter.
I accidentally slipped off the rock; but, thanks to dear
Sept., I am quite safe.

Mrs. Gale.   Come right straight up to your room, and
change your clothes.   You'll ketch your death a cold.
Come right along. (*Leads* KATE *off*, R.)

Ray. (*seizing* SEPT.'s *hand*).   Sept. Gale, Heaven bless
you! you've done a noble deed. (*Exit*, R.)

Sept.   Well, well, here's a jolly spree about just nothing at all!   But, I say, March, isn't she splendid?   Do
you know, when I pulled her from the water into my
little craft — I couldn't help it — I felt as though she
belonged to me.   Yes: rich, young, beautiful as she is,
but for the arm of the rough sailor she would now be
sleeping her long sleep beneath the waves.

March.   Well, I dunno about her belonging to you.

All the fish you pull out of the water are yours; but a woman isn't exactly a fish.

Sept. No, no, not exactly, March.

March. Sept., you're a lucky dog. That's just your luck. I might have been on the water a month without making such a haul as that.

Sept. Well, Father Gale, my little spinning Jenny, as you call her, has done good service to-day. Haven't you a little better opinion of her?

John Gale. Sept., my boy, as March says, you've had a streak of luck. But don't brag about that boat.

Sept. But I will, though. She is the fastest sailer on the coast; the neatest trimmed, and the cleanest built; and I'm proud of her. Hallo, Kitty, what's the matter?

Kitty. Oh, dear, this is an awful world! Suppose Miss Kate should have been drowned, — and she would if it hadn't been for me, — hurrying down stairs to tell —

March. After she had been saved. You're a smart one, you are.

Kitty. I couldn't help being late, could I? (*Enter* Mrs. GALE, R.)

Sept. Well, mother, all right, hey?

Mrs. Gale. Yes, Sept., all right. Come right here and kiss me. You're a dear, good, noble — (*hugging him*).

Sept. Now, don't, mother. You'll spoil me. You'll make me believe I've done something great instead of my duty. (*Enter* MR. R., R.)

Ray. Kate has quite recovered. Sept. Gale, how can I express my obligations, how reward —

Sept. Now, please, dou't Mr. Raymond. Don't say any thing about it. If I have been the humble instrument of Heaven in saving a life precious to you, believe me the consciousness of duty done is a rich reward, and I ask no other. Oh! here's Kate. (*Enter* KATE, R.)

Kate. Here I am, just as good as new. Where's my preserver? Now, don't raise your hand : I'm not going to say one word in praise of your conduct. Man was born to wait on woman ; and so, sir, you will please follow me to the rock to find my handkerchief, and see that I don't take another bath. Come along. (*Exit*, C.)

Sept. Ay! Ay! I'll watch you: never fear. (*Exit*, C.)

John. Mother Gale, it strikes me forcibly that if we are to have any dinner to-day —

Mrs. Gale. Heavens and airth! I forgot all about it. You, March, run and split me some wood ; and you, Kitty, peel me some pertaters ; and you, John — dear, dear, what a confusion ! (*Exit*, L.)

March. Come along, Kitty.

Kitty. Dear me ! If there's any thing I hate, it's peeling taters.

March. Well, you jest wait until I get my wood, and I'll fix 'em for you. Come along. (*Exit* KITTY *and* MARCH, L.)

John. It strikes me, that March has a mighty faucy for our Kitty. Who knows but what there'll be a wedding here some of these days? I say, Mr. Raymond, you'll excuse me, but I must look arter my boat. (*Exit*, C.)

Ray. Oh, never mind me ! Twenty-three years ago !

What revelation can fate have in store for me? Twenty-three years ago, I was the possessor of a young and beautiful wife. Travelling in France, I was hastily summoned to America, and obliged to leave my wife, with her infant child, to follow me: she took passage in the ship Diana, in the summer of '31: the vessel was never more heard of. Every inquiry was made, but no intelligence could be obtained. What was also remarkable, the ship Gladiator, which sailed from Havre on the same day, met a like mysterious fate. These boys found on the sands, — can they be connected with this history? Strange, strange, I never heard of this circumstance! But twenty years ago communication was more difficult than now; and that dreadful winter the fearful losses by storm were never known. New ties, — another wife, — she, too, gone, — a daughter loving and beloved, — have stilled the longings to gain tidings of the fate of the lost one: but this strange history awakens a desire to learn more. I have watched them attentively, but can see no resemblance to my lost wife in either of their faces. Yet something tells me that this strange meeting — this desolate place — the wrecks — the children — cannot be accidental. I will be calm, and watch and wait: for I believe that in one of these boys I shall find my lost son. (*Exit, R.*) (*Enter* MARCH, C., *with an armful of wood, in time to hear the last words. He drops the wood.*)

March. It's coming, it's coming! Hold me, somebody! Hold me, especially my head, for I hear strange sounds! I hear the roll of carriage-wheels, and oh, there's a piebald horse gave me a thundering kick in the

head! What did he say? " one of these boys must be
his lost son." So, so! he's got a lost son; and I've got
a lost father, somewhere. I shouldn't wonder if we
found out we were related. I've seen quite a resemblance between Mr. Raymond and myself, — the same
aristocratic air. Suppose it should be — oh! it must be,
— I never could have been left out in that cold sand,
hungry and wet, for nothing. Won't it be gay? I long
for the time when he will disclose himself. I knew he
never could have come to this desolate spot for nothing.
And now it's all out. (*Enter* Mrs. G., L.)

Mrs. Gale. Yes, it is all out, you lazy scamp! Didn't
I tell you to put the wood on the fire?

March. (*Picking up wood he dropped.*) Now, don't
scold, Mother Gale. There's a fire here (*hand on
heart*).

Mrs. Gale (*at fireplace*). I tell you, there's no fire
here. What are you thinking of?

March (*placing wood on fire*). " I dreamt that I dwelt
in marble halls."

Mrs. Gale. Marble fiddlesticks! O March, March!
you'll never set the river afire!

March. Won't I, Mother Gale? You may be sure
of one thing: I shan't try in a hurry. Shall I tell her?
no; I will keep silence, least I interfere with his plans.
(*Enter* Kitty, L.)

Kitty. Oh, dear! oh, dear! I've cut my finger with
those plaguey taters.

March. Dear me, Kitty! you are always in trouble.

Kitty. Well, I couldn't help it. My hands were
never made to peel taters.

March. No, indeed, they wa'nt. Here, let me fix it for you (*wraps cloth round it*). You shan't do it again. Fortune has at last smiled upon me : I shall soon be rich, and then —

Kitty. How long must we wait?

Mrs. Gale. How long must I wait for the pertaters?

Kitty. Oh, dear! I wish they were in the sea (*goes to door*, c.). O March, look here, quick! There's a yacht coming round the point. Isn't she a beauty?

March. My eyes! look at her! A gentleman's yacht, and headed this way.

Mrs. Gale. Mercy sakes! More visitors. Who can it be? (*All exit*, c. *Enter* RAYMOND, R.)

Ray. Confusion! That confounded Capt Dandelion, to escape whom I fled to this out-of-the-way place, is almost at the door in his yacht. His pursuit of Kate is persistent; and, but that I knew the utter selfishness of the man, I could honor him for the apparently unwearied patience with which he follows her. (*Enter* KATE *and* SEPT, c.) Well, child, you have heard of the new arrival?

Kate. A new arrival? No : who is it?

Ray. Your persevering gallant, Capt. Dandelion, is after you. That is his yacht just dropping anchor.

Kate. Now, what could have sent him here?

Ray. You don't seem pleased. Perhaps I may have been unkind in thought; but, remembering your partiality for him in the city, I feared you might have clandestinely invited him here.

Kate. Why, Father! can you think so meanly of me? Capt. Dandelion is very pleasant society in the city; but

here I can do without him. Oh! I forgot : Sept. wants
to speak to you.

Sept. Me? No I don't.

Kate. Why, Sept.! what did you tell me when we
were walking by the shore?

Sept. What did I tell you? why — that — I — what
did I tell you?

Kate. Come, come, sir.

Sept. Well, then, I said you were very beautiful.

Kate. Oh, pshaw! not that.

Sept. Yes, I did ; and I meant it ; that you were rich,
admired and courted ; that your presence here had been
like the coming of a new star in a dark night, to light
the path of us hardy fisherman ; that — that —

Kate. O father! speak to him.

Ray. Well, Sept., I'm willing to obey ; but what shall
I say? — that I fear the presence of my daughter has
made a young man forget his lowly station?

Sept. Yes, you may say that : it has. It has made
him forget that he is poor, rough, and untutored, — that
there are social bonds which hold the rich within their
circles, where the poor may not enter. He has forgot
all, all this. For the manhood within him — the love of
the beautiful implanted in his breast — has burst all
slavish bonds, and his heart has forced from his lips the
words, ' I love you!'

Ray. And you have said this to my daughter?

Sept. I have : I could not help it.

Ray. Base, — base, — base! you have taken advantage of having saved my daughter's life —

Kate. Hold, father! you are mistaken. He has taken

no advantage : I do not believe he ever thought of it. It was I who remembered that when I said, ' Sept., I am glad to hear this ; for I dearly, truly love you.'

Ray. Confound it, girl! what have you done?

Kate. Obeyed the instincts of a true woman, who, when she gains the heart of a man noble and good, accepts it fully and freely, caring not for wealth or station.

Ray. You're a pair of romantic fools. I tell you, girl, you know not what you have done. This must not, cannot be.

Kate. Oh! but it is; you are too late: the mischief is done. So, father, give your consent and make us happy. (*Enter* KITTY, c.)

Kitty. O Miss Kate! here's somebody to see you,— a real gentleman, with rings on his fingers and bells on his toes, I should say, a great mustache under his nose, and half a pair of specs in one eye ; and he says " he's deused wearwy, ah ! " (*imitating.*)

Kate. That's Capt. Dandelion, sure. (*Enter* MARCH, c., *with Captain.*)

Capt. Wall, now, wearly, what a surpwise ! You don't know, my dear fwiends, what a search I've had for you ; you don't wearly !

Ray. Well, Captain, you have found us out. I suppose it would not be polite for me to say we came here on purpose to get rid of you?

Capt. Say it, my dear fellah, say it : it's just like you ; it is, wearly ; you're always joking. But, you know, you can't affwont me, 'pon my word.

Ray. (*Aside.*) No : I wish I could.

Capt. And how is the beautiful, bewitching, adowable Miss Kate?

Kate. Quite well, thank you, Captain. How are all our friends in the city?

Capt. Miserwable, perfectly miserwable : the sun don't shine in the city when you are not there ; it don't, wearly. I couldn't live there, and so I took my wacht and sailed after you.

Kitty. (L. *to* MARCH, L.) Took his what?

Kate. Excuse me, Captain : let me present my friends. This is Mr. March Gale.

Capt. No, wearly? What a queer name ! queer fish, too, 'pon honor.

March. The Captain and I have met before. He's a a little near-sighted, and tumbled head over heels over a rock ; but I picked him up.

Kate. And this is Mr. Sept. Gale.

Capt. Oh ! wearly, a fisherman.

Sept. (*Takes Captain's hand, and gives it a rough shaking.*) Glad to see you, Captain, glad to see you : we'll make you comfortable here ; plenty of fish.

Capt. (*Grinning, and shaking his head.*) Fish ! Yes, and lobsters, too : I've felt their claws.

Kate. And this is Miss Kitty Gale.

Capt. Ah, wearly ! (*Bows, puts his eye-glass to his eyes.*) Positively bewitching ! wuwal simplicity ! Wenus in a clamshell ! (*To Kate.*) But all fishermen.

Kate. Yes, all fisherman ; and you'll find me handy with the line, too, thanks to Sept.'s teaching.

Capt. Glad to hear it ; quite a womantic place this ; so pwimitive, though it does smell hawibly of fish.

March. Yes, Captain, she's a capital fisherman. (*Aside.*) I do wish they would clear out, and give me a chance for a word with Mr. Raymond. There's something in my bosom tells me —

Mrs. Gale (*Outside,* L.). March, March!

March. Yes: there's always something telling me that. It's nothing but March. (*Exit,* L.)

Capt. By the by, Miss Kate, I have a message from a friend in the city, Blanche Allen.

Kate. Dear Blanche! give it me quick.

Capt. I declare I've left it in my wacht.

Kate. Oh! do run and get it quick. Come, I'll go with you.

Capt. Will you? that's deused kind of you, — it is wearly.

Kate. Come, come! I'm impatient to hear from dear Blanche. (*Takes Captain's arm, and exit,* C.)

Sept. She seems mightily pleased with her city friend. Well, he's an elegant gentleman, while I'm but a rough fisherman. Can I ever hope to win her! And yet she told me, but a little while ago, she loved me. (*About to exit,* C.)

Ray. (R.) Sept., a word with you.

Sept. Ay, ay, sir. (*Comes down,* L.)

Ray. John Gale has been telling me a strange story about you. You are not his son.

Sept. Ah, the story of the shipwreck. No, sir: I am not his son by birth; but he has been a true father to me, and I love him as though he were my own.

Ray. Have you no recollection of a mother?

Sept. None: I was an infant when found upon the shore.

Ray. This rough fishing life, — do you like it?

Sept. Like it! to be sure I do; for I have known no other. I was lulled to sleep in infancy by the dash of the waves upon the rocks, the whistling of the breeze among the shingles of the old house; and, winter and summer, I have been rocked upon the bosom of the only mother I know, — the ocean.

Ray. Oh! but there's danger in it.

Sept. Yes, there is danger; but who, with a true heart and a stout arm, cares for danger! Ah, that's the sport of it! To be upon the sea when the winds are roaring, and the waves are seething in anger; to hear along shore the dash of the sea upon the rocks, and to know you have a stout plank beneath you and a light bark obedient to your command, braving the fury of the tempest, — ah, that's glorious!

Ray. But it is mere drudgery. You have read some, I know. Have you never longed for other scenes, — other occupations?

Sept. To be sure I have. As I have read of great generals and their campaigns, of merchant princes, — their thrift and industry, — I have longed to be among them, to bear a hand in the battle, to test my brain, or strain my sinews with the best.

Ray. Well, why have you never tried? The city is open to all who possess industry and talent.

Sept. Ay, ay, sir. But here's father and mother Gale; age is creeping upon them: who is to take care of them? No, no! let the dream pass. They might have left me to die upon the sands: but they took me to their hearts; and, with Heaven's help, I'll be a true son to them in their old age. (*Enter* MARCH, L.)

March. (*Aside.*) Halloo! what's going on here!
Something about me.

Ray. March, — is he contented here?

March. (*Aside.*) Not by a long chalk.

Sept. March? Oh! he's a queer fish; his head is
filled with whimsical notions regarding his parentage.

Ray. Has he any clue to his parents?

Sept. No more than I have.

March. (*Aside.*) Don't be too sure of that.

Ray. Has he any recollection of a mother?

March. (*Breaking in.*) Most certainly he has.

Ray. How?

March. That is, I think I must have had one; and
my father, — I know where he is, and just what he looks
like.

Ray. You do!

March. Yes: he's rather tall, gray hair, dresses well,
and looks like me.

Ray. (*Laughing.*) A very accurate description.

March. You know him, then?

Ray. Me! how should I?

March. He's rich too.

Ray. Ah! that's good.

March. Yes; and he's got his eye on me. He's looking after me. He's only waiting to see how I take it.
He fears it will overcome me: but when he finds I am
instinctively drawn towards him; when he finds I only
wait to hear a voice say — (*Enter* KITTY, L.)

Kitty. March, I've peeled the taters.

March. Confound your taters!

Ray. Well, well, March, remember the old adage,

" Patient waiting, no loss."   Come, Sept., let's go down
and look at the captain's boat.   (*Exit with* SEPT., c.)

March.   Kitty Gale, you're enough to try the patience
of Job : just when I was on the brink of a discovery, you
must pop in, and spoil every thing.

Kitty.   How could I help it?   I did'nt know you was
on the brink of any thing.

March.   In another moment, I should have found my
father.

Kitty.   Oh,   pshaw !   you're always finding a father.
I don't believe you ever had one.

March.   You don't, hey?   I have got one, and he's
rich too ; got a fine horse —

Kitty.   Then why don't you find him?   Bige Parker
don't have to hunt for his father !

March.   Bige Parker !   Do you dare to speak his
name to me?

Kitty.   To be sure I do.   I'm going to walk with him
to-night : perhaps he'll see more beautiful rainbows.

March.   We'll see about that.   I'll just go and hunt
him up, and he'll ketch the darndest licking ever he got :
you see if he don't. (*Dashes out,* c.)

Kitty.   Now he's gone off mad.   Well, I don't care.
(*Enter* MRS. GALE, L.)

Mrs. Gale.   Come, Kitty, hurry and set the table
(*pulls table out,* c., *spreads it ; she and* KITTY *get cloth and
dishes, and lay the table, during the scene*).

Kitty.   Lord! here comes the captain back again.
(*Enter* CAPT. *and* KATE, c.)

Kate.   It's no use, Captain ; my answer is still the
same : I can never marry you.

Capt. Now, that's deused unpleasant, after a fellah has come down here in his *wacht.*

Mrs. Gale (*to Kitty*). What's he say? he's got warts! I'll cure 'em for him.

Kitty. Hush, mother! he's making love to Miss Kate.

Mrs. Gale. Land sakes! he don't look strong enough to make love to a skeeter.

Capt. Do let me entreat you to reverse your decision.

Kate. Not another word, Captain. (*Enter* JOHN GALE, L.) Ah! here's Mr. Gale. Mr. Gale, let me make you acquainted with a friend of mine, Capt. Dandelion.

Mr. Gale (*seizing Captain by hand, giving him a rough shake*). Glad to see you, Captain. I've been admiring your yacht. She's a beauty.

Capt. (*shaking his own hand*). Another fisherman. More lobsters' claws. (*Enter* RAYMOND, R.)

Ray. John Gale, I forgot one question about the wrecks. Did you find no name about them?

John Gale. Name? yes. We found the name of one on pieces of the wreck. 'Twas the Gladiator. The name of the other, on a bucket, — this one (*takes up bucket,* L., *turns it round, showing the name Diana nearly effaced*), the Diana.

Ray. The Diana? Merciful Heaven! which one was this?

John Gale. The first. The one which gave us our Sept.

Ray. Sept.?

John Gale. You seem mighty interested in these wrecks.

Ray. I am, I am, John Gale.   My wife and her
infant son sailed from Havre in that same Diana, twenty-
three years ago.   She was the only passenger with a
child : of that I have had abundant proof.   This wreck,
this name (*enter* SEPT., C.), the story of the wreck, are
convincing proofs of the presence of my lost child beneath your roof.   He can be no other that September
Gale.

Sept.   Me?   I your son?

Ray.   Yes, my boy : you are indeed my son.   You see
now, Kate, why your marriage with him was impossible.
He is your brother.

Kate.   My brother? oh, misery !

Sept.   Her brother? thus ends my dream of happiness.

Capt.   Her brother?   'Pon honor, my chance is wealy
better.

John Gale.   Well, this does beat all natur.

Mrs. Gale.   Sept.! Sept.! My dear boy, I can't lose
you.

March. (*outside,* C.).   Darn you, Bige Parker!   You
just come out here in this public highway. (*Enter* C.,
with a black eye and nose bloody.)

Kitty.   Why, March Gale !   what have you been doing?
Fighting Bige Parker?

March.   Yes, rather.

Kitty.   Did you thrash him?

March.   Does this look like it? (*Points to eye.*)

Kitty.   O March! there's been such a time here!
Mr. Raymond lost a son twenty-three years ago.

March.   Yes.

Kitty.   And what do you think?—he's just discovered
him.

March. I told you so, — I told you so! It's coming.

Kitty. He's discovered him here.

March. Yes, yes.

Kitty. And who do you suppose it is?

March. Suppose? I know, Kitty. Can I smother the paternal instinct in my bosom? It is — it is —

Kitty. Our Sept.

March. O Lord! there's another black eye for me. (*Tumbles against table, knocking it over.*)

Mrs. Gale. Heavens and airth! All my best chiny! (*Grand crash of crockery and quick curtain.*)

DISPOSITION OF CHARACTERS AT END OF ACT:

R. CAPT., KATE, MR. RAYMOND, MARCH (*on floor*), KITTY, SEPT.,
MRS. GALE, JOHN GALE. L.

ACT SECOND.

SCENE. *Same as Act 1.* (JOHN GALE, *seated at fireplace,* R., *smoking;* MRS. GALE *sitting,* L., *knitting.* MARCH *on stool,* C.)

March. Now, isn't this a nice little family party? Since Sept. found his father, the house has been about as lively as a funeral. Daddy Gale is as cross as Julius Cæsar, and Mother Gale as dumb as an oyster. Sept. doesn't seem to take kindly to his new position; and Miss Kate acts as though she had lost a mother, instead of finding a brother. Nobody seems to have any life, except Kitty; and she's busy flirting with that Capt. Dandeliou — confound him. I say, Mother Gale?

Mrs. Gale. Well?

March. Where's Sept.?

Mrs. Gale. Don'no, and don't care.

March. Daddy Gale?

John. Well?

March. Where's Sept.?

John. Don'no, and don't care?

March. Dry weather, ain't it?

John (fiercely). Now, what's the use of talking about the weather?

March. So I say : what's the use of talking at all? I like singing better (*sings*), —

"Oh, my name was Capt. Kyd."

John Gale ⎫ (*together*). Stop that confounded squalling!
Mrs. Gale ⎭ Heavens and airth, yelling again!

March. (*Aside.*) I thought that would fetch them.

Mrs. Gale. If John Gale was any kind of a man, he'd soon put an end to sich nonsense.

John. Now, what's the use of telling about John Gale? You spilt the boys! you know you did.

Mrs. Gale. Gracious goodness! the man is crazy: I spiled 'em?

John. Yes, you.

Mrs. Gale. John Gale, you're a brute.

John. You're another.

March. (*Aside.*) Hallo! it's getting squally here.

John. Here I find these 'ere lads left to die on the shore : and, in the goodness of my heart, I brings 'em home, and tries to make good, honest men on 'em ; but what have you done? You've made one a fine gentleman, that don't know us ; and the other a sassy chap, that's eternally squalling when we want peace and quiet.

Mrs. Gale. Well, I never, John Gale! if I had a skillet, I'd comb your hair for you, you brute. (*Enter* SEPT., C.)

Sept. Hallo! hallo! what's the matter now? Silent! no word of welcome for me! Well, well, what's gone wrong, father? what's gone wrong?

John Gale. Now, what's the use of calling me *father?* I *ain't* yer father. You've got a rich father, rolling in riches; and you're a great man now. Of course you look down on us poor fishing-folks: it's what we expected.

Sept. Indeed!

Mrs. Gale. Yes: poor folks must remember their station now.

Sept. Ay, mother, that they must. If they are honest and true, loving God and their fellow-men, their station is the proudest and the noblest among mankind: for the hands they raise to heaven bear the proof-marks of their kinship to Nature's first nobleman, Father Adam; and their hearts are rolls of honor, ever brightened by inscriptions of good works and noble heroism.

Mrs. Gale. Heavens and airth! do hear that boy talk!

Sept. Pray heaven, I may never forget mine, — never forget the kind benefactors who in my helplessness rescued me from the fury of the storm, who took me to their hearts, watched over me in sickness, guided my feet in the path of duty, and made a man of me. It may be as you say, — that I have found a father, one who claims me by right of birth; but my heart beats with no such feeling of love, of reverence, and of duty, towards him, as it does for the honest, true-hearted old fisherman, John Gale (*takes* JOHN GALE's *hand*).

John. God bless you, Sept.! God bless you, boy! I knew you were true as steel; but the old lady —

Mrs. Gale. Now, stop, John Gale! don't you go to slandering.

Sept. And a mother! where shall I find her? They tell me, that, long ago, she found a grave beneath the wave; but my heart tells me she is here, — here, where my childhood was passed; here among the rocks and sands, where the wild winds roar their loudest and the dark waves beat their fiercest. At the feet of her who first taught me the name of mother, I lay a son's love and duty, which she, and she alone, has right to claim (*kneels at* MRS. GALE's *feet*).

Mrs. Gale. O Sept., Sept.! my dear, dear, boy: we thought we were going to lose you now you are rich and high in the world.

Sept. Never fear, mother, never fear. Come what will, this is my home. We have weathered it together when the clouds of adversity gathered thick about, and we'l share together the sunshine of prosperity which now breaks upon us.

Mrs. Gale. Dear me, dear me! what *does* ail my glasses? I can't see. There, I've dropped another stitch; and good gracious! where's my handkercher? I declare, I've dropped it somewhere — I never did see such careless — (*Exit*, L.)

John Gale. Hang me if I don't believe something,

run into my pipe, and put it out. Well, Sept., here's my hand: you're an honor to us, and all you've got is rightly yours; you deserve it. Come, March, let's go down and look arter the boats. (*Exit*, c. MARCH, *has been sitting staring at* SEPT. *with mouth open.*)

Sept. Hallo, March, who are you staring at?

March. At a chap that's got a father. It's a wonderful curiosity to me. I say, Sept., how does it feel?

Sept. Well, March, thus far I can't say I like it.

March. Don't like it? what a queer chap you are! I wish I was in your shoes.

Sept. I wish with all my heart you were.

March. A rich father and a beautiful sister!

Sept. Sister! Ah, there's the sting!

March. Why, you don't mean to say — oh? good gracious! why, you were dead in love with her — you can't marry her now, you know.

Sept. No: all my fond dreams of happiness are dispelled by this unfortunate affair.

March. Unfortunate! well, you are a queer one. Don't I wish it was me? wouldn't I make the money fly?

John Gale (*outside*, c.). March, March, must I wait all day for you, hay?

March. Hallo! I forgot I had a job on hand. Goodby Sept., — poor unfortunate son of a millionnaire. (*Exit*, c.)

Sept. Sister! can I ever call her by that name; must I forever relinquish the hope of claiming her by a dearer title. No, no: I bear to her something warmer than a brother's love. This cannot be: this man Raymond treated with scorn my overtures for the hand of his daughter. He can have no proof that I am his son, — nothing but the fact that his infant child was a passenger in the vessel that left me on the sands. He cannot claim me upon such a mere thread as this. Perhaps it is a plot to keep me quiet until his daughter is married to some wealthy suitor ; and then how easy to discover his mistake, and cast me adrift in the world. Ah ! here is Kate. (KATE, R.) Good-morning, sister.

Kate. Sister?

Sept. It sounds strange from my lips, does it not?

Kate. Indeed, it does, Sept. : you know I have never been called so before ; and — and —

Sept. You expected once that I should use a dearer title.

Kate. Once — O Sept., Sept.! this is so strange. We were so happy yesterday, it seems like awakening from a glorious dream. That you should be fated to call me by the name of sister — it is cruel. I awoke last night, and saw the moonbeams stream in at my window. I arose, and looked out upon the night ! the waters were calm and peaceful ; the moon glistened upon the rocks, lighting the very spot where you and I sat last night, telling our future hopes. I know it was wicked ; but I was so wretched, so miserable, I wished I was sleeping calm and still beneath the waves from which you rescued me, ere I had awakened to such misery as this.

Sept. Be calm, dear Kate : all will yet be well ; I am not your brother.

Kate. Not my brother ! you jest now. My father has claimed you.

Sept. But there is something here that revolts at the kinship. Why should he claim me as his son? There are no proofs, no likeness to him, or her he calls my mother. Nothing but the mere fact that I was found after the wreck of the vessel in which his wife sailed.

Kate. No, no! Sept., he must be right. He *does* see a resemblance to his lost wife in your face. No, no! it must be true.

Sept. I will not believe it without further proof. I do not feel towards him as I know I should were he my father; and as for a brother's love, the love within my heart for you is of a higher and a holier nature than even that of brother. Kate, you told me last night that you loved me, that you would one day be my wife: will you still keep your promise?

Kate. O Sept.! it is impossible!

Sept. If this should be a trick, — a trick to rob me of you, — this claim put forward to keep me from your path until you had wed a richer suitor —

Kate. Why, Sept., you cannot believe my father so base as that: you are mad?

Sept. Yes, Kate! I am mad, — madly in love with you. Believe me, I am not your brother. This is, at the best, a mere suspicion.

Kate. Suspicion! yes: it is a suspicion, but one that must forever separate us. It may be you are right, and something at my heart tells me you are; but this suspicion will forever darken my life. No, Sept.; much as I love you, it were better we should forever dismiss the hope. For, whether further proof should be found or not, every hope of happiness would be blasted by the fear — the dread

—that you might be my brother. Sept., you shall always find in me a sister, a loving sister; ever watchful for your comfort, ever praying for your happiness; but, for Heaven's sake, no more of a warmer tie. (*Exit*, R.)

Sept. Have I lost her? What can I do? where turn to escape from this bewildering maze? Upon this I am determined: I will not accept this man's bounty, or acknowledge his claim. (*Enter* RAYMOND, C.)

Mr. R. My dear boy, I've just despatched a messenger to town with the glad tidings; and to-morrow we'll leave this barren spot, and hie to the gay scenes of city-life. Gad! boy, we'll make a gentleman of *you.* You must drop that outlandish name of September: you shall be Alden Raymond, jr.

Sept. You go to town?

Ray. Yes, to-morrow: I'm impatient to show my city friends the fine lad I found down by the sea.

Sept. I cannot share your gratification, sir, for I shall remain here.

Ray. Remain here! what for?

Sept. Because I belong here. Mr. Raymond, I am extremely obliged to you for the kind interest you have manifested in me; but I cannot accept your claim. I do not believe I am your son.

Ray. Not my son! why, boy, you are crazy. There cannot be the least doubt of it: you came in the vessel with my wife; there was no other infant on board.

Sept. That you are not certain of.

Ray. Certain! of course I am. I tell you, boy, there can be no mistake.

Sept. There may be; there must be. I do not feel

towards you the love of a son for his father; and, until some other proof is found, I shall remain here, and bear the only name to which I feel I have a right, — that of September Gale. (*Exit*, L.)

Ray. But, boy — Sept., come here. Confound him! Here's a pretty predicament. Here's an ungrateful scamp who refuses to acknowledge his father. I'll disinherit him — oh, pshaw! what does he care for that? He's a noble fellow, and he *must* be my son. (*Exit*, R. *Enter* CAPTAIN, C., *with* KITTY *on his arm.*)

Kitty. Well, I declare, Captain, you are the most delightfulest beau that ever I saw.

Capt. No, wealy: 'pon honor, you overwhelm me; you do, wealy, you dear, delightful little nymph of the sea.

Kitty. You're the sweetest man: your conversation is so sugary.

Capt. Yes, jest so: 'pon my honor, I don't know the weason, but the ladies in the city are very fond of me. I am quite a flower in the city.

Kitty. (*Aside.*) A sunflower! Oh, I do wish that March could see us!

Capt. Yaas, you should go to the city; such a beautiful cweature is wasting her sweetness on the desert air in this howid place, that smells so of fish.

Kitty. Now, do you think so, Captain? Well, I've always thought I was born for a higher sphere.

Capt. You were, weally. Your beauty would be the admiration of the whole city: it would, weally.

Kitty. O Captain! you flatter now.

Capt. Flatter? 'pon honor, no. Do let me take you to the city in my *wacht:* the trip would be delightful.

Kitty. What! (*Aside.*) I do believe the man wants me to run away with him. (*Enter March,* c.)

Capt. Yaas, we could slip away from here, go to the city, see all the sights, and return, without any of these people being the wiser.

March. (*Aside.*) Confound his picture! he's trying to run off with Kitty.

Kitty. Why, what an idea! I run off with a man! —

Capt. Who loves you to distraction; he does, weally.

Kitty. What would Miss Kate say?

Capt. Who cares what she says? 'Tis you I love, you whom I adore.

Kitty. Why, what would March say?

March. (*Coming between them.*) He'll be cursed if you do any thing of the kind.

Kitty. March! you here?

Capt. That howid fisherman!

March. Yes, that howid fisherman, you confounded old goggle-eyed sculpin! And as for you, Kitty Sands, I'm ashamed of you. A pretty pair you are! Want to run off, do you?

Capt. Come, come, sir! you're impertinent.

March. Oh! I'm impertinent, am I? Wall, I ain't near-sighted, and I don't wear eye-glasses, and I can see your nose plainly. (*Takes off his coat, and rolls up his sleeves.*)

Kitty. Why, March! what are you doing?

March. I'm just going to open your nose in the most approved style of the manly art! (*Squares off.*)

Capt. Lord, gwacious! I believe the fellah's going to fight!

Kitty. March, if you touch him, I'll call father just as loud as ever I can.

March. Well, you call: you'll get a pretty talking to, I tell you. (*Advances to Capt.*)

Capt. Here, you stop, you fellah! Stop, I say! (*Retreating towards door,* c.)

March. I'll teach you to skulk round here with your airs! (*Advances.*)

Kitty. Father, father! quick, quick!

Capt. That's right: call your father, or I'm a dead man! (*Enter,* c., *Jean Grapeau with a large bundle.*)

Grap. Ha! ze top of ze morning, gentlefolks! How you vas? how you vas?

Kitty. A peddler.

March. Hallo, Frenchy! where did you drop from?

Capt. (*Aside.*) They seem to be busy: I'll just step out. (*Exit,* L.)

Grap. Ah, sacre! I am ver mouch fatigue, ver mouch all ovar. I have travel all ze day wiz my pack, and not sell ze fust thing; and I see your door open, and I slip in to show you my goods. You pardon me ver mouch.

March. Well, old chap, sit down. I've got a little job here. Why, the Captain's gone!

Kitty. Yes, he has gone. You're a pretty fellow, you are! — scared him about to death.

March. I'll scare him if I catch him!

Kitty. No, you won't!

March. Yes, I will! Making love to you, darn him!

Kitty. Pooh! I don't care for him. I'm only amusing myself while Bije Parker's away.

March. Bije Parker? Confound him! I'll lick him, too!

Kitty. Oh! will you? You tried that once before, you know.

Grap. Sacre! what for you scold, hey? You ver mouch angry, ver mouch. Now, you jest keep yourself quiet, and I sal show you what I has in my pack. Silks for ze leetle girl and shawls for ze leetle girl, brazelets for ze leetle girl.

Kitty. Oh, do let me see them!

March. See! Why, you've got no money to buy.

Grap. Nevar mind, nevar mind. I will show zem all ze same for ze plesure I have to please ze leetle girl. Ha, sacre! I be ver mouch fatigue. My old legs, zay have what you call ze shakes. Parbleu! I remember ze time when I vas ver spry, — ver active, — ver robust. In mine own France, ven I vas young, I vas ze great acrobat. I dance on ze cord elastique, zis way, — you see, — zis way! (*Imitating.*) Oh, sacre! it is what you call no go, ver mouch. My legs be very old.

March. How long you been here?

Grap. I have ben in zis country, let me see, ten — twenty — more years ago. I have leave my own home wiz ze grand acrobatic trope zat nevar reach ze land, — nevar.

March. Acrobats! why, them's circus chaps!

Grap. Circus chaps! vat you call circus chaps, hey? I no comprend circus chaps.

March. Why, the fellers that turn flip-flaps in the tan.

Grap. Flip-flaps in ze tan? what for, hey?

March. Oh! no matter: let's see your goods.

Grap. (*Attempts to untie bundle.*) Sacre! my pack has ze ver hard knot. I must take off my coat! (*Takes off coat*). Parbleu! I am grow old ver fast ver much.

Mrs. Gale (*outside,* L.). Kitty! Kitty!

Kitty. Oh, gracious! there's mother. What shall we do? She can't abide peddlers.

March. That she can't. Old gent, you'll have to tramp.

Grap. Tramp! what for I tramp?

March. You'll get broomed out if you don't. Here's a pretty kettle of fish!

Grap. Keetle of fish? I see no keetle of fish. (*Enter* Mrs. Gale, L.)

Mrs. Gale. What! a peddler in my house! Get out of this, quick! Out of this, I say!

Kitty. It's only a poor old Frenchman.

Mrs. Gale. But he's a peddler; and I won't have a peddler in my house. Start! Where's my broom? (*Exit,* L.)

Grap. What for she get her broom, hey?

March. You'll find out: quick, run for it!

Grap. What for I run for it? Oh, sacre! I see ze old woman wiz ze broom, and I comprend, I comprend! (*Darts out door,* C. *Enter Mrs. Gale, with broom,* L.)

Mrs. Gale. Where is he? where is he? (*Darts out door,* C.)

Kitty. Hide the old gentleman's pack, March, quick! Mother will pitch it into the water. (*March carries it off,* L., *as Mrs. Gale enters.*)

Mrs. Gale. The idea of a peddler! I've had enough

4

on 'em; but they won't cheat me again in a hurry, I can tell 'em. (*Exit*, L.)

Kitty. What a blind, silly goose March Gale is!—fighting Bije Parker, and going to fight the Captain, because I encourage their attentions, and can't see that it's all to make him speak. So jealous of everybody! If he loves me, why don't he tell me so? (*Enter Capt.*, c.)

Capt. Ah, ha, my little beauty! you see I have returned.

Kitty. Like a dear, charming Captain, as you are.

Capt. Where's that howid fisherman?

Kitty. Oh! you needn't be afraid of him: he's gone.

Capt. Gone, has he? and left the coast clear? What a chawming opportunity!

Kitty. Charming opportunity for what?

Capt. To tell you, divine cweecher, how I love you.

Kitty. You've told me that a hundred times.

Capt. Let me tell you a hundred times more. (*Sees Grapeau's coat.*) Hold! what's that?

Kitty. Why, your coat,—isn't it?

Capt. Mine? what an howid idea! The idea of my wearing such a coat as that! (*Slips it on.*) And such a hat! good gracious! (*Puts on hat.*) Don't I look queer!

Kitty. Oh, my! what a queer-looking chap you are! You wouldn't feel much like making love in that suit,—would you, Captain?

Capt. Make love to you, my chawmer! Yes, in any dress.

Kitty. Oh, capital! It would be so jolly to have a lover on his knees at my feet, dressed as you are!

Capt. On my knees!

Kitty. Yes, on your knees. (*Aside.*) Don't I wish March could catch him there! Down on your knees! Quick, or I'll run off!

Capt. (L.) Well, then, here I am. (*Kneels.*) What a howid idea! (*Enter Mrs. Gale, with broom.*)

Mrs. Gale. That horrid old peddler here again?

Capt. Beautiful nymph of the sparkling sea!

Mrs. Gale. I declare, he's sparking our Kitty!

Capt. Captivating cweecher! I do love you, — 'pon my honor, I do! Your beauty charms me! your bewitching manner stwikes — stwikes — stwikes — st——

Mrs. Gale. (*Rushes at him, knocks his hat over his eyes with broom.*) I'll strike you, you tarnal varmint! Get out of my house I say!

Capt. (*Gets on his feet tries to get hat off.*) Murder! murder!

Mrs. Gale. (*Strikes his hat down again.*) Out of my house! You scamp, you villain, you cheat! (*Beats him off,* R., *the Captain yelling " Murder !"*)

Kitty. (*Sinking into chair.*) Ha, ha, ha! what a comical figure the Captain does cut! He won't make love to me again in a hurry. (*Enter Grapeau,* C.)

Grap. Whist, leetle girl! I have come back for my pack and mine hat and mine coat. Sacre! I have run ver much from ze old lady wiz ze broom. Where she be, hey?·

Kitty. (*Aside.*) Oh, dear! what shall I say? — the Captain's run off with them. (*Aloud.*) My brother has put them away somewhere: you must wait till he returns.

Grap. Sacre! I sal get me head break ver much, if I stay here.

Kitty. No, mother has just gone out.

Grap. Oh! the old lady have gone out? Parbleu! I feel all ze better, ver much; I feel quite ze comfortable. Ha, you be ver pretty girl!

Kitty. Oh, pshaw!

Grap. What for you say 'pshaw'? You know I speaks ze truth all ze time! You break ze young men's hearts all to pieces ver much.

Kitty. No, I don't, Mr. Frenchman.

Grap. Ah, ma chere, but you do, you leetle rogue! Did I not see ze young man viz ze red hair? He be ver much in love all over.

Kitty. He, — March — in love with me! You are quite mistaken.

Grap. Ah, but he be ver much. I see it in his eyes. (*Enter* MARCH, C.)

Kitty. March love me? No, sir! He's a selfish —

Grap. Take care, ma cher, — take care! You leetle rogue, you love him, — you know you do!

Kitty. I don't, one bit.

Grap. Ha, you do! Vat for you plague him so if you no love him? Ha! your eyes, — zay tell ze tale.

Kitty. I don't care if I do: he's a booby! He don't love me.

March. (*Aside.*) Don't I, though!

Grap. Vat for you say that, hey?

Kitty. Because he never told me.

March. (*Rushing down* C.) Then, by jingo! he tells you so now. Kitty Sands, you're the idol of my heart.

There's a devouring passion in my bosom that gnaws —
Oh, pshaw! I can't imitate the Captain. But, Kitty
Gale, I do truly and sincerely love you.

Kitty. Why, March Gale! you've been listening.

March. A little bit, Kitty, — just enough to find out
what a fool I've been : but it's all right now. And you'll
marry me one of these days.

Kitty. One of these days? When?

March. Well, when I find my father.

Kitty. Oh, yes, I'll marry you then, never fear.

Grap. Ha! zat is good, — zat is very much better.

Kitty. Oh, dear, March! here's mother coming again.

Grap. Ze old lady wiz ze broom? Sacre! I sall get
my head broke ver much!

March. Old gentleman, you'll have to make a run of
it.

Grap. But I have not ze coat nor ze hat. I will
catch ze death of cold in mine head! (*Sneezes.*) Sacre!
I have him now! (*Sneezes.*)

March. Where is his hat and coat, Kitty?

Kitty. I don't know, but I suspect mother has them
now.

Grap. Ze old lady wiz my coat? Sacre! zat is ver
much too bad, — ver much too bad!

March. Run and hide him somewhere, — in the wash-
room, — anywhere; for here comes Mother Gale.

Kitty. Come, old gentleman! I'll hide you. (*Exit,
with Jean,* L.)

March. What a confounded ninny I have been! If I
had known this before, I might have saved Bije Parker
the trouble of giving me the thrashing I intended for

him. But ain't it jolly! I'm so happy I could sing for
joy! (*Sings.*)

"Oh, my name was Captain Kyd."

Enter MRS. GALE, R., *with broom, which she claps upon*
MARCH's *head.*

Mrs. Gale. I'll Kyd you!

March. Mother Gale, what are you about?

Mrs. Gale. About mad. Where's Kitty? Such a
caper! Oh dear, oh dear! I've been and chased and chased
that confounded pedller way down to the water; and
when he gets there, he strips off his coat and hat, and —
would you believe it? — it was the Captain!

March. Why, Mother Gale! what have you done?
what will he say?

Mrs. Gale. He didn't stop to say any thing: he jest
gave one leap into the water, and swam for his yacht!

March. This is bad. What will Daddy Gale say?

John Gale. (*Outside,* c.) Now, what's the use of
talking about Sept.?

Mr. Raymond. (*Outside.*) But I tell you I will be
obeyed! (*Both enter,* c.)

March. Hallo! here's a breeze.

Ray. It's all your doing, you rusty old sea-horse!
You've made the boy disobey his father.

John Gale. I tell you, Sept. is his own master; and, if
he doesn't chose to go, why here he stays.

Ray. It's a conspiracy to defraud me of my son, and
I won't stand it!

Mrs. Gale. What's the matter?

John Gale. Matter? Matter enough! Sept. won't own his father: that's what's the matter!

Ray. By your advice! Now, don't tell me! I know it's your doing. You envy me the possession of such a son, and you try all you can to keep him here. (*Enter* SEPT., C.)

John Gale. Do I? Well, here's the boy now to speak for himself. Look here, Sept. Gale, you're an ungrateful young scamp! Here's a father boiling over with love, and rich as an alderman, waiting to take you to his arms. *He* says I'm trying to keep you here.

Sept. Mr. Raymond knows well you have nothing to do with it. I do not acknowledge his claim, because I see no proof. (*Enter* KATE, C.)

Kate. What's the matter, father?

Ray. Matter? Your brother refuses to acknowledge me as his father, or you as his sister.

Kate. Indeed!

Ray. Yes, indeed! But I'll find a way to make him. Hark you, Kate! Capt. Dandelion has again proposed for your hand, to *me* this time, and I have accepted him: so you can look upon him as your future husband.

Kate. Capt. Dandelion! — my husband?

Sept. Her husband! I thought it would come to that.

Ray. Yes, your husband! You cannot object to the match: he is rich and highly accomplished.

Kate. But I do object. He is rich; but, when I marry, it shall be a man, and not a money-bag.

Ray. You refuse to obey me?

Kate. In this, yes. You have ever found me an

obedient child, ready and eager to obey you : but this is
a matter in which the heart commands ; and mine bids
me obey a higher law, which not even a father has
power to set aside.

Ray.   Well, here's another!   The son refuses to
acknowledge his father, the daughter her husband!   I
tell you, girl, you shall marry this man !

Kate.   I will not!   I love another.

Ray.   And that other? —

Kate.   September Gale.

Sept.   True, true as steel.

SITUATION.

(KATE, R.   RAYMOND, R. C.   SEPT., C.   JOHN GALE,
L. C.   MARCH, L. C.   MRS. GALE, L.   *Enter* KITTY
and GRAPEAU, L., KITTY *trying to screen him as they
creep toward door,* C. MARCH *attracts* MRS. G.'s *attention, who seems inclined to turn around.*

Ray.   Your brother.   Confound it, you're all crazy!
Do you want to drive me mad?

Kate.   He is not my brother.

Ray.   But I say he is: every circumstance goes to
prove it, — "The Diana," the wreck, the child found
upon the sands.   I tell you he must be my son.

John Gale.   Now, what's the use of talking about the
wreck?   Wa'n't there two on 'em?   Couldn't there have
been a baby born on board?   Couldn't your wife have
made a mistake in the vessel?   I don't see your proof.
She might have sailed in "The Gladiator."   (GRAP.
rushes down, C.)

Grap.   "Ze Gladiator?"   What for you say "Ze
Gladiator"?

John Gale. Hallo! who's this?

March. The old Frenchman's caught.

Mrs. Gale. That plaguy peddler here! Where's my broom?

March. Hold on, Mother Gale! The old gentleman has done me a service, and I'll stand by him.

Ray. What does he know of "The Gladiator"?

Grap. "Ze Gladiator"? Sacre! I have know "Ze Gladiator" too much, — ver too much. I have sailed from my own France ever so long ago in ze ship call "Ze Gladiator."

John Gale. When was that?

Grap. Oh, sacre! ten, twenty-one, two, three years ago.

Ray. Twenty-three years ago?

Grap. Oui, oui! But, sacre? she was vat you call wreck; she all go to ze pieces on ze sands, and I have to make ze passage on ze leetle frail hencoop.

March. Oh, it's coming, — it's coming! Say, old man, — Frenchy, — look here! where was this?

Grap. Parbleu! I do not know ze place. I have sail on ze hencoop far, far away from ze wreck before I picks myself up.

March. But — O Lord! somebody hold me! — the passengers? — any babies aboard?

Grap. Babies? passengers? Oui, oui! zere vas ze passengers, — ze lady and ze little baby; but ze poor lady die before ze ship all go to ze pieces.

Ray. Died! This lady, — do you know her name?

Grap. Oh, sacre, no! ze membrance fail me ver much. Ze beautiful lady, — she was so pale and so young, mine heart feel ver much for her. Her name — sacre! — oh, it have gone from me. She was ze kind lady, for I vas ver sick. Her name — She was ze light — ze light — Oh, sacre! I have ze name. What ze sun do when he shine, — when he shine? He shoot — he shoot de — de — oh, sacre! my poor old head! — he shoots de —

Kitty. Rays?

Grap. Ha, ze little rogue, — ze pooty leetle girl! Zat vas her name, — Ray — Ray — Ray —

Ray. Heavens, man, speak! Was it Raymond?

Grap. Oui, *oui!* Ze Raymond, — ze beautiful Madam Raymond!

Ray. Gracious heavens! My wife! But the child, old man? — the child?

Grap. Ze child? ah, ze poor lady, — she have made ze grand mistake: she have engage a passage in ze oder ship vich sail ze same day; but ze stupid driver take her to ze wrong ship, too late for her too make ze change. Ze fatal mistake; for ze unlucky ship met wiz disaster upon disaster, — ze very long passage, and ze wreck at last.

John Gale. Long passage! I should think so; six months behind time!

Ray. But the child?

Grap. Oui, ze child! Ven ze poor lady die, ze capitan, he take ze leetle boy, and he say, "I do not know zis child or his mozar, but ze child sall be remembered." So, wiz ze needle and ze ink, he prick upon ze leetle arm of ze leetle boy ze leetle red anchor.

Ray. Sept. Gale, speak the truth! Have you such a mark upon your arm?

Sept. No, no, — thank Heaven, no!

March. (*Rushing to* c.) One minute! Just somebody watch me, for I know it's coming! (*Throws off his coat and rolls up his sleeves.*) It's no use trying to deceive me any longer! I am the child! See the little red anchor!

All. The anchor!

Ray. My boy, my boy!

John Gale. }
Mrs. Gale. } Our March!

Sept. Heaven be praised!

Kate. My dear, dear brother!

Grap. (*Patting March on the back.*) Ha! ze leetle baby have grown ver much, — ver much. Zis is vat you call jolly.

March. Jolly, old Frenchy? That's so, and I owe it all to you. But where's Kitty?

Kitty. (*Up stage*, c.) Here, March.

March. What are you skulking back there for? You know what you told me to-day.

Kitty. But I didn't think you'd ever find your father; and now you're rich, and I'm only a poor girl.

March. Father, you've found a son to-day, and that son has found a wife. You must take both, or neither: which shall it be?

Mrs. Gale. What! our Kitty!

John Gale. Yes, our Kitty.

Ray. Well, I don't know. I must have time to consider.

March. No, you mustn't. Speak quick, or you lose us. I wanted a father bad enough; but thus far I have done without one, and I rather think —

Ray. Now, stop! don't *you* disobey me. I'll take you both.

Kate. That's a dear father! I know I shall love Kitty dearly; and March and I have been like brother and sister, — haven't we, March?

March. Ay, that we have, — you and I and Sept. By the by, what's to become of Sept.? Where's *his* father?

Sept. Don't trouble yourself about me. I've got a father here in John Gale.

Ray. And here's another, if you'll own him. Sept., here's my daughter, who refused to obey me. I'd give her to you, only, as she has refused to obey me, and —

Kate. Dear father, I wouldn't refuse again for the world.

Ray. Then take her, Sept. You deserve her. Well, John Gale, what have you got to say to this?

John Gale. Now, what's the use talking about what I've got to say? What will the Captain have to say? (*Enter Capt.*, C.)

Capt. Quite a family party, I declare!

Ray. Why, Captain! where have you been?

Capt. I've just been aboard my yacht, to change my clothing; that's all. 'Twas a little chilly.

Mrs. Gale. Why, Captain! you looked warm enough when I saw you last.

Capt. That howid old woman! — she's poking fun at me: I know she is.

Ray. Well, Captain, I mentioned your proposal to my daughter; but she positively refuses to marry you.

Capt. I'm doosed glad of it; for I've found a beautiful cweecher, who suits me better.

Ray. Who is that, pray?

Capt. Miss Kitty Gale.

March. You're too late, Captain: she's engaged to me.

Capt. You? — a howid fisherman!

Ray. You are mistaken. This young man is my son. It's all out at last.

Capt. Well, it's doosed plain that I'm out too: so I'll get up anchor, and off for the city again in my wacht.

Grap. Ze Capitan seems what zay call ver much over ze come.

John Gale. Old lady, it strikes me, if we are to have any dinner to-day —

Mrs. Gale. Land sakes! I forgot all about it. You, March, run — Oh, dear! what shall I do without March?

John Gale. Never mind March: we've got Sept. left.

Kate. But suppose I take him away?

John Gale. O Lord! what shall we do without Sept.?

Sept. You shan't do without him. We began life here in the old shanty; and, whatever fortune may have in store for him, this is his home.

Ray. I begin to like this place. We'll set the men at work, and put up a house on the bluffs, large and roomy.

John Gale. That's right; for this union of the Gales will be likely to end in a squall.

Ray. It shall be a family house, with room enough for Sept. and his wife, March and his wife, John Gale and his wife, I and the Captain; and, once a year at least, we'll all meet there, to talk over old times, and return thanksgiving for the treasures found down by the sea.

DISPOSITION OF CHARACTERS:

R. KATE, SEPT., CAPT., RAY., JOHN GALE, MRS. GALE, MARCH, KITTY. L.

A CLOSE SHAVE.

A FARCE.

CHARACTERS.

CRUSTY (a man of means, generally considered a mean man).
TONSOR (a barber).
McGINNIS (his assistant).
ZEB (a colored apprentice).
HEAVYFACE (a hypochondriac).
SIMPER (an exquisite).

SCENE. — *Tonsor's barber-shop. Two barber's chairs,* c., *facing audience. Table,* L., *with two hand-mirrors upon it. Table,* R., *with razors, strop, shaving-cups, towels, &c.* McGINNIS *discovered dusting.*

McGinnis. Now, isn't this illigant! It's a moighty foine lift I have in the worrld, onyhow. Mike McGinnis, who's curried the horse and fed the pig, toted the hod and tinded the cows, promoted to the illigant position of a man-shaver! Oh! be jabbers, it's moighty foine intirely, — what much I know ov it, and that's moighty little. Faith, when Mr. Tonsor's assistant was took wid the faver, it was at his wit's ends he was intirely. Sez he to me, sez he, — for it's always moighty fond he was of me whin I lived wid his father, — "Mike," sez he, "did iver yer shave?" — "Is it me-

62

self?" says I : " faith, yes, — wid a pair of scissors."
" No, no!" sez he : " did ever yer shave anybody?"
·" Faith, yes," sez I — " the pig."— " Oh, murther!" says
he : " I mane a man." — " Niver a wun," sez I; " but I
could soon learn." And so he took me in here to learn
the business; but it's precious little I'm learning, for the
mashter does all the shaving : but the time must come,
and then look out for yoursilf, Mike McGinnis. (*Enter
Tonsor*, R.)

Ton. Ah, Mike! Brushing up? That's good. I do
like to see a busy man. Where's Zeb?

Mike. Faith, I don't know. It's moighty little he's
shown of his face at all, at all.

Ton. The lazy scamp! that's just like him. No doubt
he's down at the Corners dancing jigs, or turning flip-
flaps for coppers.

Mike. Faix, that's what yer might call turning an
honest penny!

Ton. Any customers this morning, Mike?

Mike. Sorra a wun.

Ton. It's a little early. They'll soon be dropping
in. Heigho, Mike! was you ever in love?

Mike. Ah! away wid yer, now! Ask an Irishman
such a silly question as that! Musha, it's nearly kilt
I am wid the love of Nora Honey. Ah! but the ould
man's got rich *peddling panuts.*

Ton. A rich father, who does not encourage your
attentions!

Mike. Sorra a bit. " Mike," sez he,—and it's moighty
winning he is in his way, — " the front uv my door is il-
ligantly painted on the outside, — much finer than the

inside; and you'd do well to examine it whin you're
passing by, — whin you're passing by, mind."

Ton. Meaning, " I won't turn you out, but you can't
stay here."

Mike. That's jest what he meant. Faith, it's well
posted yez are in the trials and tribulations uv the tinder
passion.

Ton. Yes, Mike; I can sympathize with you. I'm
desperately in love myself.

Mike. · You?

Ton. Yes, and with the daughter of a rich man, and
my love is returned. Ah, Mike! she is the paragon of
loveliness! — the otto of roses! — the pink of purity.

Mike. The shaving-cream uv perfiction, and the hair-
oil uv illigance! Oh, murther! they're all alike till
they find you've no money.

Ton. Ah! but she's entirely different, Mike. She is
willing — nay, anxious — to share my humble fortunes.
'Tis I who dread to take her from all the rich comforts
she has enjoyed. and ask her to share —

Mike. Love in a cottage, wid bacon and greens!
Faith, you're right: it's a mighty foine picter, but hard
of digestion. What says the ould gintleman?

Ton. He knows nothing about it.

Mike. And yer haven't asked his consint?

Ton. No: it would be useless. He has declared his
daughter shall marry only a rich man; that he will not
let her walk, ride, or receive the visits of any young
man; that he will cut her off with a shilling should she
marry *without his consent.*

Mike. The taring ould heathin!

Ton. He is encouraging the attentions of young Simper, whom the young lady detests, and whom he only tolerates because he has a rich father.

Mike. The miserable ould varmint! But who is he?

Ton. One of my customers, — old Jotham Crusty.

Mike. What! that ould skinflint? His consint? It's precious little he'd give onyhow.

Zeb. (*Outside,* R.) Ain't yer 'shamed yerself, yer great, overgrown? Fie! — for shame! Yer ought to be rediclcish!

Ton. Hallo! here's Zeb. What's the matter now? (*Enter* ZEB, R., *shaking his head and fighting imaginary foes outside.*) Where have you been? and what is the matter?

Zeb. Yes, well, I guess — Who-o-o-'s a nigger? Who — who's a nigger? Dar ain't no niggers now: didn't de prancepation krocklemation make 'em white folks, hey?

Ton. Here, what's the matter?

Zeb. Yes, well, I guess — a parcel of ignumramuses a-yellin' and a-shoutin' as cf dey nebber seed a tanned man afore. What does de Declamation of Indempendence say, — hey?

Ton. No matter what it says. You just take off your jacket and go to work, or you'll find out what a tanned man is. (ZEB *takes off his jacket,* R.)

Mike. Faith, Zeb, it's plaguing uv yez the b'ys have been.

Zeb. Yes, well I guess — Who's a nigger? what does the Constitution say, — hey?

Ton. Look here, Zeb! if you open your mouth again, it won't be healthy for your constitution.

Zeb. Yes, well, I guess! —

Ton. Shut up quick, and hone those razors! (ZEB *goes to table,* R.) We've had just enough of your talk. (*Enter* CRUSTY, R.)

Crusty. Oh! you're here, are you? Pretty time this is to get your place open, — ain't it? You forget it's the early bird that catches the worm.

Zeb. Worms? worms? Going a-fishing, Massa Crusty.

Ton. You Zeb! —

Zeb. By golly, I know where 'em are! — flounders as big as a slab; and eels, golly, — what whoppers!

Ton. Shut up, and mind your business! Yes, Mr. Crusty; first chance for you this morning.

Crusty. Yes, I should think so! I tell you what, Tonsor, you don't go to work right to make a fortune. Do as I did, — early to bed, and early up in the morning. You live too fast: you should sober down. Why don't you get married?

Ton. Ah, Mr. Crusty, that's the very thing I would like to do. A nice little wife, a nice home, every thing comfortable, — ah, sir! a man must be happy.

Crusty. Of course he must, and make money too. Why don't you try it? There's plenty of girls about here anxious to get a husband.

Ton. I know that, sir; but I've already made my choice.

Crusty. Oh! you have? Then why don't you get married, have a little comfort, and not poke along in this way, with no company but a thick-headed Irishman and a ball of blacking?

Mike. Faith, it's mighty complimentary is the ould gint, onyhow.

Zeb. Yes, well I guess! Ball of blacking, — blacking! What does the Declamation —

Ton. Shut up, Zeb!

Crusty. Say, Tonsor, why don't you get married?

Ton. Well, sir, you see, sir —

Crusty. Oh, bother! why don't you speak out?

Mike. Faith, Mr. Crusty, I'll be afther telling uv yez: it's mighty bashful is the masther. Ye say, sir, it's all along uv the young lady's father.

Crusty. Well, what of him?

Mike. Ye say, sir, he's wealthy and concaited, and manes the daughter shall niver marry anybody but a rich man.

Crusty. Not when such a likely young man as Tonsor offers? The mean old scamp!

Mike. That's thrue for yez, sir. He won't let her go wid a young man, or have a young man come uv court-in' her.

Crusty. The miserable old scoundrel!

Mike. And swears by all that's blue that he'll cut her off widout a shilling if she marries widout his consent.

Crusty. The miserly old vagabond! Look here, Tonsor, you must marry this girl directly.

Ton. Marry her!

Crusty. Marry her? — yes! Confound you! don't you want to?

Ton. But her father —

Crusty. Who cares for him? The mean old scamp! I'd like to play him a trick, and I will too. Here, you just take my chaise, — it's at the door, — get the young lady, go down to Hobson, get a license, and then be off to Parson Sanborn, and get married at once.

Ton. But, Mr. Crusty, her father will not consent to this.

Crusty. Confound her father! Who cares for him or his consent? I give mine, and that is enough. I'm the richest man in the place; and, if anybody complains, let 'em sue me for damages. I won't have such a confounded mean old cuss —

Ton. Take care, Mr. Crusty!

Crusty. — tomer in town!

Ton. You will back me in this?

Crusty. Back you? — of course I will! Do you suppose I'll stand by and see youth and honesty and worth given the go-by, by an old, mean —

Ton. Don't, Mr. Crusty, — don't call him names.

Crusty. Here, I'll give you a note to Parson Sanborn, and another for old Hobson. They'll help you along. I'll tell the parson to tie the knot strong. (*Goes to table.* R.) A mean, contemptible scamp!

Zeb. By golly, the old man's crazy sure for sartain! See him eyes roll!

Ton. Mike, I've a great mind to take the old man at his word.

Mike. If yer don't, yer a goose. He gives his consent, and ye'll have it in writin', too. Go it, honey!

Crusty. There you are: there's a note for the parson, and another for old Hobson. Give my regards to the lady, and tell her she's a goose if she misses such a chance of getting a husband.

Ton. Thank you, Mr. Crusty. I'll be off at once. Mike, you look after the shop. Don't let old Crusty out of here for half an hour, mind.

Crusty. Come, come! I want that horse and chaise in half an hour.

Ton. All right, sir. I'll be back before then. Mike, give the old gentleman a shave. Good-by! I'm off. (*Exit,* R.)

Mike. Good luck to yez! Here's an old shoe for luck. (*Throws a shoe off,* R., *which hits* ZEB *in head.*)

Zeb. Stop, yer fool — will yer? By golly, you almos' broke my jaw!

Mike. Faith, if I had, 'twould been a savin' for the shop.

Crusty. The young man's off. Good joke on the girl's father! Well, it won't cost me any thing; so I can afford to give my consent. (*Takes off handkerchief and dicky.*) Now, my man, I'll trouble you for a shave.

Mike. A shave! (*Aside.*) Oh, murther! how could I go to work to shave this ould rhinoceros?

Crusty. Come, be lively! I want to get out of this at once. I'm wanted at the house.

Mike. Oh, murther and Irish! at the house is it? (*Aside.*) Faith, that 'll niver do. (*Aloud.*) Here, sit down here, sir.

Crusty. (*Sits in chair,* R. C.) A close shave, mind!

Mike. A close shave is it? (*Aside.*) By the blissed St. Patrick, what's that? (*Enter* SIMPER, R.)

Simper. Now, weally,' tis disgustingly vulgaw, — it is

weally,—the ideah of a wefined gentleman being compelled to cutaw such a howid place, to have his chin
shaved, and his whiskaws twimmed : it is weally!

Mike. Your turn next, sir : take a seat.

Simper. My turn next? Do you weally mean to say
that I must wait? Aw!

Mike. Faith, honey, you must : there's niver a wuu
to shave you at all, at all!

Simper. But I can't wait,—I can't weally. I have
a pwessing engagement. A dear, delightful cweecher is
fondly waiting my coming,—she is weally.

Crusty. (*Aside.*) Then all I've got to say, she's got
a job. Here, you slow coach! am I never to have a
shave?

Mike. In a minit, sir : the wather's could. (*Puts
wrappers, towel, &c., round him.*)

Simper. Yes, weally, you must attend to me. The
dear cweecher will die : I know she will.

Crusty. Then let her die, or shave yourself!

Mike. Faith, sir, I can't help it. Oh, murther! that's
Zeb. It's high time he had his hand in. Here, Zeb!
shave that giutleman.

Zeb. What dat you say, hay?

Mike. Oh, bother! Shave that giutleman.

Zeb. Shabe him,—shabe him? me shabe him? By
golly! in coose,—in coose! (*To* SIMPER.) Dar's de
cheer. Hist yerself,—hist yerself!

Simper. Do what?

Zeb. Hist yerself, honey! Discompose yerself iu
dat are cheer.

Simper. Now, weally, the ideah of placing myself iu

the hands of such a howible cweecher! It's too bad, —
it is weally. (*Sits in chair, &c.* ZEB *puts wrapper and
towel about him.*)

Simper. Now, Mr. Bawbaw.

Zeb. Mr. Which?

Simper. Use despatch.

Zeb. Yes, well, I guess not; we use razors hea, we
do.

Crusty. Come, come, hurry up.

Mike. Yes, sir, intirely, sir. (*Lathers him.* ZEB *lathers*
SIMPER, *putting it plentifully in his mouth.*)

Simper. Ph — ph — ph — ! deuse take you; do you
want to choke me with your nasty soap?

Zeb. Yes, well, I guess not. It's jest as wholesome as
flap-jacks and sirup. (*To* MIKE.) I've got him lathered:
what will I do with him now?

Mike. Do, you spalpeen? — do wid him as I do wid
de *other* chap. (*Takes the razor.*) Now for my first
attimpt at shaving. Blessed St. Patrick, befrind me, or
I be afthir cuttin' his wizen.

Zeb. (*Goes to table, taking razor.*) I'm to do as Mike
does: golly, I kin do dat jist. (*During the next speeches
he runs between the two chairs, watching* MIKE, *and shaving* SIMPER.)

Simper. Now, bawbaw, do your neatest; for, in a
few minutes, I shall be at the feet of a divine cweecher.

Zeb. Screecher! does she play on de banjo too.

Simper. Be careful now, don't destwoy the symmetwy
of my whiskaws.

Zeb. (*aside*). Sim — sim — sim — what am dat?
By golly, Mike's taking de whiskers off dat chap of
his'en.

Simper. I say, bawbaw: in a few minutes I shall thwow myself at the feet of this divine cweecher; and I shall say —

Crusty. Confound you, stupid, you've cut me —

Mike. Oh, murder! it was the razor. Bedad, I wish I was well out of this.

Simper. Oh! — murder! — murder! you've cut me hawwibly!

Zeb. By golly, so I has. (*Aside.*) Must do jes as Mike does.

Simper. Be careful, bawbaw: don't spoil my complexion; for it would be hawwible to meet my chawmew, the divine Kate Cwusty, with a howwid cut.

Crusty. Kate! this must be Simper. (CRUSTY *and* SIMPER *having their heads back in the chairs are supposed not to see each other.*)

Simper. Yes, bawbaw, the rich Miss Kate Cwusty. Her fathaw's immensely wich, — a gay old boy, who likes to save his money; but we'll teach him better when we are mawwied.

Crusty. (*Aside.*) Will you? confound you! we'll see about that.

Simper. Bawbaw, be a little more gentle, if you please; handle my ambwosials very carefully.

Zeb. Ambrose who? Ambrose! by golly, I used to know an Ambrose down Souf, — a molasses-darkey, about your complex —

Simper. Why, you, bawbaw, do you mean to compare me to a negwo?

Zeb. Molasses-color, molasses-color! dat's all.

Simper. Why, you infuwual nigg —

Zeb. Hey! what's dat you call? Hey! what's dat, what den's the Constitution say. Hey! (*flourishing razor.*)

Simper. Good gwacious! put down that wazor!

Zeb. What did the 'mancipation krocklamation do, hey? (*Flourishing razor.*)

Simper. Dear me! will you put down that wazor?

Zeb. Nigah! by golly, if you ain't dark complexed yourself I'd — I'd —

Simper. Help! murdew! put down that wazor!

Mike. Faith, Zeb, if yer not quiet, out yer go.

Zeb. Ob course, ob course! what's the dec —

Mike. Oh! whist wid yer blarney, and shave the man.

Crusty. Come, come, hurry up: will you never get through?

Mike. In a minute: aisy, aisy, sir! (*Enter* HEAVY-FACE.)

Heavy. Oh, yes! of course: all full, just as I expected! That's the way the world over: there's nothing but disappointment; every thing goes against me.

Mike. Your turn next, sir.

Heavy. Now, I suppose you call that consolation. I tell you the world is all going wrong; there's nothing but misery and deceit in it. (*Takes a chair, and seats himself between the two barber's chairs.*) A man's got no real friends in this world: your riches are deceitful, your dearest friend may be your foe. Now, I suppose you two chaps feel perfectly comfortable in those chairs, with a pair of grinning fiends standing over you with razors, ready at the slightest provocation to plunge them in your throats.

Simper. Oh, hawaws!

Crusty. What do you mean? } *Together rising up.*

Mike. (*Pushing back* Crusty.) Aisy, now, honey: it's all right; don't be timorous.

Zeb. (*Pushing back* Simper.) It's all right, all right! don' be timbertoed.

Heavy. Oh, yes! of course they say it's all right, and you believe them; but I tell you it's all wrong: wickedness and deceit are hid beneath the most smiling faces. I've heard horrible stories of barbers: they have been known to murder their customers in their chairs.

Crusty. } *Starting up.* { Goodness, gracious!
Simper. } { Oh, hawwible!

Mike. Now, do be aisy: I'll finish you directly.

Crusty. No, you won't! I object to being finished by you. Put down that razor: I've had quite enough. You've been long enough on my face to plough an acre of land.

Mike. (*Aside.*) Faith! it's about as tough a job, — but I haven't finished.

Crusty. Well, then, you shan't; wipe my face! quick! quick, do you hear? (Mike *wipes face.*)

Simper. Bawbaw, I've had quite enough: wipe my face, and give me a mirraw. (Zeb *wipes face.*)

Zeb. All right, massa! all right!

Heavy. Quite enough! I should think you had! Men generally do get enough in this world of misery! nothing but misery! We're all going to the bad. There's that barber, Tonsor, instead of attending to his customers, he is off on a spree. I met him with a young woman, and I'll bet he's off to get married. He's bound for perdition.

Crusty. Good, good, good!

Heavy. Good! suppose he's run off with somebody's daughter!

Crusty. I know he has!

Heavy. You know he has? You are a pretty man, — you are! perhaps you aided and abetted him. How should you like it if it was your daughter, instead of old Crusty's?

Crusty. (*Starting up.*) My daughter?

Simper. Old Cwusty's daughtaw?

(*They both start up, and speak together.* CRUSTY *has one side of face shaved clean of whiskers, the other untouched.* SIMPER *has one of his whiskers and half of his mustache gone; they sit, and look at each other.* HEAVYFACE *between,* ZEB, L., *and* MIKE, R.)

Heavy. Well, you're a pair of beauties, — you are!

Simper. Old Cwusty here — as I'm alive! it's all up with me. (ZEB *hands him mirror.*)

Crusty. My daughter! I see it all! What a confounded fool I've been! gone and helped that Tonsor to run off with my daughter. It's horrible! I shall be the laughing-stock of the whole village!

Simper. (*Looking in mirror.*) Good gwacious! horwible! what do I see! my whiskaws and my beautiful mustache totally wuined! totally wuined!

Crusty. After all the money I have spent for her education!

Simper. Good gwacious! after all the hair-oil I've poured ovaw them!

Crusty. The masters I've given her!

Simper. The care I've bestowed upon them!

Crusty. Every accomplishment has been given her!

Simper. They've been twimmed and curled day aftew day!

Crusty. And to lose her thus! It's too bad!

Simper. And to be shorn and mangled thus! It's hawwible!

Crusty. (*Sees his face in the glass.*) What's this? my whiskers gone! O you idiot! you infernal scoundrel, what have you done?

Mike. Faith, it's the bist I could do: it's mighty little I'm acquainted round here.

Crusty. I'll teach you to mangle me in that way, you scoundrel! (*Runs after MIKE, who gets under table.* L.)

Mike. Aisy, Mr. Crusty: yer wanted a close shave; and, 'pon my word, I'd a 'gin it to yer if you'd waited!

Zeb. By golly! Mike's under de table. Well, I guess I better look out for squalls. (*Gets under table,* R.)

Simper. Where's that horrid bawbaw? (*Sees ZEB under table,* R.) The scoundwel! you black imp! —

Zeb. Hold yer hush! hold you hush! what dous the Declamation —

Crusty. Come out of that, or I break the table about your head.

Mike. If you plaze, Mr. Crusty, I'd rather stop here. (*Enter TOSSOR,* L.)

Crusty. Oh! you're back, — are you? Now, you villain, what do you mean by running off with my daughter?

Ton. I beg your pardon, sir; but I couldn't help it: I was tempted.

Crusty. Tempted by who?

Ton. The writer of this note (*reads*). " Dear Parson, Marry this couple quickly, and marry them strong. The young man is worthy of any young lady in the place. The father of the lady, an ugly old scamp, objects ; but I'll give my consent and will pay all damages. Yours, Jotham Crusty." These were my instructions, which I have carefully obeyed. I've brought back your chaise ; and you'll find my wife in it ready to thank her dear father for his thoughtful attention in giving her the husband of her choice.

Heavy. (*Who has taken barber's chair vacated by* CRUSTY.) Crusty, you are slightly done.

Crusty. Oh, yes ! this is nuts for you, you sour old hypochondriac. You think you are going to crow over me ; but you shan't. I've lost a daughter, but I've found a son. Here, Tonsor, here's my hand : the old man's sold, and must own up. Sell out this business, shut up shop, and come home.

Ton. Thank you ! I'll sell at once. Here's Mike : he shall have it.

Crusty. He ! why, look at my face !

Ton. We'll set him up in business with Zeb.

Simper. That horrid bawbaw ! look at my ambwosials.

Mike. Faix ! I go into business wid dat black son of Africa ?

Zeb. Hold yer hush ! hold yer hush ! dare's no brack, now. What doz the Declamation of Indecempeudence say ?

Ton. No matter what it says : you shall have the business. So, after thanking all here for their kind attention to my business while away, I will retire, as there is only one thing I require, — their kind plaudits.

Crusty. Hold on, Tonsor: there's something else. Here's Simper: he's lost a wife and half his whiskers; I've lost a daughter and half mine; so I'll take the chair.

Heavy. Hold on! hold on! it's my turn next!

Crusty. Why, you've just been railing at barbers and razors and the wickedness of the world: will you put yourself in their hands?

Heavy. To be sure I will. We're all going to the bad. I'm reconciled, and they can't hurt me.

Crusty. Well, have your turn; and, after you get through, I'll see if I can't have what I came here for.

Ton. What was that, father-in-law?

Crusty. A clean shave.

DISPOSITION OF CHARACTERS.

R., ZEB, SIMPER, CRUSTY, TONSOR, HEAVY, MIKE, L.

CAPULETTA;

OR,

ROMEO AND JULIET RESTORED.

AN OPERATIC BURLESQUE.

CHARACTERS.

CAPULET, a Gentleman of Verona.

ROMEO, } Gay Lords of Verona.
MERCUTIO, }

JULIET, Capulet's Fair Daughter.

Costumes to suit the taste of the performers.

SCENE 1. *Garden in front of* CAPULET'S *house. Door,*
C. *Balcony (the balcony is a shed with poles and lines
filled with clothes drying),* R. C. *Set bushes or trees,*
L. C. *Enter* CAPULET, C., *in dressing-gown, carrying a
lantern.*

Cap. Now is the winter of my discontent
Made glorious summer by this dark night sent,
And all the troubles gathering o'er my house
In inky darkness I may bid *varmouse.*
Now on my brows my night-cap sets at ease ;
My bruised arms no more my *fire*-arms seize ;
No stern alarms to wake me from a nap,

79

To spring wild rattles, and revolvers snap;
Stern visaged war — Why, what am I about?
I did not come out, Richard III. to spout.
I am the father of a daughter dear, —
Dear! yes, she costs a thousand pounds a year.
They call her fair, they praise her auburn tresses,
And go in raptures o'er her handsome dresses.
Her hats outdo Verona's richest lasses —
So small they can't be seen without opera glasses.
She sports in silks and satins of the best
That can be made by Madam Demorest.
Verona's gallants seek to flirt and flout
With this dear *gal*, when'er her *aunt* is out.
They'd like to catch her with a wedding-ring;
And so they come at night to spout and sing.
But I won't have it: under lock and key,
This floating *belle* shall *ring* for none but me.
I am her father; and my lawyer knows,
Paying for her dresses, I can keep her *close*.
All's safe to-night, and so I'll tramp to bed —

                    (*Moon rises.*)*

What's that? the moon is rising overhead,
And coming up in such a smashing way,
It rival's the Museum's famous Peep o'Day.
So I'll to bed, and should marauders roam,
Let them beware; for Capulet's at home.   [*Exit*, C.

---

* Half a cheese box covered with cotton cloth, on which is painted a
very jolly face, with the letters S. T. 1860 X. upon it, illuminated by
a candle placed behind, and drawn up by a pully and string, is the
original moon prepared for this piece.

JULIET *appears on balcony with a jar of pickled limes.*

Song, "Juliet." Air, "No one to Love."

No one to woo, none to address
A tender young maid in the greatest distress.
Hard is my lot; beaux I have none;
On this piazza I'm sitting alone.
No gentle man, no tender lad,
Comes here to woo: 'tis really too bad.
No one to woo, none to address
A tender young maid in the greatest distress.
Hard is my lot, beaux I have none;
On this piazza I'm sitting alone.

Jul. Ah, me! Ah, me! Ah, me! Oh, my!
I cannot sleep, nor tell the reason why.
'Tis now the very *witching* hour of night,
Which is to say, it would be if 'twas light.
Why, there's the moon, quite dear to me, I'm sure:
I never felt she was so *near* before.
O beauteous queen! descend from thy high sphere,
And taste a pickled lime with me, my dear.
I'll tell thee lots of scandal and of fashion,
And whisper in thine ear my tale of passion;
For I'm in love; in love with a dear feller
I met one night while seeing Cinderella.
Oh, such a dear! dear me, I'm in a flutter.
He's young and rich, and sweet as fresh June butter:
His name is Romeo; he's the idol of the town;
I'll sing his praise. Prythee, dear, come down.

ROMEO (*outside*), L. *sings.*

We won't go home till morning,
We won't go home till morning,

6

We won't go home till morning,
Till Juliet doth appear.

Enter ROMEO *and* MERCUTIO, L.

Mer. Shut up, old chap, this strain will never do:
'Twill get us both locked up in Station Two.

Rom. Mercut*h*, old chap, I'll own I'm rather airy,
And feel as limber as a Black-Crook fairy.
'S all right, old fel', I'm deuced glad you're here:
Fact is, I hardly know which way to steer.

Mer. Oh, ho! I see King Lager's been with you,
And on his beer you're settled fast and true.
He is the Dutchman's idol, and he puffs
In shape as monstrous as Jack Falstaff's stuffs.
His throne's a monstrous cask of his own brew,
With courtiers drawing him by two and two.
His crown Dutch cheese, his sceptre's a Bologna.
His subjects — well, they're *mustered* in Verona.
His drink is Bock, his food is sour krout,
Pretzels his lunch, his night-cap, gin, without.
And in this guise he keeps a jolly pace,
Shaking his sides, a grin upon his face.
Great in our land as is our famous eagle,
He sings in opera, and he fights mit Sigel.

Rom. Steady, my boy, your really getting dry.
My stars! old fellow, what's that in the sky?

Mer. The moon, of course —

Rom. But I see two, I'll swear.

Mer. Then you see double.

Rom. There's the other there (*points to Juliet*).

Mer. Another? Bless me! 'tis too brilliant far.
Call that a moon? It is a glorious star.

Rom. Call that a star? by what arrangement, pray?

Mer. Why, don't you know? The star of our new play.

Rom. You speak in *meteor*-phor, now pray have done. What is't o'clock?

Mer.   Four-quarters after one.

Song, " Juliet.*" Air, "* Five o'clock in the Morning.*"*

> My father is snugly in his bed,
> Taking his morning nap;
> My aunt has stuffed her waterfall
> Under her snow-white cap;
> The crickets are singing merrily;
> While I, all danger scorning,
> Sit quietly eating pickled limes,
> At two o'clock in the morning.
>
> Then what care I for costly gems,
> Or silks and satins fine?
> I know full well when daylight comes
> That those will all be mine.
> Alone on my father's balcony,
> Far, far, from fashion's warning,
> I'm happier far with my pickled limes,
> At two o'clock in the morning.

Rom. Mercutio, it's really getting late:
You know that your mamma for you will wait;
You'd better go.

Mer. Oh, no! I thank you, chum!
My ma will look for me when I'm to *hum.*
I'll stay a while.

Rom. Mercutio, listen now,
'Tis not the time of night to pick a row.

There's an old proverb, really 'tis well done,
That two is company, and three is none.
Now, pray consider —
 Mer.   You are right, 'tis so:
As two is company, you'd better go.
 Rom. Oh, pshaw! Mercutio have no more such fun.
 Mer. He's scared at jests who never made a pun.
 Rom. But, soft! what light in yonder window lies?
It is the (*y*)east.
 Mer.   There's something on the rise.
 Rom. It is the east, and Juliet is the sun —
Arise! fair sun.
 Mer.   Oh, murder! do have done;
Of grammar you are making fearful slaughter.
What gender makes a son of Capulet's daughter?
 Rom. Arise, fair sun, and kill the envious moon —
 Mer. You are getting to the killing part too soon.
 Rom. Who is already sick and pale with grief—
 Mer. Then give it a dose of Radway's Ready Relief.
 Rom. She speaks, yet she says nothing —
 Mer.   Nary word;
Upon my life, such silence ne'er was heard.
 Rom. See how she leans her cheek upon her hand!
 Mer. Because she's tired: can't you understand?
 Rom. Oh! would I were some gloves upon thy —
 Mer.   *Pause!*
Or else old Capulet 'll have us in his claws.
 Rom. That I might print a kiss upon that cheek!
 Mer. Hold on a moment ere you further speak:
You're getting cheeky with you're warm address.
If you must print, go try the printing-press.

Jul. Ah, me! ah, me! ah, me! oh, my!

Rom.   She speaks.

Mer. She's got a meteor in her eye,

Rom. Oh, speak again, bright angel!

Mer.   So I will:
You'll catch the rheumatism by standing still.

Rom. Shut up; she speaks.

Jul.   O Romeo! Romeo, say
Wherefore, oh, wherefore art thou Romeo, pray?

Rom. Well, really, madam, that's a poser, rather:
I really think you'd better ask my father.

Song, " Romeo."   Air, " Pat Molloy."

At fourteen years of age I was a tall and strapping lad:
My father had the oil-fever, and had it awful bad.
" I'm hard up, Romeo," says he, " and cannot raise the tin:
" My copper stocks are getting low; I really must give in."
He put my best clothes in a bag, and put it on my back,
And, with his knotty walking-stick, gave me a parting whack.
" Get out of this, my boy," says he, " and remember, as you go,
Old Montague's your daddy, and your name is Romeo."

Jul. Deny thy father, and refuse thy name,
Call thyself Smith or Jones, 'tis all the same;
Or, if thou art inclined to give it me,
I'll pack my trunk and go along with thee.

Rom. Shall I hear more, or had I better —

Mer.   Wait,
Give her a chance, she'll pop the question straight.

Jul. What's in a name?

Mer.   Why, often there's a letter.

Jul. Pickles by any other name taste all the better,
And so would Romeo—

Mer.   Oh, dear! here's a row:
She's got you in a precious pickle now.

Jul.   Romeo, doff thy name now, that's a dear;
For Mrs. Montague would sound so queer:
I do not like it; for thy name mine take;
A better bargain you did never make.

Rom.   I'll take thee at thy word: I'll change my
        nature,
And get my name changed by the legislature.

Mer.   Not in *our* General Court can you, I'll swear:
They change not names, but only color, there.

Jul.   What lads art thou beneath my window met?

Mer.   Lads! With a ladder we'd be nearer yet.

Rom.   I know not how, dear saint, to tell you that,
Because my name is written in my hat,
And you don't like it. I would rub it out,
If there was any rubber here about.

Jul.   Whist! how came you here, and why?
My father's fence is very sharp and high,
And should he find you here —

Mer.   The ugly cuss
Would straight salute us with a blunderbuss.

Rom.   With love's light wings did I the fence o'er-
        leap
On sounding pinions —

Mer.   Ain't you getting steep?

Jul.   I cannot hear you; pray come nearer, love.

Rom.   Oh! that I had wings to mount above.

Mer.   Wings? Pshaw! a stouter platform you will
        need
If that fond purpose in your eye I read.

(Rolls in barrel of flour from L. *; places it beneath balcony,*
and assists ROMEO *to mount it.)*

Here is the article, and just the size,
Placed in your east, 'twill help you to *arise.*
Now mount, my hero, spread your softest talk,
And, while you're busy, I'll go take a walk.
Be careful of your feet, or, by the powers,
Our next tableau'll be " love among the *flours.*" *Exit,* L.

   Jul. By whose direction found you out this spot?

   Rom. 'Tis put down in the Directory, is it not?

   Jul. If you are found here, you'll be murdered
    straight,

So pray begone —

   Rom.   I think I'd rather wait.

Fear not for me my jewel, on my word,
Your eyes cut deeper than the sharpest sword.
Oh! beauteous Juliet, fairest of the fair,
Within my heart a roaring flame I bear.
I'm over ears in love within this hour. *(Stumbles on*
   barrel.)

   Jul. Be careful, you'll be over ears in flour.

   Rom. If thou wouldst have me paint the home

To which I'd bear thee when our nuptials come,
Listen. In a deep vale where huckleberries grow,
And modest sun-flowers blossom in a row,
Where blooming cabbage rears its lofty head,
And fragrant onion spreads its lowly bed,
A yellow cottage, with a chimney tall,
Lifts to eternal summer its shingled wall.
From out a bower made musical with frogs,
Who chant their wild lays in the neighboring bogs,

At noon we'd sit beneath the arching vine,
And gather grapes to make our winter wine;
And when night came we'd guess what star
Should next attract us to the op — era;
And then —

    Jul.   Oh, pshaw! give o'er,
Your yellow-covered cottage is a bore;
For cabbages and onions find new names:
I mean to have rooms at the new St. James.
And if you love me it is surely fair —

    Rom.   Lady, by yonder blessed moon I swear —

    Jul.   Oh! swear not by the moon.

    Rom.   Well, then, I won't.
What shall I swear by?

    Jul.   Swear not at all, my dear.

    Rom.   What! not a swear? Oh, this ain't love, 'tis
clear!

    Cap. (*outside*).   Ho, Juliet! Juliet, are you there?
I cannot find my nightcap anywhere.

    Rom.   Who's that?

    Jul.   My father. Oh, the deuse's to pay!

    Rom.   I wish the old man was *farther* any way.

    Cap. (*outside*).   Juliet!

    Jul.   Coming, coming soon.

    Rom.   I wish old Capulet was the man in the moon.

    Jul.   Good night, dear Romy; tie your ears up tight.

    Rom.   And wilt thou leave me so unsatisfied? 'taint
right.

    Jul.   What satisfaction canst thou have, my blade?

    Rom.   Why, that of giving you a serenade.

    ("*Mocking Bird,*" *Whistling serenade, by* ROMEO.)

Song, " Juliet."   Air, " Listen to the Mocking Bird."

My father now has spoken, has spoken, has spoken,
My father now has spoken,
And the whistling lad is ringing in my ear.
I feel like one heart-broken, heart-broken, heart-broken,
I feel like one heart-broken,
For my Romey can no longer linger here.
Listen to the whistling lad,
Listen to the whistling lad,
The whistling lad who pipes his merry lay.
Listen to the whistling lad,
Listen to the whistling lad,
Who whistles where the yellow moonbeams play.

I'm dreaming now of Romey, of Romey, of Romey,
I'm dreaming now of Romey,
And the tender, tender words he spake to me.
To the opera he shall beau me, shall beau me, shall beau me,
To the opera he shall beau me,
And I the happiest maid in town will be.
      Listen to the whistling lad, &c.

Cap. (without).   Juliet, I say, ho! Juliet, do you
hear?

Jul.   Coming, papa ; and now good-night, my dear.
Exit.

Rom.   Good-night, good-night ; parting were such
sweet sorrow,
I'll come again and try it on to-morrow.   *Exit*, L.

Enter MERCUTIO, L.

Mer.   Is this a bottle which I see before me?
The nozzle towards my mouth.   Come, let me pour
thee.
I have thee not ; and yet I'll swear I saw

Thee just as plain as this which now I draw.   (*Draws
  bottle from his pocket.*)

Song, " *Mercutio.*"   Air, " *Rootle tum, tootle tum ta.*"

> Mercutio, you have been told,
> Was a gay boy of old :
> One Shakspeare his story has told
> In a humorous sort of a way.
> He was fond of a nice little game, —
> Any game you can name,
> Would see you, and go it again.
> Rootle tum, tootle tum tay.
> For frolic or fighting quite ready,
> You could hardly, I think, call him steady.
> Rootle tum, tootle tum, tootle tum, tootle tum,
> Tootle tum, tootle tum tay.
>
> Of his virtues we oft have been told
> By this wise bard of old ;
> But his vices he didn't unfold,
> But just kept them out of the way.
> A patron he of the race-horse,
> And the turf, — what is worse,
> Was given to betting, of course.
> Rootle tum, tootle tum tay ;
> So a moral to put if you're willin ,
> I'll make him a sort of a villain.
> Rootle tum, tootle tum, &c.

Ha ! ha ! ha ! this Romeo, silly looney,
Has, on old Capulet's daughter, got quite spooney ;
And now to wed her he is nothing loth.
Ha ! ha ! he'll find my fingers in the broth.
He's ordered cards for Wednesday — Park-st. Church :
Mayhap his bride will leave him in the lurch ;
I'll marry her myself, or rot in prison.

Why should'nt she be mine as well as his'n?
I do remember an apothecary, or rather orter,
Who, somewhere hereabouts, sells soda-water.
I'll hie to him, and high this bottle fill,
With laughing gas. Ha! ha! my heart be still.
We'll block this little game, that's very plain;
Conscience, avaunt! Mercut*h*'s himself again.

Turns and meets CAPULET, *who has entered from door,* C.,
with revolver.

Cap. So, so, my early bird you've caught a worm;
Keep still, you stupid, don't begin to squirm;
Explain this early visit if you can.
  Mer. " Pity the sorrows of a poor old man."
  Cap. Oh! that won't do, shut up, you silly elf:
I do the old man's business here myself.
Your business here? My name is Cap —
  Mer.   —You let
Me off, and I won't come again, you bet.
I came to look at yon revolving moon.
  Cap. You'll get a taste of my revolver soon.
  Mer. You have a daughter —
  Cap.   What is that to you?
  Mer. Nothing, but she is very fair to view:
Her name is Juliet —
  Cap.   I knew that before.
  Mer. You did? Well, you're a smart old man, I'm
    sure.
A pretty name; what is her dowry, pray?
  Cap. A hundred thousand on her wedding-day.
  Mer. The noble Plaster Paris seeks her hand?

Cap.　　Yes, and to marry him is my command.

Mer.　　O wild old man! I came to ope your eyes,
To save you from a fearful sacrifice.

Cap.　　How, now? speak out! you rouse my wildest
　　fears!

Mer.　　Hush, hush, old man! they say the walls have
　　ears.
To save you fifty thousand dollars, I agree,
If for one moment you will list to me.
Paris to take her gets a hundred thousand plum:
I'll marry her for just one-half the sum.　　　*Exit*, L.

Cap.　　Get out, you scamp! I am completely sold:
I'll back to bed, for it is bitter cold,
And I've been bit already; but to-morrow
I'll give that girl a taste of early sorrow;
Pack up her crinoline, and off she'll go
To Di——o Lewis, or Professor Blot.　　　*Exit*, R.

　　　　　　Enter JULIET *from house.*

Jul.　　O Romeo, Romeo! I forgot to say —
Why, he is gone — oh! for the trumpet's bray,
The watchman's rattle, or the fire-alarm,
To lure him back —

Enter MERCUTIO, L. (*wrapped in a domino*), *eating a
　　　　　　　sandwich.*

Mer.　　　　　　It's really getting warm.
How tender sweet taste sandwiched tongues by night
To hungry stomachs! — now I feel all right.

Jul.　　Romeo —

Mer.　　　　　　　　　　My sweet.

Jul. When shall we wedded be?

Mer. What's that? when wedded? Dear me, let me see.

Hush! love, a fearful tale I have to tell,

That but a moment since on me befell.

Your father swore point blank that you should marry

Only that spooney, the young Plaster Paris.

Jul. Never! I'll be an old maid first.

Mer.   Now, don't you fret:

I'll fix his flint; we may be happy yet.

Just take this bottle, wrap your shawl around,

And hie you off to Capulet's burying-ground.

Jul. What is it, ketchup or Peruvian dye?

Mer. No matter, dear: just ketch it up and fly.

When you get there, imbibe a goodly dose,

Then near the tomb of Capulet hide you close.

Just read the label, sweet, before 'tis taken:

My precious jewel, it must be well shaken.

Hush! I hear a voice, a footstep too, beware!

Remember, burying-ground and gas, you'll find me there.

Duet, " Mercutio and Juliet."   Air, " We Merry-hearted Marched Away."   (Grand Duchess.)

Jul.   Well, well, my love, I'll start away,
           Your strange request to quick obey;
           Equip myself in hat and shawl,
           And meet you 'neath the church-yard wall.

Mer.   She don't suspect — it is all right;
           I'll be a happy dog to-night;
           Rob Romeo of his darling spouse,
           And 'neath the church-yard wall carouse.

" *I Love the Military.*"

Both Oh, $\left.\begin{array}{l}\text{I'll}\\\text{you'll}\end{array}\right\}$ run for $\left.\begin{array}{l}\text{my}\\\text{your}\end{array}\right\}$ millinery,

Run for $\left.\begin{array}{l}\text{my}\\\text{your}\end{array}\right\}$ millinery, run for $\left.\begin{array}{l}\text{my}\\\text{your}\end{array}\right\}$ millinery ;

Oh, yes, $\left.\begin{array}{l}\text{I'll}\\\text{you'll}\end{array}\right\}$ quickly run and get $\left.\begin{array}{l}\text{my}\\\text{your}\end{array}\right\}$ shawl.

(*Repeat, and Dance off*, R.)

Enter ROMEO, L.

Rom. My sweet, my dove.

Enter JULIET, R.

Jul. What, back again so soon?
Why, you're as wayward as the silver moon.
Rom. My dear, I came to fix our wedding-day.

CAPULET *appears at door*, C., *with pitch-fork.*

Cap. I'll fix you !
Rom. Murder !
Jul. Don't, father, pray.
Rom. Oh, dear !
Jul. Oh, my !
Cap. Well, sirrah, how is that?
Rom. Help, help, Mercutio !
Cap. You are cutting fat.

Enter MERCUTIO, L.

Mer. Holloa, old man ! 'tis time you were in bed :
Just let me fix your night-cap on your head.

Pulls his night-cap over his eyes.

Chorus. Air, " Sabre du mon père."

Pull on your night-cap, your night-cap, your night-cap!
Pull on your night-cap, and take yourself to bed.

(Repeat.)

(Quick change.)

Scene 2. *A Wood.*

*(Should it be found necessary to drop the curtain, scene 2
and scene 3 can be run into one.)*

Enter Mercutio, L.

If I had a beau for a soldier would go,
Do you think I'd marry him? No, no, no!
And so must not Miss Juliet, that is flat,
Bestow her hand, her money, and all that,
On such a reckless, foolish, soft young man
As Romeo, who would join the Klux Klux Kahn
Because old Capulet, o'er his gin and water,
Has vowed he shall not carry off his daughter.
Such carryings-on are very bad, no doubt;
And so my little game I'll carry out.
Oh, ch!—this midnight roaming suits not me,
This influenza shall not influence me,
Ah, ch— would I were safe in bed!
There's cold without and cold within my head.
'Tis time this little maid should be along:
I'll while away the time with a ch — ch — song.

Song, " Mercutio." Air, " French Sneezing-Song."

I'm really very stiff and cold
As you can very plainly see;

This mild spring weather here, somehow,
Has raised the very deuse with me.
My eyes are getting red and weak,
My nose appears inclined to freeze;
And, when I seek to raise my voice,
I only raise a sneeze, suceze, sneeze.
    Too ral la, too ral la, &c.

O Juliet Capulet! my love,
To keep me waiting 'tis a sin :
This May-day weather will, I fear,
Put out the flame of love within.
My heart with love is burning high,
My bones with cold are like to freeze :
For you I seek to raise a sigh,
But only raise a sneeze, sneeze, sneese.
    Too ral la, too ral la, &c.

Mercutio, you're a silly goose
To choose a maid so very cruel :
This midnight prowl for you, I fear,
Will end in rheumatiz and gruel ;
And then, should Romeo cross your path,
Prepare to face another breeze :
He'd cut you down in his great wrath,
Nor give you time to sneeze, sneeze, sneeze.
    Too ral la, too ral la, &c.

SCENE 3.. CAPULET's *burying-ground. Tomb,* C., *on which is written,* " *No one allowed to pick here without permit of the proprietor.*" *Graves,* R. *and* L., *with headstones facing audience. On* R. *is painted,* " *To be occupied by* JULIET CAPULET ;" *on* L., " *To be occupied by* RO-MEO MONTAGUE.*"

Enter JULIET, L.., *with basket, bottle, and candle.*

Jul. Here is the place (*dog barks*), our plaguy *Spot,*
  I say.

You should not follow your mistress in this way.
(*Clock strikes.*) One, two, 'tis now the very time, I think,
When I was bid this sleeping draught to drink.
Oh, dear! suppose this should not work at all;
Suppose this evening Romeo should not call;
Suppose, suppose — oh! I'll leave off supposing,
For really I begin to feel like *dozing:*
And so I'll take a *dose* (*drinks*). Why, this is queer!
What new-found sherry-cobbler have we here?
Narcotic music in my head is ringing
Such blissful airs, I cannot keep from singing.

> *Song, " Juliet." Air, " O Mio Fernando."*

> Oh mio Romeo, my galliant lovericr!
> My father's house I've slipped for to meet thee;
> But oh! my ducksey, do you be tenderer
> Or else a broken-hearted maid I'll be.
> If by this cup my senses be capsized
> When I have drank this sherry-cobbler down,
> Oh! do not, dearest, do not, be surprised,
> But wake me gently, Romeo, from my nap.

Jul. To bed, to bed! it's really getting late. (*Knock.*)
What knocking's that? The watchman's at the gate.
What is undone can't be done up, 'tis said.
My hair is down, and so to bed, to bed!

Lies down on grave, blows out candle, R. *Enter* MER-
CUTIO, L.

Mer. Rest, my maid, lie still and slumber:
Now for my carriage. I've forgot the number:
That is too bad, I ne'er can find mine,
So many are ordered for just half-past nine.

7

What's to be done?   I'm getting in a muss,
I know.   I'll take her off instanter in a buss.
Halloo, halloo!   Why, here's the deuse to pay, —
Man with a light, and coming down this way!
I'll step aside and of this light keep dark.   (*Hides* R.)

Enter ROMEO, L., *dragging child's carriage, containing a
large bottle of* Mrs. WINSLOW's *Soothing Syrup.*

  Rom.   Bah!   I'm chilled through, and hungry as a
    shark.
I do remember where an oysterman did dwell
Who opened Providence Rivers passing well,
Concocted luscious stews and toothsome roasts
And "Fancys," which are oysters laid on toast.
I would that I to-night within his stall
Might seat myself, and for a good roast call;
But I'm forbid, for I to-night must stir up,
My fainting soul with Winslow's Soothing Syrup.
My Juliet, poisoned, in this churchyard lies;
And I, poor silly fellow! — I — I — cries.
I'll weep no more, but to my Juliet flee.

     Knocks down gravestone at head of JULIET.
Get out, you pale-faced slab, make way for me!

      Enter MERCUTIO, R.
  Mer.   Halloo, my gallant youth, is that the way
You with old Capulet's costly marbles play?
  Rom.   What wretch art thou that thus beseemst the
    night?
  Mer.   Why, wretch yourself! it seems to me you're
    tight.

Rom. Are you Mercutio's kinsman, Plaster Paris?
Or are you Villikins?

Mer.   Thank you, I am nary;
But I am Mercutio, who, upon my life,
Had nearly made that maid there be my wife
But for your coming. Now that you have come,
And I'm not wanted, I think I'll go home.

Rom. Stay, vile Mercutio, I see what you're about:
With this 'ere maid you tried to cut me out;
But you shall find that I can cut as well.
A game of turn him out, we'll have, my swell.
You are a sneak, so be a little bolder:
Let's see you knock that chip from off my shoulder.

(Mercutio blows chip off.)

A blow. We'll try the manly art.

Mer.   The manly art? — oh, no!
We can't do that: it's not for us, you know.
Our legislators keep it for their public play:
'Tis *More-easy* taught in Washington to-day.
Talking of cutting you out here with this lass
I call an insult; but we'll let that pass.
I'll have a pass, and with a cutlass too,

Produces a pair of cutlasses from side.

Draw, villain, draw! I'll have a bout with you, —
The old stage combat, that's the sort,
With an accompaniment on the piano-forte.   ·   ·

Combat to the tune of, " *Wood up.*" Mercutio's *stuck.*

Hold on! I'm stuck, as narrow as a church-pew,
And hardly deep enough: well, it will do.

Ask for me to-morrow, if you will ;
And, if I'm not gone, I'll be here still.
I'm *peppered* sore, and nearly *mustered* out.
Now, gentle Romeo, mind what you're about !
You have a country house, and one in town :
A plague on both your houses ! burn 'em down !
Have you a cigar?   I think I've got a match.

ROMEO *gives* MERCUTIO *a cigar, and holds up his foot, on
which* MERCUTIO *strikes a light, and then lights his
cigar.*

Thank you, you are a perfect hen to scratch.
From all the many ills of married life
I would have saved you, carried off your wife ;
But that's all over, wish you joy, I'll swear.
Good-by !   I'm going home to die — my hair.

                                        Exit, L.

   Rom.   So young to die !   Farewell, my gentle friend :
Now to my business I will straight attend.
Here lies my love so snugly covered up,
And near her sits the fatal poisoned cup.
Eyes, look your last ; but do not look too long.
If 'twon't disturb you, love, I'll sing a song.

         Song, " *Romeo.*"   *Air,* " *Captain Jinks.*"

         My Juliet at last I've found,
      .   Stretched out at full length on the ground :
            She shows no signs of coming round,
            Which causes me much trouble.
            But I've a qui:tus, you see,
                  tus you see,
                  tus you see

And Winslow's Soothing Syrup for me
Will soon end all my trouble.
It will be a story to tell the marines
That we were driven to such extremes,
And came to our end by poisonous means,
Through drinking too much of the balmy.

Rom. Come, fatal syrup, soothe my aching breast;
Come, Mrs. Winslow, come and give me rest.
Here's to my love, hip, hip, hip, hurray!

Tumbles on grave, L.

That's given me a settler any way.

Enter CAPULET, L., *ringing a bell.*

Cap. Lost, lost, lost, strayed, stolen, or run away!
A daughter, anybody seen her, pray?
Robed in a muslin dress, a tender maid,
Of all male creatures very much afraid.
I cannot find her: I am tempest tossed,
And so I toss this bell — lost, lost, lost!

Trio: Air, " Dear Father come home." JULIET, ROMEO,
and CAPULET.

Jul. Father, dear father! go home, will you, now?
  You'll get a bad cold in your head:
  I've put out the candle, and, covered up warm,
  I'm resting so nicely in bed!
Rom. You'd better clear out, old Capulet, now,
  There hardly is room here for you;
  Disturb not the rest of a poisoned young pair,
  But clear out instanter, now, do!
Jul. { Come do, now do, dear father, sweet father, go home!
Rom. { Will you, will you, old buffer, old buffer, go home?
Cap. Now, do hear the words of this pair,
  Which his fingers* repeat as they roam.

---

* The pianist or leader of the orchestra.

I'll be blessed if such nonsense I'll stand, any way,
No, looneys, I will not go home.

Jul. { Come father, dear father, go home.
Rom. { Old buffer, old buffer, go home.

Cap.   Well, here's a pretty kettle of fish, I'll swear.
Juliet Capulet, what are you doing there?

Jul.   (*Sitting up.*)   I'm poisoned, waiting here for
Romeo.

Rom.   (*Sitting up.*)   Well, here I am : I guess we'd
better go.

Song, " Romeo and Juliet." Air, " Billy Taylor."

Rom.   Now, Juliet, that we're free from poison,
               We will quickly wedded be.
               The loveliest maid man ever set his eyes on
               I'll marry in style, quite gorgeously.
               Tiddy, iddy, iddy, iddy, ol, lol, li, do,
Jul.   Tidy, iddy, iddy, iddy, ol, lol, la.
Rom.   Tiddy, iddy, iddy, iddy, ol, lol, li, do.
Tombs.   Tiddy, iddy, iddy, iddy, ol, lol, la.

Jul.   O Romeo ! though you're my deary,
               Prithee, listen unto me.
               When I go to get my wardrobe, I shall feel quite
                  scary
               If it's under lock and key.
                    Chorus. — Tiddy, iddy, &c.

Cap.   Humbug ! Do you two young ones 'spose
I'll have this billing under my very nose?
Vile Montague, begone, or you shall sweat !
I'm on my native heath, my name is Capulet.

Jul.   Give me my Romeo, or I shall die :
I'll cut him up in little stars —
    Rom.   Oh, my !

Cap.   No, no, my child, you'll cut up no such capers:
Do you want to figure in the Boston papers?
Go home and sew, and so your morals mend:
This fool I'll straight about his business send.
If you two marry — why, then, I'm a noodle,
Who dare dispute me —

Song.   Tomb opens, and MERCUTIO *appears as Yankee
Doodle.   (Allegorical dress of America.)*

Mer.   Only Yankee Doodle!
Old man, within my home across the water,
I've had my eye upon your handsome daughter,
And sighed to think that two fond lovers here
Should find a home within a tomb so drear.
And so I've opened it to have it aired:
Really, old gent, you should have it repaired.
Being on a yacht race in "The Henrietta,"
To give you a passing call, I thought I'd better.
I'm of a race that likes to see fair play:
My fair one, can I serve you any way?
  Rom.   Why, that's Mercutio!
  Mer.   Shut up, will you, now!
I've only doubled, don't you make a row.
  Rom.   But you were killed —
  Jul.   And now have come to life.
  Mer.   Some one spoke, I think —
  Rom.   It was my wife.
  Mer.   Don't puzzle yourselves, I'll straightway make
    it clear.
You know the Spiritualists hold meeting here;

You rapped me, and I went, is that not plain?
So with another *wrap*, I come again.

   Cap.   Entranced youth, you are not wanted here,
So quickly you had better disappear.
I want my daughter —

   Mer.   So does Romeo too ;
And he shall have her straight, in spite of you.

   Cap.   Come, sir, you meddle!   Mind what you're
     about!
I'm a belligerent —

   Mer.   Oh! that's played out.
It will not do all wrongs to redress :
You'll find America in any mess.
So, Romeo, take your wife, and pack your bag :
We'll give you shelter 'neath a starry flag.

   Rom.   What say you, Juliet? shall we westward go?
Speak up, my darling, do not color so.

   Jul.   I like those colors well, I do confess :   ·
Those stripes are just the style of my new dress.

   Rom.   To seek that blissful land, I think we'd orter.

   Jul.   But I'm so horrid sick upon the water!

   Mer.   Come, Capulet, your blessing I command ;
Then pack up trunks, and off for Yankee land.

   Cap.   What! end a tragedy without a death?
It's horrible : you take away my breath!

   Mer.   Then we shall have one sure, let's move along :
We'll end our tragedy with a yachting song.

  Finale, " A Yankee Ship and a Yankee Crew."

     A Yankee yacht and a Yankee crew,
     Tally, hi, ho, you know,

Can beat the world on the waters blue.
Sing high, aloft and alow.
Her sails are spread to the fairy breeze,
The spray sparkling as thrown from her prow;
Her flag is the proudest that floats o'er the seas;
Her way homeward she's steering now.

Chorus. — A Yankee ship and a Yankee crew, &c.

Curtain.

THE GREAT ELIXIR.

CHARACTERS.

WALDIMER WIGGINS (the seventh son of a seventh son).
GUNNYBAG GREENBAX, }
NERVOUS ASPEN, } Wiggins' patients.
MAJOR FINGERS (a discontented Bridegroom).
CHARLES FREEDLEY (a dissatisfied heir).
HARRY QUILLDRIVER (an author).
HERBERT EASEL (his friend).
DENNIS McGRATH (the Doctor's help).
BOB (the Doctor's boy).

COSTUMES.

Wiggins. — Eccentric gray wig, with cue, white necktie, crimson vest, dressing-gown, and slippers.

Greenbax. — Long brown coat, gray wig, broad brimmed hat.

Aspen. — Brown wig, nankeen pants and vest, dark coat, hat and cane.

Fingers. — (Very short man.) Undress uniform.

Freedley, Quilldriver, and Easel. — Modern costume.

Dennis. — Red wig, white jacket, yellow vest, dark pants.

SCENE. — *Wiggins' Office. Table,* C. *Chairs,* R. *and* L. *of table. Entrances,* R. *and* L. *Letters and bottles on table.*

Enter WIGGINS, L.

Wiggins. I am a lucky man! I should like to know how many times an hour, by the most approved rules of computation, that sentence escapes my lips; to how

108

many mirrors have I uttered those memorable words; how many sheets of paper have been devastated with that *multum in parvo* of sentences, I am a lucky man? Look at me, Waldimer Wiggins, seventh son of Waldimer Wiggins, the blacksmith, who was the seventh son of Wigglesworth Wiggins, the cooper. I, who have been knocked about the world like a shuttlecock, buffeted by everybody and everything; who never saw but one schoolhouse in all my life, and that from the outside, — here am I puzzling all the learned doctors, creating a frenzy among the apothecaries, and setting the whole town to taking medicine by the pint, quart, and even demijohn, and hauling greenbacks into my capacious pockets with an agility and velocity that would astonish the father of greenbacks. I am the lucky possessor of the greatest remedy of modern times, — a medicine that will cure anything and everything, anybody and everybody; and where there is nothing to cure, will make something, and then cure that. Men praise it, women dote on it, and children cry for it. I am the lucky possessor of this treasure, and yet I never received a diploma, or even amused myself with the graceful but rather monotonous exercise of the pestle and mortar. As I before suggested, it's all luck. I'll tell you all about it *(seats himself familiarly before the audience)*. Like Byron, that beautiful but dyspeptic poet, " I had a dream." It was one night after I had partaken of oysters. I generally indulge in a light supper before retiring. Upon this occasion it consisted of cold chicken, mince pie, pigs' feet, and, as I before remarked, oysters. I had retired to my downy couch, when the following striking tableau was presented in a vision. I beheld

the great Barnum, surrounded by greenbacks. On his
right were the Albino woman and Joyce Heath, on his
left, Tom Thumb and his Bride; while the "What is
it?" a little elevated, was crowning the great showman
with a wreath of posies. Of course my attention was
first attracted to the free exhibition of curiosities, but
after a careful examination of them, my eyes were fixed
upon the great "Supporter of the Moral Drama," by
whom I was greeted with this characteristic original
remark, "How are you, Wiggins?" to which I answered, as is customary in all polite circles, "How are
you, Barnum?" "Wiggins," said he, "do you want to
make a fortune?" to which I responded, "I do." "Then
look in 'The Daily Slungshot,' outside, first column,
top line, and obey the injunction there given." I
thanked the great man, signified to him that I thought
him an immense individual, but that he could not keep
"The Aquarial Gardens." He pronounced my remark
very of *fish* ous; and with this scaly joke, vanished. I
awoke, purchased "The Slungshot," sought the desig-
nated spot, and read this cabalistic word, "Advertise."
It was enough. I remembered a recipe an Indian
woman had given me when a child. It was for curing
corns. I resolved to make a fortune from that. Now
everybody is not afflicted with corns; so, to have a striking effect on all diseases, I call my medicine "The Great
Elixir," and warrant it to cure everything. I might
easily show you how all diseases are first taken into the
system through the medium of corns, but as it would
take some time to convince you, I will not make the
attempt. Advertising has done the business for me, and
now everybody is taking The Great Elixir and blessing

the name of Waldimer Wiggins. *(Rises takes a seat at table* R., *and opens letters, making memorandums on each as read.)* Now, here is a string of correspondents that would puzzle a regular physician, but which I, with my superior skill, can dispose of in a very few moments. *(Reads.)* Hm! an old lady has fits. *(Mem.)* Take The Elixir three times a day. *(Reads.)* An old gentleman with a bald head wants his hair to grow. *(Mem.)* Apply The Elixir externally and internally three times a day. *(Enter* DENNIS, L.) Well, Dennis, what is it?

Dennis. Faith, I don't know; there's the kitchen fire don't burn at tall, at tall, and there's a gintleman wants to say the dochter.

Wiggins. Show the gentleman in here, and put "The Great Elixir" on the fire. If that wont make a blaze, then nothing will. *(Exit,* R., *with letters.)*

Dennis. Faith it's an illigant man is the dochtor. It's the — the learning he has onyhow, and it's the fine physic he makes. The Great Elixir. Put it in the fire? by my sowl, I will do that same; and — and in the blacking and in the soup. It's meself that has a mind to take a wee dhrap meself, for the sthrong wakness I have for Judy Ryan. Bless her purty face! *(Enter* CHARLES FREEDLEY, L.)

Charles. Did you tell Dr. Wiggins I wished to speak with him?

Dennis. Indade I did, sir, and he'll say yez in a minute. *(Exit,* L.)

Charles. So this is the office of the Great Doctor. Great Fiddlesticks! He's no more a doctor than I am, and he shall own it, too, before I've done with him. There's my Aunt Hopkins, whose heir I expect to be, crazy about this Dr. Wiggins. Calls his "Great Elixir" delightful, and vows she will leave him a legacy. Now I have set my heart on possessing all the property of Aunt Hopkins, and have no idea of parting with it to such a humbug as this; and here I am on a voyage of discovery, which will, I hope, end in the unmasking of this quack. (*Enter* WIGGINS, R., *slowly, his eyes fastened on an open book in his hand.*)

Wiggins. Why is the privacy of the Seventh Son of the Seventh Son thus intruded upon?

Charles. Privacy? Why, aint you a regular physician?

Wiggins. I am, very *regular*. My office hours are from 10 A. M. to 2 P. M. The balance of my time is devoted to the study of the human system; to poring over the open book of nature, or to gazing in quiet, tranquil solitude upon the sublime spectacles performed by stars of the first magnitude.

Charles. Oh! you mean at the theatres.

Wiggins. Theatres, sir! No, sir, the study of the heavens is enough for my inquiring mind. What want you with me?

Charles. I have a very painful malady.

Wiggins. What is it?

Charles. An itching sensation in my hand. (*Aside.*) Itching to get hold of you.

Wiggins. Let me look at it (*offering to take it*).

Charles (*raising his arm quick, hits the doctor in the stomach*). It hurts me when I raise it thus.

Wiggins (*jumping back*). Oh! confound you! Then why in the deuce do you raise it thus?

Charles. I want it cured.

Wiggins (looking very wise). Let me see. Mars in the seventh heaven, and Jupiter in an eclipse, Venus in a brown study, and Mercury in the blues. Young man, the stars tell me you can be cured.

Charles. Much obliged to the stars. How?

Wiggins (speaking very quick, as though repeating an old story). By a plentiful application of "The Great Elixir," which will cure coughs, colds, burns, bruises, consumption, fits, fevers, earache, heartache, headache, toothache, corns, bunions, etc., etc. Whose virtues are known and appreciated from one end of the continent to the other. Prepared under the special directions of the stars, and sold by all respectable druggists at the low price of one dollar a bottle.

Charles (aside). Just as I thought, an ignorant quack. *(Aloud.)* I will procure a bottle, and give it a fair trial. *(Aside.)* I'd sooner take poison than his infernal stuff. *(Exit, L.)*

Wiggins. It is thus that science blesses her devotees with the glow of success. *(Looking at watch.)* 10 o'clock! We must prepare for the patients. Here, Dennis *(enter* DENNIS, L.*),* prepare the paraphernalia.

Dennis (puzzled). The what is it?

Wiggins. Prepare the paraphernalia.

Dennis. Yis, sir, directly *(going, L.).*

Wiggins. Where are you going?

Dennis. For the razor, sir.

Wiggins. Razor! What do you want of a razor?

Dennis. To pare your nails ouv course. You wouldn't expect me to bring an axe.

Wiggins. Oh, pshaw! Set out the table and put the instruments upon it; it is time to receive patients.

Dennis. Oh, yis, sir. *(Aside.)* Why don't he spake his mother tongue in the first place *(sets table in* c., *takes from a drawer in the table a long carving-knife, a saw, and other instruments, places them upon the table. Wiggins seats himself at back of table pompously. Bell rings outside).*

Wiggins. Our first patient. Show him in, Dennis.

Dennis. Yis, sir. *(Exit,* L.)

Wiggins. Talk about your colleges! What is the good of them while there's newspapers to advertise in, and people with throats large enough to swallow anything. *(Enter* DENNIS *with* GREENBAX, L.) Hallo, who's this?

Dennis. Here you are, sir; that's the doctor; be quick, for he's awful busy.

Greenbax. Dizzy! I should think so; it's enough to make anybody dizzy climbing so many stairs. Where's the doctor?

Dennis. There he is in his place!

Greenbax. Wrong place! Why didn't you tell me so before?

Dennis. What a stupid ould man.

Wiggins (coming forward). Here's a queer customer. What do you want?

Greenbax. Hey?

Wiggins. Do you want the doctor?

Greenbax. Of course I do *(going).*

Wiggins. Hold on, I am the doctor.

Greenbax. Hey?

Wiggins. I am the doctor.

Greenbax. Yes, yes, I want the doctor.

Wiggins (very loud). I am the doctor. Stupid!

Greenbax. No,. no! Dr. Wiggins, not Dr. Stupid.

Wiggins (shouting). I am Dr. Wiggins. Who are you?

Greenbax (holding out his hand). Pretty well, I thank you; a little deafness for you to cure, that's all.

Wiggins. How long have you been so?

Greenbax. Yes, it does look like snow, but I think it will turn to rain.

Wiggins. How long have you been in this condition?

Greenbax. Awful bad condition. I went over shoes in mud getting here.

Wiggins. Oh, pshaw! what's to be done with him? *(Still louder.)* Does your deafness increase?

Greenbax. Hey?

Wiggins (shouting). Do you keep getting worse?

Greenbax. Oh, yes! I keep a horse, — fast one, too.

Wiggins. I am speaking about your ear.

Greenbax. Yes, I've had him about a year. He has the heaves a little.

Wiggins (shouting). I'm talking about you — you — you!

Greenbax. Me! oh, no! I never had the heaves.

Wiggins. Oh, dear, dear! what shall I do? *(Shouting.)* Have you ever tried The Elixir?

Greenbax. No, sir, I never do. The hostler he licks her sometimes.

Wiggins (desperately takes bottle from table). Here, take this three times a day.

Greenbax. Certainly, with pleasure. I'll take it to Mr. Day. Go right by his house.

Wiggins (shouting). No, no; take it yourself.

8

Greenbax   Oh, yes; for my ear.   .

Wiggins.   Apply it externally and internally.

Greenbax (looking at bottle).   It does have an infernal look.   Oh, I've tried this, it wont do.   Must have something stronger, — something to shake me up.

Wiggins.   I must try something else.   What shall it be ?   I'll mix something to warm him up.   I will return in a moment.   *(Exit, R.)*

Dennis.   What an ould heathen ! he's as deaf as ould Mother Mullin's cow, that was so deaf she couldn't say straight.   What's the matter wid his ears ?   they're long enough onyhow.   *(To Greenbax.)*   Servant, sir !

Greenbax.   Hey ?

Dennis.   It's a fine day, sir.

Greenbax.   No.   Nothing to give away.   Go to the poorhouse.

Dennis.   Poor house, is it, you thaif !

Wiggins (outside).   Dennis !

Dennis.   Coming, sir.   Away wid yez, you deaf ould haddock.   *(Exit, R.)*

Greenbax.   So many beggars about.   Strange the police will allow it.   *(Re-enter* DENNIS, *R., with a phial.)*

Dennis.   I'm to give the deaf fellow, then, this bottle, and he's to follow the directions.   What's that ?   *(Reads label.)*   "To be well shaken before taken."   Faith, my boy, I'll do that same for yez.   *(Seizing Greenbax and shaking him.)*   Ye'd have me go to the poorhouse, would yez ?

Greenbax.   Murder, murder !

Dennis (shaking him).   Howl away, ye spalpeen. 'Twill help the circulation.

Greenbax. Murder, murder!

Dennis. Once more, ould man, and then ye'll do.

Greenbax. Murder, help, murder! *(Enter* Wiggins, R.)

Wiggins. What are you doing, you scamp?

Dennis. Faith, obeying orders, to be sure. "To be well shaken before taken."

Wiggins. You stupid blockhead! I meant the medicine, and not the patient.

Dennis. Oh, murder! I thought it was the ould man.

Wiggins (shouting). I'm sorry this happened; 'twas all a mistake.

Greenbax. Yes. It was a pretty good shake.

Wiggins. My man will be more careful in future. *(Gives him phial.)*

Greenbax. Shall I take this?

Wiggins. Yes, morning and night.

Greenbax. Oh, no! I wont get tight. I belong to the temperance society. Good-by. *(Exit, L.)*

Wiggins. There's one disposed of. Who's the next, Dennis?

Dennis. Mr. Aspen, the shaky gintleman.

Wiggins. Oh, yes! Show him in, Dennis. *(Exit* Dennis, L.) My nervous patient; we must shake *him* up a little. *(Re-enter Dennis with Aspen, who is very nervous; drops first his hat, in picking that up drops his cane, and then his gloves (to be continued). Wiggins takes his seat at back of table. Dennis sits R. of table, and during the scene with Aspen flourishes the carving-knife, scrapes it on the table, etc., to frighten Aspen.)*

Wiggins. Good-morning, Mr. Aspen. Take a seat. How do you feel this morning?

Aspen (sits L. *of table).* Oh, I don't know, I guess — I think — I should say — I must be-er — kind-er — sort-er — I don't know.

Dennis. Faith ! he's getting no better very fast.

Wiggins. A decided improvement. How much of the Elixir have you taken?

Aspen. Two dozen bottles.

Wiggins. Not enough. You must take a gross.

Dennis. Not enough. You must take a gross *(flourishing knife).*

Aspen (shaking). A gross? Oh, dear!

Wiggins. Perhaps a barrel.

Dennis. A barrel *(flourishing knife).*

Wiggins. Your nervous, bilious organization is completely prostrated by sudden and repeated attacks of dorrammomphia, and an enlargement of the ambigular excrescences in the influctions of the cornicopia.

Dennis. D'ye mind that now? *(knife.)*

Wiggins. You must continue the Elixir night and day, and in six or seven years you will be entirely cured.

Dennis. Yes, skewered *(knife).*

Aspen. But it makes me so horrid sick.

Wiggins. What if it does?

Dennis. What if it does? *(knife.)*

Aspen (rising). Well, no matter, I'll take it. Take a barrel of that nasty stuff. Oh, dear! *(Exit with Dennis,* L.*)*

Wiggins. That is one of my best patients. With a little moral suasion, I shall be able to make him swallow a hogshead of the Elixir. *(Enter Dennis, l.)* Well, Dennis, who now?

Dennis. Major Fingers, sir. *(Exit Dennis, l.)*

Wiggins. Major Fingers! who the deuce is Major Fingers? It must be a military man. I'm afraid of those chaps. I'll tell Dennis I can't receive him. *(Starts for door, l., and nearly upsets Major Fingers, who enters.)* Excuse me, sir, I didn't see you.

Major (fiercely). Didn't see me, stupid, swords and bayonets! Is this the way you receive patients?

Wiggins. Excuse me, sir; but you are so diminutive.

Major. Diminutive, sir! Look at my face! look at that moustache! Is there anything diminutive about that? I'd have you know, sir, that I am the equal of any man, in intellect, sir.

Wiggins. I really beg your pardon. To what do I owe the honor of this visit?

Major. My name is Fingers. I called to see you about my wife.

Wiggins. Your wife? You mean your mother.

Major. Swords and bayonets! sir, what do you mean? My wife, I said. Didn't you know I was married? I thought everybody knew it. Married in New York. Great *eclat*. Everybody turned out. Married in style, style. Yes, sir, style.

Wiggins (aside). What a young bantam.

Major. Now, sir, I have come to you on a very important matter. No listeners about, hey?

Wiggins. Not a soul.

Major. Then listen. When I was married I took a beautiful young lady of my own size. Perhaps you'd like to know the reason. I had been my own master so long that I could not bear to have a woman rule over me, so, although I have had many ladies at my feet, I waited until I met my " Vene."

Wiggins.   Your Vene?

Major.   Yes, my " Vene," — short for Lavinia, my wife.

Wiggins.   Oh ! I see.   Short wife, short name.

Major (fiercely).   Sir !

Wiggins.   Oh, no offence intended.

Major.   Well, sir, soon after my marriage, my " Vene " undertook to tell *me*, her lord and master, that if I stopped out after ten o'clock, she would turn the key on me.   Think of that !

Wiggins.   It's outrageous.

Major.   Now, sir, seeing the advertisement of your " Great Elixir," I have called to see if it will do what it pretends, — a miracle, — and make a tall man of me.

Wiggins.   Make a tall man of you?   *(Aside.)* Here's a job.   What's to be done ?   I must get him for a customer; he's rich.   *(Aloud.)*   Yes, sir, the Elixir will cause you to grow right out of your boots.   You shall see a specimen of its working.   Dennis !   *(Enter Dennis,* L.)   Where's Bob ?

Dennis.   Down-stairs, sir.

Wiggins.   Send him up.   *(Dennis going.)*   And hark you, Dennis.   *(Whispers.)*

Dennis.   All right.   I understand.   *(Exit,* L.)

Wiggins.   Be seated, major, and you shall see a specimen of the miraculous effects of the Elixir.   *(Enter Bob, with a long cloak on his shoulders and a fur cap on his head.)*   What are you doing in that rig ? Do you think it is winter ?

Bob. Please, sir, I can't help it. I've got the influ-
endways awful, and I'm so cold.

Wiggins. I'll soon warm you. (*Takes bottle from
the table.*) Here, show this gentleman its power as a
growing medicine. (*Bob takes the medicine and
grows.*) *

Bob. Oh, dear! oh, dear! Stop me, — stop me!
Give me air, — give me air! (*Exit, L.*)

Wiggins. Well, major, what do you say to that?

Major. It's wonderful. But will it do the same
for me?

Wiggins. Certainly it will.

Major. Then send a dozen bottles to my hotel, at
once. Oh, "Vene," "Vene," you shall find *I* am the
head of the family. (*Struts out, L.*)

Wiggins. That's a queer case; first of the kind on
my list. Hope it will prove a success. (*Enter Dennis, L.*)

Dennis. There's two snobs want to see the doctor.

Wiggins. Snobs? Come, come, sir, a little more
respect.

Dennis. Well, then, gents.

---

* This feat of growing is performed by a well-known trick.
Bob's cap is fastened to the cloak behind; he carries a long stick
concealed beneath the cloak, one end of which is placed in the
cap; after drinking, he turns his back, goes to the wall, and gradually raises the stick, of course raising the cap and cloak. Com-
mencing at R and going towards the L., raising and lowering the
stick, bobbing here and there, it has the appearance of a growing
man; when he reaches the door, L., he suddenly lowers it and exits.
Should this be found too difficult to perform, the piece is so arranged as to admit of "cutting" by leaving out the characters of
Major Fingers and Bob, of course, omitting all the "lines" of
Wiggins and Dennis referring to this scene.

Wiggins. Bring them in, and I will see them in a moment. (*Exit*, R.)

Dennis (*calling*, L.). Hallo, you, this way. (*Enter Harry and Herbert*, L.) The doctor will see you in a jiffy. (*Exit*, L.)

Herbert. So, Harry, you have at last followed the fashion and been caught by the advertisement of a quack?

Harry. Not caught, as you imagine. The fact is, Herbert, I want something novel for my new play, and hearing this fellow pretends to be an astrologer, I want to know what he can tell me through the medium of the stars.

Herbert. Stars? I should think you were pretty well posted regarding them. By the way, what is the plot of your new piece?

Harry. About as usual. A man who possesses a secret, another who would go through fire and water to find it out.

Herbert. Blood and thunder school?

Harry. Rather. But my villain, — he's a character, — he does the murder admirably.

Herbert. Murder! (*Enter Wiggins*, R.)

Wiggins. Murder! (*Starts back and conceals himself*, R.)

Harry. Listen. (*In melodramatic style recites.*) "He possesses the secret by which I might obtain gold! gold! gold! He keeps me from that secret. But I have him in my power. I am now beneath his roof. I know all the secret windings of the various passages, and at the dread hour of midnight I will steal to his apartment, and with my dagger over his head will shout in his ear, Blood! Blood! Blood! and bury it in his heart. Then the secret is mine and mine alone." Sh! (*Enter Wiggins*, R.) The doctor.

Wiggins (aside). Oh, dear! I see it all. I'm a doomed man. It's all up with me. But I must appear calm. (*Trembles violently.*) Wh-wh-wh-at d-d-d-o you w-w-want?

Harry. Are you the physician?

Wiggins. Yes. That is — no — no — oh! Blood! Blood! Blood!

Harry. Blood? I thought it was Wiggins.

Wiggins. It is. It is Wh-Wh-Wh-ig-ig-ins.

Harry. I have a nervous affection for which I wish to be doctored. A spasmodic moving of the arm at times.

Wiggins. Yes, I know. "At the dread hour of midnight."

Harry. What shall I do for it?

Wiggins (fiercely). Go home, put your head in a basin of gruel — no — no; put a basin of gruel on your feet and — The dread hour of midnight! Oh! oh! (*Sinks into a chair.*)

Harry. Why, what's the matter?

Wiggins (jumps up). Matter? Murder, robbery, cold steel! That's what's the matter. Go home; stay at home. Your disease is fatal if you stir from home for the next fourteen years, especially (*aside*) at the dread hour of midnight. (*Sinks into chair.*)

Harry. But the remedy, your great secret?

Wiggins (aside). There it is, my great secret

(jumping up). Go home, I say. Do as I tell you, or your life isn't worth a lucifer match.

Harry. This is a very queer doctor. Come, Herbert, let's go. I will call again, when you are more calm and quiet. *(Exit Harry and Herbert,* L.)

Wiggins. Yes, I know, "at the dread hour of midnight." What's to be done? This sanguinary ruffian who is bound to obtain the secret of "The Great Elixir." I always had an idea that I should be martyred for the knowledge I possess. I wish I was rid of the Great Elixir. Oh, Wigglesworth Wiggins, I wish you had been in the seventh heavens, ere you had made me the seventh son of a seventh son! *(Enter Dennis,* L., *with lunch on a waiter).*

Dennis. Here's your lunch, sir *(places it on table).*

Wiggins. Lunch! A pretty time to think of lunch. *(Aside.)* I must make a confidant of Dennis. Perhaps he can assist me. Dennis!

Dennis. Yes, sir.

Wiggins. What would you do to get hold of such a secret as that of the Great Elixir?

Dennis. Faith! I'd go through fire and water to get a hould of it.

Wiggins (aside). Oh, murder! Suppose he should forestall the ruffians! Would you shed blood, blood, blood?

Dennis. No, no, no, divil a hape.

Wiggins (aside). He can be trusted. Dennis, my life is in danger. Two ruffians are coming here at the dread hour of midnight, shout blood, blood, blood in my ear, and then murder me.

Dennis. Murder and Irish! An' will they wake yez afterwards?

Wiggins. What's to be done?

Dennis. Divil a bit do I know, onyhow. Fasthen the door.

Wiggins. But they know a secret entrance.

Dennis. Then fasthen the gate and throw the kay down the well.

Wiggins. No, no! *(Fingers heard outside crying.)* Who is that?

Dennis (going to door, L.) It's Major Fingers in trouble. *(Enter Major Fingers, L., rubbing his eyes and bawling. Exit Dennis, L.)*

Major. Oh, dear! Doctor, what shall I do? — what shall I do? I went home and took a dose of your Great Elixir, and then, oh, dear! I was a goin' to take another, when "Vene," sh-sh-she took it away from me and th-th-threw it out of the window, and then boxed my ears. What shall I do? — what shall I do?

Wiggins. Do? Why, get a divorce.

Major. So I will, see if I don't. I'll never sleep, drink, eat — *(spies doctor's lunch on table)*. Hallo! what's that? *(Seizes lunch.)* Cake, oh, my! *(Stuffs it into his mouth.)*

Wiggins. Come, come, sir, that's my lunch.

Major. Can't you allow me a little comfort after I've been abused by "Vene"? *(Continues eating. Enter Dennis, L., hurriedly.)*

Dennis. Oh, murder, murder! Here's a row. Here's a shindy. Doctor, you're a dead man.

Wiggins. Oh, Lord! What's the matter now?

Dennis. Mr. Freedley, who took the prescription

this morning, took the Great Elixir, and then was took crazy intirely. He's left his house, and his friends have jist been here after him.

Wiggins. Why here?

Dennis. Because he's raving about the doctor, and swearing he'll have his life.

Wiggins. Oh, horror! What's to be done? Oh, that infernal Elixir!

Charles (outside, L.). Where is he? Where is the destroyer of my peace?

Wiggins. Here comes the madman. *(Gets R. Dennis runs behind the table, seizing the carving-knife. Major Fingers crawls under the table with the lunch. Enter Charles, L., in pantaloons and white shirt, with a sheet draped about his body. A wreath of straw " à la King Lear " on his head, his face whitened).*

Charles (gesticulating wildly). There he is! Grinning demon, why do you defy me? *(makes a dash at Wiggins, who escapes to L.)*

Wiggins. Please, sir, I don't know. I am an unfortunate man.

Charles. Liar! You have robbed me of that which time can never restore.

Dennis. Somebody's stole his watch.

Charles. Villain, destroyer of my peace, vile caitiff, thou must die! I will have thy heart's blood. *(Makes another dash at Wiggins, who escapes to R.)*

Wiggins. Here's another wants blood, blood. blood!

Charles. Silence, demon! Where's my wife?

Major. Oh, dear, me! where's mine?

Charles. My wife, my wife, my wife!

Dennis. That's three wives. That fellar's a Mormon.

Charles (seizing Wiggins and dragging him to centre.) Now, demon, I have thee in my grasp, and if ever you escape, it shall be with the everlasting curses of Black Ralph.

Wiggins (on his knees). Murder! He will strangle me.

Dennis. Watch! Watch!

Major. Barnum! Barnum!

Charles. Villain, confess your sins at once.

Wiggins. Please, Mr. Black Ralph, I haven't got any.

Charles. 'Tis false! Confess yourself a vile impostor.

Wiggins. Well, well, I am.

Charles. Your Great Elixir is —

Wiggins. A humbug. *(Enter Greenbax and Aspen, L.)*

Charles. Repeat it before these gentlemen.

Wiggins. I am a humbug. My Elixir is a humbug, and everything is a humbug. Now let me go *(rises).*

Aspen. Have I been deceived? Oh, you villain !

Greenbax. What ails the doctor ?

Dennis. His nerves are a little shaken.

Greenbax. No, no! I don't want to be shaken.

Major. What ! sha'n't I be a tall man ?

Dennis. Nary at all, at all.

Major. Wont " Vene " make me pay for this ?

Charles. Now, Mr. Doctor, you can go *(removing wreath).* You see I have recovered my senses. I have exposed your quackery. I'll give you three hours to leave town; if you are not gone then, I'll hand you over to the police.

Wiggins (aside). What a fool I've been! *(Enter Harry and Herbert,* L.) There are the ruffians. Seize them! I charge those two individuals with a conspiracy to murder me at the dread hour of midnight. Blood! blood! blood!

Harry. Why, Charley, what does this mean?

Charles. That I have exposed a quack, and saved my Aunt Hopkins from making a fool of herself.

Wiggins. But I charge these villains with an attempt to murder me. Did you not a short time since, in this very room, concoct a vile plot to murder me at the dread hour of midnight?

Herbert. Ha, ha, ha! Harry, your new play has evidently made an impression on the doctor.

Wiggins. Play?

Harry. Yes, play. Waiting for you, I entertained my friend, here, with an extract from my new play. Would you like to hear it again?

Wiggins. No, I thank you. Fooled again. Here's a pretty kettle of fish. The Great Elixir exploded and its great inventor obliged to leave town by rail or on a rail. What shall I do? Mr. Greenbax, — you like my Elixir; don't you?

Greenbax. Hey?

Wiggins. You like my Elixir; don't you?

Greenbax. Oh, yes, I use it in my house.

Wiggins. You hear that, gentlemen?

Charley. What for, Mr. Greenbax?

Greenbax. To kill rats. It's a dead shot.

Wiggins. But you like it, Mr. Aspen?

Aspen (shaking). No, no, it's villanous.

Dennis. Bedad, if it's like you, it's no great shakes.

Wiggins. Major, I can still depend upon you for a customer ?

Major. Not much. " Vene " called you a quack.

Dennis. Faith, " Vene " ought to know, for she's a duck herself.

Wiggins. All forsake me. " The Great Elixir " is doomed. No, it isn't. *(To audience.)* Ladies and gentlemen, you have had a dose of it to-night; may I hope that you will recommend it. It may not perform all the wonderful cures it pretends. What medicine can ? If it has pleased you, and you are inclined to take another dose, my purpose here is accomplished, and I shall still have great faith in the power of The Great Elixir.

n. Dennis, Fingers, Aspen, Wiggins, Herbert, Harry, Greenbax. L.

THE MAN WITH THE DEMIJOHN.

A TEMPERANCE SKETCH.

CHARACTERS.

ZEKIEL SHORT (Corresponding Secretary of the Rocky-valley Teetotalers).

PHIL CARSON, } anti-teetotalers.
NED HUNTER, }

CHICK (an infantile darkey).

COSTUMES.

Zeke. — Long white overcoat, checked pants, light wig, white hat.

Phil. }
Ned. } Seedy clothes, red noses, and slouched hats.

Chick. — Woolly wig, blackened face, overalls, and checked shirt.

SCENE. — *Back street in Boston. Should it not be convenient to have scenery, a very good substitute can be obtained by spreading upon the wall at the back of the stage a variety of posters, show-bills, advertisements, &c.*

Enter PHIL, L.

Phil. Well, if this isn't particularly pleasant! I've been roaming round town ever since the break of day, longing and waiting for my bitters. Dead broke, bank closed, and credit exhausted. Nobody asks me to take a drop. The landlords won't treat, and I can't find a copper in the gutter. I have begged of everybody I met; but it's no use. One man said he would give me a loaf of bread. Bread!—do I look like a man that wants bread? No, I want something to drink : when I can't get that, I'll begin to think about bread. Another man said he would give me a breakfast if I would work for him an hour. Work! I never did work, and I don't think I shall begin now. I'm one of the aristocracy; they don't work; society takes care of them when they're unfortunate : so let society take care of me. I wish I could find a dollar, or a half a dollar, or a quarter, or a ten-cent bit, or— (*Enter* NED, R.) Halloo, Ned! is that you?

Ned. Yes, all there is left of me! What are you doing down there?

Phil. Looking for my diamond pin. But what's the matter with you? You look as though, like me, you hadn't had your bitters this morning.

Ned. No, I haven't had my bitters; and that's what's the matter. This is an ungrateful country! Why don't it take care of its " bone and sinew " better. There's those chaps at the State House mighty civil to you just before election. Plenty of liquor then, — enough to float us all.

Phil. That's why we are called the floating population, — hey, Ned?

Ned. But no sooner is election over than they shut themselves up, won't treat themselves, and go to making laws against selling liquor, which prevents their constituents from obtaining the necessities of life. There's gratitude for you.

Phil. Put not your trust in princes, Ned.

Ned. Trust! I wish I could find somebody to trust me. I wasted my valuable time last night in Steve Foster's bar-room, laying round to get asked to drink; and I was asked. And Steve Foster made money by my being there; and now this morning, when I ask him for a drop of gin, he says, "Where's your money?"—"Ain't got any," was my reply; and then, before I had time to explain things, he gives me a lift, and sends me into the gutter. I say this is an ungrateful country, where a hard-working man like me is used in this way.

Phil. Hard-working man you are! What do you work at?

Ned. Yes, hard-working indeed. Don't I inspect liquors that go into Steve Foster's cellar, to see that they are genuine?

Phil. How, pray?

Ned. By smelling round his cellar windows. Do you think I don't *nose* good liquor?

Phil. Well, I guess we don't either of us "nose" much liquor this morning.

Ned. Look here, Phil: when I was in Steve Foster's just now, a greenhorn was buying some liquor. I don't know what it was; but it was put up in a demijohn. There he is now (*pointing*, L.), coming this way. If we can only manage to get possession of that demijohn, we're safe for one drink at least.

Phil. Good! let's try it on,—pass ourselves off for State constables, give him a scare.

Ned. All right, stand back, here he is! (*They retire back. Enter* ZEKE, L., *with demijohn.*)

Zeke. I declare I feel about as mean as old Deacon Smithers did when he split his bran-new, brass-button, Sunday-go-to-meeting coat clean up the back while he was on his knees to Aunt Nabby's darter Susan, popping the question, and she wouldn't have him neither? Here am I Zekiel Short, Corresponding Secretary to the Rocky-valley Teetotalers, sneaking through the streets of Boston with a demijohn in my hand. I daren't look a decent man in the face; and as for the gals — Christopher! the sight of one on 'em makes me blush way up to the roots of my hair. Catch me in such a scrape again! Got all my groceries and fixin's up to the cars fust-rate, all ready for a start, when I happened to think that our apothecary wanted me to bring up something for him to make matrimonial wine of — no, that ain't it; antimonial wine, — something for sick folks: and he wanted to get the poorest and cheapest stuff that I could scare up; and I rather think I have something that will suit him. I can smell turpentine way through that demijohn; and I shouldn't wonder if it eat its way out afore I got home. I shouldn't like to have any of our folks see me in this pickle, they'd have me up for backslidin' sure as preaching. (*Phil and Ned have been prowling round Zeke during this speech eyeing him and the demijohn.*) Neow, what's them are chaps eyeing me for? I wonder if they're State constables. How do you do, sir?

Phil. Sha'n't I assist you with that demijohn, Mr. Johnson?

Zeke. No, I thank you; and my name ain't Johnson, nor demi-Johnson either.

Ned. Sha'n't I assist you, Mr. Eh—— Mr. Eh——?

Zeke. Well, I guess not; and my name ain't Mr. Eh——.

Phil. Do let me take it for you, you look fatigued.

Zeke. Do I? well, so do you. You look kinder peaked, as though you'd slept on the top of the meeting-house steeple, and had to shin down the lightning-rod afore breakfast, with nary a streak of lightning to grease your way.

Ned. You'd better let my friend carry it for you. He's used to carrying such things.

Zeke. Well, I haven't the least doubt of that. You both look as though you could carry a great quantity of this article. I'll carry it myself; but I'm just as much obliged to you; and, to show my gratitude, won't you take something?

Ned.
Phil. } *eagerly.* Yes, yes!

Zeke. Well, s'pose you take a walk.

Phil. Look here, Mr. What's-your-name. There's just enough of this. I'll take that demijohn. I'm a State constable.

Zeke. A what?

Ned. A State constable. So am I. Our orders are to arrest all suspicious persons with demijohns.

Zeke. Sho, are you, though? State constables! well, I declare, I never should have thought it!

Phil. So I'll thank you for that demijohn.

Zeke. *State constables!* Well, I declare! Want

my demijohn too?   Do you know where I came from?

Phil.   Yes: from the Rural District.

Zeke.   Rural? where's that?   No, sir: I'm from Rocky-valley District; and, when a constable asks us for a demijohn in that style, we say, "Where's your warrant?"

Phil.   Oh! you do, do you?   Well, a warrant isn't necessary here; so give up your demijohn.

Ned.   Come, give it up, and save further trouble.

Zeke.   Look here, State constables, I'm a peaceable citizen.   I'm also a plain-spoken individual.   You're a couple of State constables?   Where's your uniform?   There's nothing uniform about you, except your red noses, which are pretty well matched.   Look here! (*Takes off his coat.*)   That demijohn is under my protection.   I'm mighty ashamed of its company; but I'm bound to take it home with me, if it don't burn up on the way; and, if you want it, come and take it. (*Backs up stage, squares off, and shows fight.*)

Phil (*coming forward*).   We sha'n't get it that way.

Ned.   No, sir.   State constables won't do.   We can't take it.   Ah! a lucky thought.   There's that little darkey Chick playing by the water.   Go push him in quick.

Phil.   What's the joke?

Ned.   No matter, go and do it; and then come back yelling for help.

Phil.   Ah! I see it. (*Exit, L.*)

Zeke (*resuming his coat*).   Well, as there doesn't seem to be any very great danger of a raid, I'll move along towards the cars.   Them chaps want my demijohn pretty bad. (*Phil cries outside, Help! Help!*") Halloo! what's that? (*Enter* PHIL, L.)

Phil. Ned, can you swim?

Ned. Swim? not a stroke. What's the matter?

Phil. A little darkey has just fallen into the water there. I tried to reach him with a pole, but failed; and I mustn't go into the water: my physician said it would be the death of me.

Zeke. You cursed fools! is that the way you chatter when a fellow-creature is drowning? Where is he?

Ned. Can you swim?

Zeke (*throws off his coat*). Of course I can. Where is he, I say?

Phil. Right off there: you can see his head just going under for the last time. Do save him!

Zeke. I'll save him if the wool holds. (*Exit* ZEKE, L.)

Phil. And I'll save your demijohn! (*Both Phil and Ned rush together to the demijohn.*)

Phil. Let's take it home at once.

Ned. Hold on, I must have a drop.

Phil. Be quick, then; he'll be back. Let me have the first pull.

Ned. No, no: that brilliant idea by which we obtained it was mine.

Phil. But I executed it, and nearly executed the darkey at the same time.

Ned. Well, well, hurry, hurry!

Phil. Then here goes (*drinks and spits out*). Oh! murder, what stuff! Do you suppose it is poison?

Ned. It came from Steve Foster's. You ought to know the taste of every thing in his place.

Phil. But this is horrible.

Ned. No matter, down with it! "Beggars shouldn't be choosers," you know.

Phil. Here goes (*drinks, and hands the demijohn to Ned*). I've given my stomach a surprise-party, I guess.

Ned. Ah! "this is the nectar that Jupiter sips (*drinks, and spits out*). Phew! concentrated essence of all that is horrible! What stuff!

Phil. Here comes the Yankee.

Ned. Then here goes! (*Drinks, and then* PHIL *and* NED *separate and get in* R. *and* L. *corners of the stage, leaving the demijohn in the centre. Enter* ZEKE, L. *dragging* Chick.)

Zeke. There, you little specimen of ball-blacking, try and keep out of the water! What sent you there?

Chick. Donno, Massa: spec it was a conwulsion.

Zeke. Where would you have gone to if I hadn't pulled you out?

Chick. Donno Massa: spec I'd gone to Dixie.

Zeke. Well, go and lay down there and dry yourself.

Chick. Spec I will, massa.

(*Chick goes back, and, during the next dialogue, manages to get at the demijohn, and take a drink.*)

Zeke (*putting on his coat*). Halloo! where's my demijohn? Ho, ho! I didn't leave it there. The "State constables" have been at it, have they? (*Lifts it.*) How light it is! Those chaps have helped themselves while I was pulling out the darkey. If they don't have a convulsion in their insides, then I'm a Dutchman. Here's a chance for a speculation. I'll try the effects of a little "moral suasion," and see if I can't add a couple of names to the temperance pledge. (*To Phil.*) Look here, you've been at my demijohn?

Phil. I, sir? Why, I am a member of the temperance society, twenty years' standing.

Zeke (*aside*). Are you? well, you're a-lying now. (*To Ned.*) Did you trouble my demijohn?

Ned. Me, sir? No. I'm a reformed drunkard.

Zeke (*aside*). All but the reformed. (*Aloud.*) Well, I'm glad it wasn't you; for whoever did touch it is a dead man. Do you know what's in that demijohn?

Ned (*aside*). Oh, dear, how queer I feel! (*Aloud.*) No.

Phil (*aside*). Good gracious! what's the matter with me? (*Aloud.*) No.

Zeke. That demijohn contains — (*Pause.*)

Ned (*aside*). Oh, murder! my vitals! (*Aloud.*) Well, well, what does it contain?

Zeke. That demijohn contains — (*Pause.*)

Phil (*aside*). Oh, my insides! (*Aloud.*) Well, well, speak quick.

Zeke. That demijohn contains —

Ned (*aside*). I'm burning up.

Phil (*aside*). I shall howl, I know I shall.

Zeke. That demijohn contains — Did you ever hear of Butler's New-Orleans Syrup?

Ned. } Oh, oh!
Phil. }

Chick. Ow, ow, ow!

Zeke. Well, it isn't that. Did you ever hear of Sherman's Rebel Rat Exterminator?

Phil. } Oh, oh !
Ned. }

Chick. Ow, ow, ow !

Zeke. Well, it ain't that. Did you ever hear of—

Phil. } Oh, oh !
Ned. }

Chick. Ow, ow, ow !

Zeke. Well, it ain't that.

Phil. Oh, horror ! What is it?

Ned. Oh, murder ! What is it?

Zeke. The what-is-it? No : it isn't that. That's one of Barnum's curiosities.

Ned. For mercy's sake tell me what is gnawing at my vitals. I feel my strength failing me. I'm sure I'm a dead man. (*Kneels,* R. *of* ZEKE.) I confess it was I who drank your filthy stuff.

Phil (*kneels,* L. *of* ZEKE). And I confess too. I did drink your poison. What shall we do? Save us if you can.

Chick (*kneels in front of* ZEKE). O massa ! I spec's I's a goner.

Zeke. Halloo, little nig, what's the matter with you?

Chick. Dunno, massa, spec's there's a yearthquake inside me.

Zeke. Did you drink from that demijohn?

Chick. Yes, massa : spec I did. You tole me to lay down and get dry ; and, by golly ! I got dry so fast, I couldn't help drinking. Sartin sure, hope I may die, massa.

Zeke. Well, you are a handsome group, you are ! Feel puty sick, don't ye?

Phil.
Ned. } Oh, oh !

Chick.   Ow, ow ! want to go to de horsefiddle.

Zeke.   You want to know the remedy?

Phil
Ned } *eagerly.*   Yes, yes ! the remedy.

Chick.   Yes, massa, de remember me.

Zeke.   Well, here it is. (*Produces pledge.*)   Here's the pledge of the Rocky-valley Teetotalers, whereby the signers promise to indulge in no spirituous liquors. Sign this, and I'll save you.

Ned.   What, promise to drink no more liquor!   I'll die first.

Phil.   What, sign away my liberty!   Death first.

Zeke.   All right, liberty or death.   You have swallowed poison, deadly poison : it's slow, but sure.   Goodby.   I'll send the coroner for you in an hour.

Ned.
Phil. } Oh ! give us the pledge.

Zeke.   All right; here you are. (*Turns* PHIL *round, and places paper on his back while* NED *signs; then places paper on* NED's *back while* PHIL *signs; both groaning during the operation.*)   Now, then, the best thing you can do is to make a bee-line for that apothecary's, and get an emetic. (NED *and* PHIL *start,* R.)   Hold on! The nature of the poison you have swallowed is such, that, should you ever take a drop of liquor into your stomach, the old symptoms will return.

Phil.
Ned. } Oh, oh !

Zeke.   So look out ! beware of any thing in the shape of liquor.

Phil. I'll beware of Yankees, you be sure. Oh !

Exit, R.

Ned. Yes, keep clear of the man with a demijohn.
Oh !

Exit, R.

Zeke. Well, Chick.

Chick. Well, massa, ain't you gwine to make a tea-kettle of me?

Zeke. By and by, Chick ; but for the present you
shall be demijohn-bearer to the coresponding secretary of
the Rocky-valley Teetotalers. You've had a little too
much of water to-day, and I think a little too much of
spirits.

Chick. Ow, ow, by golly, I feel him now !

Zeke. Well, take up the demijohn and go with me.
I've added two names to the temperance pledge. I
haven't much hope of their sticking ; but I rather think
they'll have good cause to remember this day, and their
adventure with the man with the demijohn.

Exit ZEKE *and* CHICK, R.

Curtain.

AN ORIGINAL IDEA.

A DUOLOGUE

FOR A LADY AND GENTLEMAN.

IN TWO PARTS.

CHARACTERS.

FESTUS, a rejected suitor.
STELLA, the cruel rejecter.

SCENE. — *A handsomely furnished apartment in the house of* STELLA. *Table,* C., *with rich cover, books, flowers, &c. Téte-à-tête,* R. C., *armchairs,* R. *and* L. *of table,* C. *Entrances,* R., L., *and* C. *Enter* FESTUS, L., *in evening costume.*

Festus. "Thus far into the bowels of the land have we marched on without impediment." Here am I once more in the place from which, but one short week ago, I made an unceremonious exit as the rejected suitor of a young, lovely, and talented lady. Rejected suitor! — those words slip very smoothly from the lips, as pleasantly as though they were associated with some high-

140

sounding title of nobility. There is nothing in the sound of them to conjure up the miserable, mean, contemptible, kicked-out feeling which a man experiences who has received at the hands of lovely woman that specimen of feminine handicraft, — the mitten. All my own fault too! I'm a bashful man. Modesty, the virtue which is said to have been "the ruination of Ireland," is the rock against which my soaring ambition has dashed itself. I have sat in this room, evening after evening, upon the edge of a chair, twirling my thumbs, and saying — nothing. I couldn't help it. I have brought scores of compliments to the door, and left them in the hall with my hat. I wanted to speak; I kept up "a deuce of a thinking;" but somehow, when I had an agreeable speech ready to pop out of my mouth, it seemed to be frightened at the sight of the fair object against whom it was to be launched, and tumbled back again. It's no use: when a man is in love, the more he loves, the more silent he becomes; at least it was so in my case. And when I did manage, after much stammering and blushing, to "pop the question," the first word from the lady set me shivering; and the conclusion of her remarks set me running from the house utterly demoralized, — "I shall always be happy to see you as a *friend*, your conversation is so agreeable." Here was a damper, after six weeks of unremitting though *silent* attention. But she likes me, I'm sure of that. It is my silence which has frightened her. I only need a little more variety in my style of conversation to make myself agreeable to her. I have an original idea; and I advise all bashful men to take warning from my past

experience, and profit by my future.   I will *borrow* language in which to speak my passion. There's nothing
very original in borrowing, financially speaking; but to
borrow another man's ideas by which to make love, I
call original.   And, as luck would have it, I have an
excellent opportunity to test my new idea.   Lounging
in the sanctum of my friend Quill, the editor of " The
Postscript," a few days ago, he called my attention to an
advertisement which had just been presented for insertion.
It ran thus: " Wanted, a reader, — a gentleman who
has studied poetic and dramatic compositions with a
view to delivery, who has a good voice, and who would
be willing to give one evening a week to the entertaining
of an invalid.   Address, with references, ' Stella,' Postscript Office."   I recognized the handwriting as that of
the lady to whom I had been paying attentions, the sig-
nature as the *nom de plume* under which she had written
several poetic contributions for the press ; and I had no
trouble in guessing the meaning of the advertisement,
knowing she has an invalid uncle.   " There is a tide in
the affairs of men, which, taken at the flood, leads on
to fortune."   I felt that it was high tide with me, and
boldly launched my canoe ; answered the advertisement
under the assumed name of " Festus," and waited for
a reply.   It came: " Stella is satisfied with the references of Festus, and will give him an opportunity to test
his ability as a reader Tuesday evening next," * &c.
You will naturally conclude that my heart bounded
with rapture on receiving this favorable answer.   It did
nothing of the sort : on the contrary, the *rebound* almost

* Or the evening of the performance.

took away my breath. I began to shiver and shake, and felt inclined to retreat. But " love conquers all things." I determined to persevere; and here I am, by appointment, to test the practicability of my original idea. The lady is a fine reader. I am well acquainted with her favorite authors; and, if I can but interest her in this novel suit, may at least pass a pleasant evening if I am *not* unspeakably happy. I was told to wait for Stella. (*Takes a book from table, and sits* L. *of table, with his back to* R.) Shakspeare, ah ! Let me draw a little courage from the perusal of this. (*Enter* STELLA, R., *in evening costume, with flowers in her hair.*)

Stella. My maid said Festus was in this room. Ah ! there he is, deep in a book: that's so like these literary gentry ! No sooner are their roving eyes fastened on a book than it is seized with the avidity with which a starving man grasps a loaf of bread. He seems happy: I will not disturb him. (*Sits on tête-à-tête.*) What a strange idea ! Here am I to pass the evening listening to the voice of one whom I never saw before. This is one of my uncle's whims: he fears I am working too hard to entertain him with readings from his favorite authors, and so determines to employ a reader to relieve me. Dear uncle, with all his pain and suffering he has a sharp eye: he notices my want of spirit, and thinks it is caused by weariness. He little knows that the true cause is that stupid lover of mine, who sat here evening after evening as dumb as an oyster, until, out of spite, I started him off. What could have ailed the man ? Nothing could he say but " Yes, ma'am," " No, ma'am," " Fine evening," " Good-night." I never was so plagued

in all my life, for I should have liked the fellow if he
had only tried to make himself agreeable; but he was
as silent and stupid as — Festus here. (FESTUS *rises,
gesticulating with his hand, his eyes fastened on the book.*)
What can the man be about?

Festus. (*Reading.*) "Is this a dagger which I see
before me? the handle towards my hand? Come, let me
clutch thee! I have thee not, and yet I see " — (*Turns
and sees* STELLA. *Drops book, and runs behind chair very
confused.*)

Stella. Good gracious! you here again?

Festus. I beg your pardon. You are — I am —

Stella. I thought, sir, I was to have no more of your
agreeable society.

Festus. I beg your pardon, madam: you seem to be
in error. I am Festus, — Festus.

Stella. You Festus?

Festus. Oh, yes: I'm Festus! I came here by appointment.

Stella. What do you mean, sir? I expected a gentleman here to read.

Festus. Exactly! Pray, are you the invalid?

Stella. Sir, you are insulting! You will be kind
enough to leave this room at once. I thought the last
time you were here —

Festus. Excuse me for interrupting; but you evidently mistake me for some other person. I never was
in this house before.

Stella. Is the man crazy? Do you mean to say you
did not make a proposal of marriage to me in this very
room a week ago?

Festus. Madam, you surprise me. To the best of my knowledge and belief, I never saw you before.

Stella. Was there ever such assurance? Is not your name —

Festus. Festus; and yours Stella. Am I not right?

Stella. Sir, this is very provoking; but, if you are Festus, what is your object in calling here?

Festus. To entertain you.

Stella. To entertain me! With what, pray? Sitting on the edge of a chair, and twirling your thumbs?

Festus. (*Aside.*) That's a hard hit. (*Aloud.*) With readings, if you please.

Stella. Readings! Pray, what do you read? Ovid's "Art of Love"?

Festus. Madam, I answered your advertisement, being desirous of securing the situation of reader to an invalid.

Stella. You won't suit.

Festus. You haven't heard me.

Stella. No, but I've seen you; and your silence cannot be excelled by your reading.

Festus. Will you hear me read?

Stella. No: you will not suit.

Festus. Very well: then I *claim* the trial. Remember your promise, — " Stella is satisfied with the references of 'Festus,' and will give him an opportunity to test his ability as a reader Tuesday evening," &c., &c.

Stella. Oh, very well! If you insist upon making yourself ridiculous, proceed. (*Sits in chair*, R. *of table, and turns her back on* FESTUS.)

Festus. But will you not listen to me? I cannot read to you while you sit in that position.

Stella.   I told you I did not wish to hear you read: you insist.   Proceed: I am not interested.

Festus.   Oh, very well!   My first selection shall be from the writings of one well known to fame, — a lady whose compositions have electrified the world; whose poetic effusions have lulled to sleep the cross and peevish infant, stilled the noisy nursery, and exerted an influence upon mankind of great and lasting power; one whose works are memorable for their antiquity, — the gift of genius to the budding greatness of the nineteenth century. (*Producing a book from his pocket.*)   I will read from Mother Goose.

Stella.   (*Starting up.*)   Mother Goose!

Festus.   Yes: are you acquainted with the lady?

Stella.   (*Sarcastically.*)   I have heard of her.

Festus.   (*Reads in very melodramatic style.*)

> "'We are three brethren out of Spain,
> Come to court your daughter Jane.'
> 'My daughter Jane she is too young:
> She is not skilled in flattering tongue.'
> 'Be she young, or be she old,
> 'Tis for her gold she must be sold.
> So fare you well, my lady gay:
> We will return another day.'"

How do you like that?

Stella.   (*Fiercely.*)   I don't like it.

Festus.   No?   Perhaps you prefer some other style of delivery.   (*Reads with a drawl.*)

> "'We awe thwe bwethwen aw-out of Spain,
> Come to court-aw your dawtaw Jane-aw.'"

Stella.   Oh, do read some thing else!

Festus.   Certainly.

> "Hi diddel diddel! the cat and the fiddle!
> The cow jumped over the moon" —

Stella.   (*Jumps up.*)   Pray, sir, do you intend to read that nonsense the whole evening?

Festus.   Oh, no!   I think I can get through the book in about an hour.

Stella.   Sir, you have forced yourself here, an unwelcome visitor: you insist upon my hearing such nonsense as Mother-Goose melodies for an hour.   Do you call that gentlemanly?

Festus.   Madam, you advertised for a reader.   I have applied, with your permission, for the situation.   Under the circumstances, I naturally expected to have your attention during the reading of such selections as I should offer; instead of which, you turn your back upon me, and very coolly bid me proceed.   Do *you* call that ladylike?

Stella.   Frankly, no.   You have asked the trial: you shall have it.   For an hour I will hear you; and, though I strongly suspect the situation of reader is not the object of your visit, you shall have no reason to complain of my inattention.   Is that satisfactory?

Festus.   Pray go a step farther.   You are said to have fine elocutionary powers.   May I not hope to have the pleasure of hearing your voice?   Grant me your assistance, and my hour's trial may perhaps be made agreeable to both.

Stella.   Oh! not quite certain of your ability, Mr. Festus?

Festus.   Not in the presence of so fine a reader.

Stella.   A compliment!   Well, I agree.

Festus.   Let me hear you read : that will give me courage to make the attempt myself.

Stella.   Oh, very well!   Remembering your partiality for juvenile literature, you will pardon me if I read a very short but sweet poem.   (*Produces a printed handkerchief from her pocket.*)

Festus.   Ah, a pocket edition!

Stella.   (*Reads from the handkerchief.*)

> " Who sat and watched my infant head
> When sleeping on my cradle-bed,
> And tears of sweet affection shed ?
>   My mother.
>
> When sleep forsook my open eye,
> Who was it sang sweet lullaby,
> And rocked me that I should not cry ?
>   My mother.
>
> When pain and sickness made me cry,
> Who gazed upon my heavy eye,
> And wept for fear that I should die ?
>   My mother."

There, sir! what do you say to that?

Festus.   It's very sweet. , But that child had too many mothers.   Now, I prefer Tom Hood's parody.   (*Reads "A Lay of Real Life," by Thomas Hood.*)

A LAY OF REAL LIFE.

> Who ruined me ere I was born,
> Sold every acre, grass or corn,
> And left the next heir all forlorn ?
>   My Grandfather.

Who said my mother was no nurse,
And physicked me, and made me worse,
Till infancy became a curse?
> My Grandmother.

Who left me in my seventh year,
A comfort to my mother dear,
And Mr. Pope the overseer?
> My Father.

Who let me starve to buy her gin,
Till all my bones came through my skin,
Then called me "ugly little sin"?
> My Mother.

Who said my mother was a Turk,
And took me home, and made me work,
But managed half my meals to shirk?
> My Aunt.

Who "of all earthly things" would boast,
"He hated others' brats the most,"
And therefore made me feel my post?
> My Uncle.

Who got in scrapes, an endless score,
And always laid them at my door,
Till many a bitter bang I bore?
> My Cousin.

Who took me home when mother died,
Again with father to reside,
Black shoes, clean knives, run far and wide?
> My Stepmother.

Who marred my stealthy urchin joys,
And, when I played, cried "What a noise!" —
Girls always hector over boys —
> My Sister.

Who used to share in what was mine,
Or took it all, did he incline,
'Cause I was eight, and he was nine?
                    My Brother.

Who stroked my head, and said, " Good lad,"
And gave me sixpence, " all he had ; "
But at the stall the coin was bad?
                    My Godfather.

Who, gratis, shared my social glass,
But, when misfortune came to pass,
Referred me to the pump? Alas!
                    My Friend.

Through all this weary world, in brief,
Who ever sympathized with grief,
Or shared my joy, my sole relief?
                    Myself.

Ste'la. That is very amusing; but, Mr. Festus, if this is the extent of your elocutionary acquirements —

Festus. Oh, I beg your pardon! By no means! With your permission, I will read something a little more sombre, — Edgar Poe's " Raven."

Stella. That is certainly more sombre. Proceed.

Reading. " *The Raven,*" *by Edgar A. Poe.* FESTUS.

Stella. Excellent! Mr. Festus, you are certainly a good reader. But this seems to affect you.

Festus. It does, it does; for I, too, have lost one —

Stella. A raven?

Festus. Pshaw! Come, madam, I believe you are to read now, and I to listen.

Stella. Certainly. I will read, with your permission, Whittier's " Maud Muller."

Festus. I should be delighted to hear it.

Reading. " *Maud Muller.*" STELLA.

Festus. Beautiful, beautiful ! Madam, this, too, affects me.

Stella. How ?

Festus. When I think " it might have been."

Stella. Then I wouldn't think of it, if I were you. What shall we have now?

Festus. Suppose we read together.

Stella. Together?

Festus. Yes, a scene from some play. There's " The Marble Heart."

Stella. Oh, there's nothing in that but love-scenes !

Festus. It's a favorite play with me ; and I have been thinking, while you were reading, that the character of " Marco " is one in which you might excel.

Stella. Indeed ! I have studied the character.

Festus. (*Aside.*) I should think so. (*Aloud.*) Let us attempt a scene. Come, you shall have your choice.

Stella. Thank you. Then I will choose " the rejection scene."

Festus. (*Aside.*) Of course you would ! (*Aloud.*) Very well.

Stella. Do you know, Mr. Festus, I think there is something very odd in your attempting a love-scene ?

Festus. Do you? I have attempted them, and with success too.

Stella. Ah ! I remember there was one attempted here.

Festus. Indeed !

Stella.   Yes ; but the gentleman's name was not Festus.

Festus.   Shall we try the scene?

Stella.   You must prompt me if I fail.

Festus.   Fail! "In the bright lexicon of youth, there's no such word as fail."

Stella.   Ah! but, in attempts at acting, there are many failures.

Festus.   True ; but yours will not be one of them.

Stella.   (*Aside.*) Another compliment! I begin to like the fellow.

Festus.   Now, then, the scene! (STELLA *takes a bouquet from the table, sits on tête-à-tête,* R.)

SCENE FROM "THE MARBLE HEART."

(*Arranged for this piece.*)

Marco, STELLA.   *Raphael,* FESTUS.

Raph.   I have endured the sarcasms of Monsieur de Veaudore, the disavowal of your love, the reproaches and anger of my only friend, who insulted me in my last adieu : for your sake, I have become a coward, a crawling, abject wretch, without heart, without mind, without shame. (*Throws himself into chair,* L., *and covers his face with his hands. A pause.* MARCO *pulls the bouquet to pieces.* RAPHAEL *raises his head, looks at her, and endeavors to speak with firmness.*) What did that man say to you? I have a right to ask.

Marco.   (*Smiling in derision.*) Right!

Raph.   Yes, Marco, the right of a man, who, knowing he is to die, would learn the time and manner of his death. He told you he loved you?

Marco.   (*Carelessly.*) Perhaps he did : what then?

Raph.   (*Violently.*) You accepted his love?

Marco.   I will not answer you.

Raph.   But you must, you shall!

Marco.   (*Disdainfully.*) Shall!

Raph. He offered you his hand? (*A pause.*) Speak, Marco, speak : in mercy let me knew the worst.

Marco. He did.

Raph. And you accepted?

Maro. (*Coldly.*) Yes.

Raph. (*Greatly agitated.*) O Marco, Marco! (*Violently, rising.*) You shall not marry him !

Marco. (*With contempt.*) Who shall prevent me?

Raph. (*With a burst of fury.*) The man you have wronged! (*Suddenly losing all command over himself, and throwing himself at her feet in an agony of grief.*) No, no! Pity, pity for the wretched maniac who cannot live without you — humanity — remorse —

Marco. (*Taking away her hand, and rising, with contempt and rage.*) Remorse! I am weary of this persecution, these clamors, these maledictions. You think me a monster of falsehood, inconstant as the wind, perfidious as the ocean, the incarnation of caprice, selfishness, and cruelty? And why? Because I am too wise to rush headlong to ruin, and too proud to be pitied.

Raph. Pitied, Marco !

Marco. Yes (*vehemently*), pitied, insulted, and despised. Look at me now, surrounded with every luxury that art can invent and gold can purchase. Everybody bows to me. I am a queen. Divest me of these gilded claims to the world's respect, and what am I? (*Bitterly.*) The dust — the friends who now follow my carriage, and fight for my smiles, will mock me, spurn me, and trample upon me.

Raph. Marco, Marco! in mercy —

Marco. I have known poverty, and have suffered such tortures in its hideous grasp that my heart sickens and my soul shudders at facing it again. You will perhaps laugh at my fear, and say there is happiness in poverty. (*Laughing in scorn.*) Yes, for those who are born to it; but to have known better days, and fall! Oh the misery, the heart-desolation, the despair ! My father was rich and proud, the descendant of a noble family. He lived in splendor, and brought me up to despise every thing but wealth. He showed me its power : it surrounded him with friends and flatterers, and made life a perpetual summer. An evil day arrived : he speculated, and was reduced to his last crown. Where were his friends? (*Laugh-*

ing in scorn, and speaking in a hoarse voice.) They passed him in the street without recognition, they maligned, they despised, they forgot him. (*Sinks into a chair, sobbing, and wiping her eyes.*)

Raph. Forbear, Marco, forbear !

Marco. Ten years (oh, how long the days and months !) we lived in poverty, — abject, squalid, starving poverty. I saw my father in the prime of his life grow old, decrepit, and insane. In his ravings he had but one thought, "Money, money, money ! " 'Cling to it, my child," he would say to me with glaring eyes and grinding teeth, — " cling to it, Marco, as you would to a raft in shipwreck : it is the all in all of our existence. See what the loss of it has brought to me. Let your heart be marble to *every thing* but gold, gold, gold ! "

Raph. O misery !

Marco. My father died, and I was left dependent on the charity of my relations. (*With savage scorn.*) Charity ! I wore their cast clothes, waited on their will, — their servant, their encumbrance, their hopeless slave. One happy day, Providence came to my relief: I was left a small fortune. (*Rising.*) From that moment I became a statue. The recollection of my days of misery extinguished the glowing impulses of my youth ; and I lived on the surface of the world, mixing in all its gay pleasures, caressed and *fêted*, the idol of the hour, hating and despising the smiling monster, and devising means to secure my independence. A wealthy marriage was the only course ; and for that I have devoted myself, heart and mind ; for that I have been cruel, false, and pitiless ; for that I am deaf to reproaches, dead to remorse. (*Sits.*)

Raph. (*In amazement.*) I hear you, Marco, and disbelieve my ears : I see you, and doubt my eyes. Those fearful words, those evil looks, — is it possible such hideousness can dwell in such a heavenly shrine ? (*Growing gradually frantic.*) But I am glad, very glad, you have at last been candid with me : it relieves me from a world of sorrow, it rescues me from despair. Yet I hoped you had some regard for me, some little regret for — Ah, well ! it was my accursed vanity. How could I ever hope to ? — (*Laughing hysterically, and speaking in a hoarse whisper.*) I, too, am a deception : I have pretended to devote to you my heart, my life, my soul — no such thing! I, too, wore a mask — ha, ha, ha! When my eyes looked fondest, my heart was plotting treachery; when I swore you were my happiness, I felt you were my curse; when I vowed I could not live without you, I was devising means to break with you — ha, ha, ha! We owe each other nothing; we are both demons : but the comedy is over now, and the actors have returned to their every-day costumes and natures. I wish to be a gentleman, like Monsieur Veaudore. Mademoiselle Marco, I ask pardon for having annoyed you so long. I leave you to your pleasures. (*He endeavors to kiss her hand; but she recoils, alarmed by the wildness of his tone and looks.*) What do you fear? (*With a burst of maniac laughter.*) There is no venom on my lips : it is in my heart! (*Kisses her hand.*)

Marco. (*Alarmed, trying to pacify him.*) Come, come, Raphael, let us be friends.

Raph. (*With a vacant stare.*) Friends! — oh, yes! delighted! (*Bowing with cold politeness, in the manner of his first introduction.*) Mademoiselle Marco, I believe — beautiful, very beautiful, but (*shaking his head mournfully*) false, false, fatally false. (*Sighing, and putting his hand to his head.*) Ah, yes! and now we are friends (*shaking both her hands, and looking at her earnestly*), — yes, yes, real friends ; for we no longer love, no longer deceive each other.

Marco. Raphael!

Raph. We thought we were happy. (*Laughing.*) Vain delusion! we were breaking our hearts. (*With a sudden alteration of tone and countenance conveying that the recollection of his home had suddenly come to his mind.*) Yes, yes (*with a tremulous voice*), breaking our hearts; but we were not the only sufferers. No, no : there were other hearts breaking, others (*in an agony of suppressed grief*) I had forgotten. But my absence is desired, and some older friends claim my politeness. Adieu! (*Going.*)

Marco. You will call and see me sometimes in Paris?

Raph. (*Gayly bowing with affected politeness*) You are very kind; but I fear I shall not often be able to profit by your politeness, for my work — you understand — it is necessary that I should repair the time I have lost; and besides, when I and the persons who reside with me have recovered our happiness, it would be indiscreet to revive recollections that might jeopardize it.

Marco. (*Coldly.*) Well, then, at least you'll try ? (*Sits on sofa.*)

Raph. (*Suffocating with suppressed emotion.*) Yes, yes : I will try. (*Puts his hand hastily to his heart with an exclamation of acute pain.*)

Marco. (*Alarmed.*) Raphael !

Raph. (*After a violent effort to calm himself.*) 'Tis nothing, 'tis nothing ! (*Staggering to go off*, L.)

Marco. Are you going to Paris ?

Raph. Yes, yes, oh, yes ! Don't you know — they are waiting for me.

Marco. Take my carriage.

Raph. (*With scorn.*) No, no (*with a maniac smile*) : I shall walk, walk. (*Bitterly.*) Poverty should walk : the weather is superb (*endeavoring to be gay*) — and (*his forces nearly abandoning him*) — my heart — is so light — I — I (*staggering to table, and taking his hat*) — Adieu, Mademoiselle Marco, adieu (*faintly*) — adieu, adieu ! (*Staggers off*, L.)

Marco. (*Rising from sofa, and looking after him with deep emotion.*) O Raphael, Raphael ! my heart is not quite marble ; no, no, not quite ! (*Falls back on sofa, covers her face with her handkerchief, and weeps.*)

Re-enter RAPHAEL.

Marco. (*With a smile, holding out her hand.*) Thank you for returning ; thank you for not taking my follies in earnest : this goodness endears you to me more than ever. (RAPHAEL *stands fixed, looking at her with a cold, immovable countenance.*) You love me still ? (*Trying to draw him to her.*) Yes, yes : I see you do ; and you will pardon me ! (*She is about to put her arm round his neck : he looks sternly at her, and repels her by extending his arms with an action of disdain.*) Oh ! do not look at me thus : you frighten me —

Raph. (*With terrible calmness.*) Give me my portrait. (*Pointing to it on her neck.*)

Marco. Nay, I am sure —

Raph. (*Sternly.*) Give it me ! (MARCO *gives it him.*) Don't be alarmed, it is only the painting I reclaim. (*Taking it from the frame.*) I leave you the diamonds. (*Gives back the frame and chain.*)

Marco. Raphael !

Raph. Marco, shall I tell you why for a moment you have love on your lips and in your eyes ? 'Tis because you have learned that in recalling me you could break another heart: the feeling which guided you was not the happiness of Raphael, but the despair of Marie. (MARCO *starts.*) Now, adieu. But first give me your wreath.

Marco. My wreath?

Raph. (*Approaching.*) I would have it.

Marco. (*Recoiling alarmed.*) Are you mad?

Raph. (*Wildly.*) Take it off, take it off! White roses are the symbols of purity; they make *you* hideous: they are only for the brows of innocence and truth. (*Tears the crown from her head, and dashes it on the ground.*)

END OF PART I.

———◆———

PART II.

SCENE. — *Same as before.* *Enter* FESTUS, C.

Festus. It *is* astonishing how much a little borrowed plumage becomes a bashful man. The ice once broken by the inspiring thoughts and words of the love-sick "Raphael," I feel now almost equal to the composition and delivery of an energetic and passionate appeal that shall carry the heart of the lady by storm; but then, having once been refused, I dread a second attempt. "A burnt child fears the fire;" and a singed lover trembles before the blazing eyes of the object of his adoration. I have yet a short time before the expiration of my hour of trial, and the character of "Sir Thomas Clifford" from which to borrow courage. (*Enter* STELLA, C.)

Stella. Well, mysterious "Festus," what new fancy is agitating your fertile brain?

Festus. Madam, to tell you the truth, I was — thinking — of you.

Stella. Of me, or of your future salary?

Festus. Both.

Stella. What of me?

Festus. (*Very awkward and confused.*) That I think — I think — that you — you — are — are —

Stella. Well, what am I?

Festus. (*Abruptly.*) A very fine reader.

Stella. Oh! is that all?

Festus. All worth mentioning.

Stella. Sir!

Festus. That is all I am at liberty to mention.

Stella. What if I should grant you liberty to say more?

Festus. Oh! then — then I should say — I should say —

Stella. Well, what would you say?

Festus. It's your turn to read.

Stella. (*Aside.*) Stupid! (*Aloud.*) Well, sir, what shall I read?

Festus. Oh! oblige me by making your own selection.

Stella. There's "The Bells," by Poe. Do you like that?

Festus. Oh, exceedingly!

Stella. But I don't know how to read it: it's very difficult.

Festus. Perhaps I can assist you. (*Aside.*) I'll provoke her a bit; see if she has a temper.

Stella. Well, you are very kind. (*Aside.*) I'll see if I can make him talk.

Festus. Well, then, you take the book, and read. (*Hands her copy of Poe.*) When I think you need correcting, I will speak.

Stella. Very well. (*They sit,* c. STELLA *reads in a very tragic tone, emphasizing the words in italics.*)

> " Hear the sledges with the *bells,*
>   Silver *bells !* "

Festus. Oh, stop, stop, stop ! Dear me ! that's not the way to read. There's no silver in *your* bells. Listen : —

> " Hear the sledges with the bells,
>   *Sil*-ver bells ! "

Very silvery, don't you see?

Stella. Oh, yes ! excuse me. (*Reads in a very silly tone.*)

> " Hear the sledges with the bells,
>   Sil——ver bells ! "

Festus. Oh, no, no ! that's too *silly.*

Stella. Sir !

Festus. I mean, there's too much of the *sil* in *silver.* (*Repeats his reading. She imitates it.*)

Festus. Ah ! that's better. Thank you : you are charming. (*She looks at him.*) That is, a charming reader. Go on.

Stella. (*Reads.*)

> " What a world of merriment their melody foretells !
>   How they tinkle " —

Festus. (*Interrupting.*) I beg your pardon : " twinkle."

Stella. No, sir : " tinkle."

Festus. But I am sure it is " twinkle."

Stella. Can't I believe my own eyes?

Festus. Not unless they " twinkle."

Stella. Look for yourself. (*Shows him the book.*)

Festus. My stars! it is " tinkle." I beg your pardon.
Go on.

Stella.   " How they tinkle, tinkle, tinkle,
                      In the icy air " —

Festus. No, no: frosty, — frosty air.

Stella. No, sir: it's icy air.

Festus. You are mistaken : " frosty."

Stella. Am I? Look for yourself.

Festus. Well, I declare! It is, *I see, icy.* I beg
your pardon. Go on.

Stella. I see, I see. You are bent on interrupting
me. What do you mean, sir?

Festus. What can you expect, if you don't know how
to read?

Stella. Sir, this is provoking. I don't know how to
read?

Festus. Not " The Bells," I know.

Stella. Oh! do you? Well, sir, I know you are no
gentleman ; and I know, if you want " The Bells." read
(*starts up, and throws book at him*), read it yourself.

Festus. Madam, what am I to understand by this?

Stella. That your presence is no longer agreeable to
me.

Festus. Oh, very well, very well! I understand you
wish me to go. (STELLA *stands,* R., *with her back to him.*)
You wish me to go. I will intrude no longer. (*Very*

loud.) Since you — wish — me — to — go— (*Aside.*) Confound it, I believe she does! (*Aloud.*) Very well, madam, very well. Good-evening. (*Exit*, L.)

Stella. He'll be back in three minutes. (*Enter* FESTUS, L.)

Festus. I forgot my hat. You'll excuse me if I take my — (*Aside.*) Confound it, she won't speak! (*Stands irresolute a moment, then approaches her.*) Madam, — Stella, — I was wrong. You can read "The Bells" divinely. I hear them ringing in my ears now. I beg your pardon. Read "The Bells" in any manner you please : I shall be delighted to listen.

Stella. Oh, very well! Since you have returned, I will read.

Reading. "*The Bells*," *Poe.* STELLA.

Festus. Splendid, splendid!

Stella. Now, sir, I shall be happy to listen to you once more.

Festus. Your "Bells" have stirred the fires of patriotism within my heart ; and I will give you, as my selection, "Sheridan's Ride."

Reading. "*Sheridan's Ride*," *Reid.* FESTUS.

Stella. Excellent! Mr. Festus, you are a very spirited rider, — I mean reader. Now, suppose, for variety, we have another scene.

Festus. With all my heart. What shall it be?

Stella. Oh! you select. Pray, Mr. Festus, did you have any design in selecting the scene from "The Marble Heart"?

11

Festus. Well. I like that. You selected it yourself.

Stella. But the play was your selection; and you were very perfect in the part of " Raphael."

Festus. Well, I selected what I thought I should most excel in.

Stella. *You* excel in love-making! That's good. But I must say, you act it well.

Festus. Yes — that is — I think that circumstances — occurring — which would make — circumstances — perfectly — that is, I mean to say that — circumstances — indeed —what were you saying?

Stella. Ha, ha, ha! O mighty Festus! you've lost your place ; but, as you have a partiality for love-scenes, what is your next?

Festus. What say you to a scene from " The Hunchback " ? " The secretary of my lord"? You know the scene, — " Julia " and " Sir Thomas Clifford."

Stella. Oh, yes! I am familiar with it ; but I think, as an applicant for a situation, you are making me perform more than my share of work.

Festus. Oh ! if you object —

Stella. Oh ! but I don't object. Proceed. (*Sits, L. of table.* FESTUS *exits,* L.)

SCENE FROM "THE HUNCHBACK."

(*Arranged for this piece.*)

Julia, STELLA.   *Sir Thomas Clifford,* FESTUS.

Jul. (*Alone.*) A wedded bride?
Is it a dream ?
Oh, would it were a dream!
How would I bless the sun that waked me from it !
I am wrecked

By mine own act! What! no escape? no hope?
None! I must e'en abide these hated nuptials!
Hated!—ay, own it, and then curse thyself
That mad'st the bane thou loathest for the love
Thou bear'st to one who never can be thine!
Yes, love! Deceive thyself no longer. False
To say 'tis pity for his fall, — respect
Engendered by a hollow world's disdain,
Which hoots whom fickle fortune cheers no more!
'Tis none of these: 'tis love, and, if not love,
Why, then, idolatry! Ay, that's the name
To speak the broadest, deepest, strongest passion
That ever woman's heart was borne away by!
He comes! Thou'dst play the lady, — play it now!

(*Enter* CLIFFORD, L).

Speaks he not?
Or does he wait for orders to unfold
His business? Stopped his business till I spoke,
I'd hold my peace forever! (CLIFFORD *kneels, presenting a letter.*)
Does he kneel?
A lady am I to my heart's content!
Could he unmake me that which claims his knee,
I'd kneel to him,—I would, I would! Your will?
   Clif. This letter from my lord.
   Jul. Oh, fate! who speaks?
   Clif. The secretary of my lord. (*Rises.*)
   Jul. I breathe!
I could have sworn 'twas he!

(*Makes an effort to look at him, but is unable.*)
So like the voice!—
I dare not look lest there the form should stand.
How came he by that voice? 'Tis Clifford's voice
If ever Clifford spoke! My fears come back.
Clifford, the secretary of my lord!
Fortune hath freaks, but none so mad as that.
It cannot be!—it should not be! A look,
And all were set at rest. (*Tries to look at him again, but cannot.*)
So strong my fears,

Dread to confirm them takes away the power
To try and end them.   Come the worst, I'll look.
                    (*She tries again, and is again unequal to the task.*)
I'd sink before him if I met his eye!

Clif. Wilt please your ladyship to take the letter?

Jul. There, Clifford speaks again! Not Clifford's breath
Could more make Clifford's voice; not Clifford's tongue
And lips more frame it into Clifford's speech.
A question, and 'tis over! Know I you?

Clif. Reverse of fortune, lady, changes friends:
It turns them into strangers. What I am
I have not always been.

Jul. Could I not name you?

Clif. If your disdain for one, perhaps too bold
When hollow fortune called him favorite,
Now by her fickleness perforce reduced
To take an humble tone, would suffer you —

Jul. I might?

Clif. You might.

Jul. O Clifford! is it you?

Clif. Your answer to my lord. (*Gives the letter.*)

Jul. Your lord!

Clif. Wilt write it?
Or, will it please you send a verbal one?
I'll bear it faithfully.

Jul. You'll bear it?

Clif. Madam,
Your pardon; but my haste is somewhat urgent.
My lord's impatient, and to use despatch
Were his repeated orders.

Jul. Orders? Well (*takes letter*),
I'll read the letter, sir. 'Tis right you mind
His lordship's orders. They are paramount.
Nothing should supersede them. Stand beside them!
They merit all your care, and have it! Fit,
Most fit, they should. Give me the letter, sir.

Clif. You have it, madam.

Jul. So! How poor a thing
I look! so lost while he is all himself!
Have I no pride?
If he can freeze, 'tis time that I grow cold.
I'll read the letter. (*Opens it, and holds it as about to read it.*)
Mind his orders! So!
Quickly he fits his habits to his fortunes!
He serves my lord with all his will! His heart's
In his vocation. So! Is this the letter?
'Tis upside down, and here I'm poring on't!
Most fit I let him see me play the fool!
Shame! Let me be myself! (*She sits awhile at table, vacantly
gazing on the lettre, then looks at* CLIFFORD.)
How plainly shows his humble suit!
It fits not him that wears it. I have wronged him!
He can't be happy — does not look it — is not!
That eye which reads the ground is argument
Enough. He loves me. There I let him stand,
And I am sitting! (*Rises, and points to a chair.*)
Pray you, take a chair. (*He bows as acknowledging and declining the
honor. She looks at him awhile.*)
Clifford, why don't you speak to me? (*Weeps.*)
Clif. I trust
You're happy.
Jul. Happy? Very, very happy!
You see I weep I am so happy. Tears
Are signs, you know, of naught but happiness.
When first I saw you, little did I look
To be so happy. Clifford!
Clif. Madam?
Jul. Madam!
I call thee Clifford, and thou call'st me madam!
Clif. Such the address my duty stints me to.
Thou art the wife elect of a proud carl
Whose humble secretary sole am I.
Jul. Most right! I had forgot! I thank you, sir,
For so reminding me, and give you joy
That what, I see, had been a burthen to you

Is fairly off your hands.

 Clif. A burthen to me?
Mean you yourself? Are you that burthen, Julia?
Say that the sun's a burthen to the earth!
Say that the blood's a burthen to the heart!
Say health's a burthen, peace, contentment, joy,
Fame, riches, honors, every thing that man
Desires, and gives the name of blessing to!—
E'en such a burthen Julia were to me
Had fortune let me wear her.

 Jul. (*Aside.*) On the brink
Of what a precipice I'm standing! Back,
Back! while the faculty remains to do't!
A minute longer, not the whirlpool's self
More sure to suck thee down! One effort! (*Sits.*) There!
   (*Recovers her self-possession, takes up the letter, and reads.*)
To wed to-morrow night! Wed whom? A man
Whom I can never love! I should before
Have thought of that. To-morrow night! This hour
To-morrow,—how I tremble!
At what means
Will not the desperate snatch! What's honor's price?
Nor friends, nor lovers,—no, nor life itself!
Clifford, this moment leave me! (CLIFFORD *retires up the stage out*
 of her sight.)
Is he gone?
Oh, docile lover! Do his mistress' wish
That went against his own! Do it so soon,
Ere well 'twas uttered! No good-by to her!
No word, no look! 'Twas best that so he went.
Alas the strait of her who owns that best
Which last she'd wish were done! What's left me now?
To weep, to weep! (*Leans her head upon her arm, which rests upon
 the table, her other arm hanging listless at her side. CLIFFORD
 comes down the stage, looks a moment at her, approaches her, and,
 kneeling, takes her hand.*)

 Clif. My Julia!
 Jul. There again!

Up, up! By all thy hopes of heaven go hence!
To stay's perdition to me! Look you, Clifford!
Were there a grave where thou art kneeling now,
I'd walk into't and be inearthed alive
Ere taint should touch my name! Should some one come
And see thee kneeling thus! Let go my hand! —
Remember, Clifford, I'm a promised bride —
And take thy arm away! It has no right
To clasp my waist! Judge you so poorly of me
As think I'll suffer this? My honor, sir!

(She breaks from him, quitting her seat.)

I'm glad you've forced me to respect myself:
You'll find that I can do so.

   Clif. There was a time I held your hand unchid;
There was a time I n ight have clasped your waist:
I had forgot that time was past and gone.
I pray you, pardon me.

   Jul. (*Softened.*) I do so, Clifford.

   Clif. I shall no more offend.

   Jul. Make sure of that.
No longer is it fit thou keep'st thy post
In's lordship's household. Give it up! A day,
An hour, remain not in it.

   Clif. Wherefore?

   Jul. Live.
In the same house with me, and I another's?
Put miles, put leagues, between us! The same land
Should not contain us.
O Clifford, Clifford!
Rash was the act, so light that gave me up,
That stung a woman's pride, and drove her mad,
Till in her frenzy she destroyed her peace!
Oh, it was rashly done! Had you reproved,
Expostulated, had you reasoned with me,
Tried to find out what was indeed my heart,
I would have shown it, you'd have seen it, all
Had been as nought can ever be again.

   Clif. Lov'st thou me, Julia?

Jul.   Dost thou ask me, Clifford?
Clif.   These nuptials may be shunned —
Jul.   With honor?
Clif.   Yes.
Jul.   Then take me! Hold! — hear me, and take me, then!
Let not thy passion be my counsellor;
Deal with me, Clifford, as my brother.   Be
The jealous guardian of my spotless name.
Scan thou my cause as 'twere thy sister's.   Let
Thy scrutiny o'erlook no point of it,
And turn it o'er not once, but many a time,
That flaw, speck, yea, the shade of one, — a soil
So slight not one out of a thousand eyes
Could find it out, — may not escape thee; then
Say if these nuptials can be shunned with honor!
Clif.   They can.
Jul.   Then take me, Clifford —

Festus.   Stop one moment.   (*Looks at watch.*)   Time's up.

Stella.   So soon?

Festus.   The tone of your voice expresses regret. What is your decision?

Stella.   My decision?

Festus.   Upon my application for the situation of reader.   Shall I have it?

Stella.   Perhaps the terms will not suit.

Festus.   Madam, I am willing to serve you on any terms.   Allow me to throw off the mask of " Festus," which of course you have seen through, and offer myself for a situation under the name of —

Stella.   Stop: you are not going to pronounce that name before all these good people?

Festus.   Of course not.   But what shall I do?   Stella,

I feel that " Raphael" and " Sir Thomas Clifford " have inspired me to attempt love-making on my own account. Grant me the opportunity to make application for the situation made vacant by my unceremonious exit the other night. Let " Festus " apply once more.

Stella. What shall I say? (*To audience.*) Would you? He seems to have found his tongue; and who knows but what he may make an agreeable beau? I think he had better call again; for to have a lover who can make love by borrowing, is, at least, — under the circumstances — under the circumstances — what is it, Festus?

Festus. Circumstances? Why, under the circumstances, I should say it was "*An Original Idea.*"

CURTAIN.

NOTE. The " Readings " and " Scenes " may be varied to suit the taste of the performers. " The Garden Scene " in " Romeo and Juliet," scenes from " Ingomar," " The School for Scandal," &c., have been used with good effect.

"MY UNCLE, THE CAPTAIN."

CHARACTERS.

Mr. Sol Hanscomb, Jr. (landlord of "The Fatted Calf").
Capt. Nat Skillings (skipper and owner of the "Jemima Matilda").
Sam Skillings (his nephew).
Pete White (a colored waiter).
Steve Black (a white waiter).
Bobby Small (a boot-black).

COSTUMES.

Hanscomb.—Modern.
Nat Skillings. — Sailor rig; blue pants and shirt, pea-jacket, old fisherman's hat, gray wig.
Sam Skillings. — Dark mixed pants, blue coat with brass buttons, white hat, shawl, red wig.
Pete and Steve. — Waiters' dress, white aprons, wigs to suit.
Bobby Small.—Red shirt, black pants rolled up, glazed cap.

Scene. — *Room No. 86, "Fatted Calf" Hôtel. Table and two chairs, c. Entrances, R. and L.*

Hanscomb (outside, L.). Steve, Pete, come, come, hurry, hurry, wake up! *(Enter, L.)* This is really encouraging. The Fatted Calf, just opened, is rapidly filling up, and such customers, too; real upper crust, — nabobs, millionnaires, heiresses, generals, majors, captains, colonels, and all sorts of stylish people! Now let's look at the situation. I have on my books already thirty permanent boarders at five dollars a day. Pretty high for the times, but that draws the style. Of these thirty, ten will pay up promptly, ten wont pay at all, and the other ten will be obliged to leave their baggage to settle the bill. Well, I think that will pay. We must give a wide margin for profit, and in course of time may make a fortune, or manage to fail for seventy-five or a hundred thousand, either of which will create a sensation. Where can those waiters be? Ah, here's Steve at last, as stiff and pompous as one of the nabobs whom he delights to wait upon. *(Enter Steve, L.)*

Steve. Mr. Hanscomb, allow me to present for your inspection this document just left at the bar, with the compliments of the landlord of the Hotel Bullock. *(Gives Hanscomb printed handbill.)*

Mr. H. What is it? *(Reads.)* "Stop, thief! Nab him! Strayed from the Hotel Bullock an individual passing by the singular name of John Smith." John Smith? I think I've heard that name before.

Steve. It has a very *distangue* air.

Mr. H. "Tall, red hair, pale, ferocious-looking countenance; wore, when last seen, dark mixed pants, blue coat with brass buttons, white hat, and a shawl. A reward of one cent will be given for the arrest of the missing individual, and fifty dollars for the recovery of one dozen silver spoons, which said individual, probably accidentally, took with him." So, so, a hotel thief. Mr. John Smith will no doubt pay me a visit; so, Steve, just keep a sharp look-out for this spoony. *(Enter Pete, R., muttering and shaking his head.)* Well, what's the matter with you?

Pete. Mr. Hanscomb, I don't wish to be *troubulous,* — I don't wish to be *troubulous,* Mr. Hanscomb, but dar are t'ings, Mr. Hanscomb, dat stir de heart of man, as Deacon Foster eloquentially distresses himself, and — and — and — well, what I mean — rile him — rile him.

Mr. H.   What's the matter, stupid?

Pete.   Mr. Hanscomb, you're my massa.

Mr. H.   Well, well?

Pete.   You're my massa, Mr. Hanscomb, and I s'pose you can call me what you please.

Mr. H.   Of course I can.

Pete.   Ob course, ob course, kase I look upon you as my equel.

Mr. H.   Well, I'm much obliged —

Pete.   Don't apologize; no matter 'bout nuffin; but dat ar hostler down dar, he's an ignoramus, down dar, he is, down dar; he's low and insultin', he is. By golly! de imperance of dat feller is distressin'. He says I'm bound to *asswociate* wid him kase he's a man and a brudder.   Guess not, Mr. Hanscomb, — guess not; don't asswociate wid people dat smell ob de stable.

Mr. H.   You attend to your business, and he shall not trouble you.

Pete.   Dat's all I ask, Mr. Hanscomb, — dat's all I ask.   Jes' you keep hisself to hisself, and I wont say nuffin.   I's perfectly dissatisfied, but if he jes' trubble me, I'll brush him off — brush him off.

Mr. H.   Well, well, you go about your business.

Steve (at door, L., looking off).   Here's a queer-looking customer, and I'm not sure but what it is our friend, John Smith, of the spoon adventure; just the dress, even to the shawl.

Mr. H.   Ah, so soon?   Now, boys, look sharp and catch him in the act, — in the act, mind. (*Exit,* L. *Pete about to follow.*)

Steve.   Where are you going, Pete?

Pete.   Going?   Going after de axe, ob course.

Steve. After the axe! What do you want of the axe?

Pete. Cotch dat ar spoon feller. Didn't massa say be sure and cotch him wid de axe?

Steve. Well, you *are* an ignoramus.

Sam (outside, L., in Cockney dialect). Up this way, eh? Oh! never mind, Mister, I'll find the way. First turn to the right, second to the left, and then keep straight on, and here you are. *(Enter, L.)* So this is eighty-six, first floor from the roof. It's airy, anyhow. *(Steve, L., Pete, R., step up each side of Sam with the exclamation, "Take your baggage!" One seizes umbrella, the other carpet-bag, and start for entrances, R. and L.)* Here, you African, bring back that umbrella, and you, Mr. Upstart, bring back that valise. I choose to have them under my own observation.

Pete. Don't you want your wardrobe aired?

Sam. No, I don't want it aired. What's your name, African?

Pete. My name, massa, am White; dey calls me Pete.

Sam. And what's your name, Upstart?

Steve. My name is Black; I am called here Stephen.

Pete. " Steben, Steben; don't you bleeb 'im." He's called Steeb, short Steeb.

Sam. Well, you cut short, African, and cut off. Do you see that entrance? Well, you both get outside that entrance instantly. *(Steve and Pete go to entrance, L.)*

Steve. Pete, that is John Smith.

Pete. No! De spoon feller?

Steve. The same. Don't you see the pants and the coat and the shawl? 'Tis the pettifogger.

Pete. Petti who ? I fought it was Smiff,— John Smiff.
Steve. So it is ; look out for spoons. Sh ! *(Exit,* L.)
Pete. Look out for de spoons. Sh ! *(Exit,* L.)

Sam (during this speech busies himself taking off his shawl, brushing his clothes, smoothing his hair, etc.). What ails them objects ? They look at me awful hard ; they are evidently not accustomed to the presence of so elegant an individual in this hotel. So this is an hotel ; this is the first time that ever I was in one. I declare, it's quite elegant. And this is Boston, the hub of the universe, as Artemus Ward says. I wonder I have ever lived to get here, after having been cooped up in that horrid hole, Dismaltown. It is refreshing to get among civilized individuals. I've passed my whole life in that place without ever seeing anybody or anything, and I should be there now but for my uncle, the captain ; and somehow I do feel quite homesick when I think of my Annastasia ; but then my Annastasia is not there ; she is nearer to me in Boston than in Dismaltown, for my Annastasia is now on a visit to her aunt in Brighton. I have received epistles often from the object of my heart's adoration, and the last one was particularly interesting. She invited me in the name of her aunt to come and spend Christmas with her. I was particularly overjoyed at first, but how was I to get there ? The people of Dismaltown never go anywhere, and I should never have got here but for my uncle, the captain. My uncle has always been called captain, though he never went to sea, but for years has been behind the counter of the little grocery at Dismaltown, where he made some money. Well, my uncle took it into his head to buy a sloop; so he bought a sloop; it was a very good sloop for a second-hand one. The sloop was well sold, and so, they said, was my uncle, the captain. My uncle bought her, and then was bent on going a voyage in her as skipper, and so he invited me to go with him on his first voyage to Boston. He never went to sea before, and don't know anything about a sloop, and he was awful sick all the way, but he had a good mate, and he is a beautiful skipper; he talks such sea lingo, and swears so beautifully, though people do say that he knows no more about the sea than an owl; but that is all envy. Well, after I got aboard, I happened to think of one sentence in Annastasia's letter, which read, " Be sure to learn how to carve before you come, as uncle is away, and aunt will expect you to carve the Christmas goose." What an idea! they might as well ask me to carve an ox or an alligator. However, when I reached Boston, I bought a little book on the art of carving, and came up to this hotel to have a little practice. Look here, African. (*Pete and Steve have been bobbing in and out of the door,* L., *during the speech, watching Sam. Enter Pete,* L.) Do you know what a goose is?

Pete. Yes, massa; one ob dem two-legged fellers dat flops his wings jes' so — dis way — so.

Sam. Well, I want one of them.

Pete. One ob dem flappers? Live one?

Sam. No, ignorance, — roasted.

Pete. Yes, massa. (*Calls,* L.) Roast goose for 86.

Sam. No, no, stupid! Not for eighty-six; I only want it for one.

Pete. It's all right, massa; dat's what I fought, —

dat's what I fought. Dar wont but one goose come up here, so decompose yourself, — decompose yourself. *(Exit, L.)*

Sam. What horrid grammar that African does indulge in! *(Capt Skillings outside — "Ship ahoy! ahoy!" through speaking-trumpet.)* There's my uncle, the captain. *(Enter Captain, L.)*

Capt. Shiver my timbers, blast my eyes, and keel-haul *me*, if this here craft ar'n't the biggest seventy-four that ever I saw in all my cruisings. Such a climbing up hatchways and over bulkheads is trying to the narves of a tar with his sea-legs on.

Sam (aside). Now, isn't that beautiful language? It sounds so briny! *(Aloud.)* But I say, uncle, where's your tar?

Capt. Blast my eyes! Shiver my timbers! Do you mean to insult me? Aint I the skipper of the "Jemima Matilda," as stanch a craft as ever sailed out of harbor, with spanker jib-boom hauled taut, and foretop main-truck flying at the mast-head?

Sam (enthusiastically). Oh, aint he a spanker?

Capt. Now, look here, nevy, none of your jokes, or, shiver my timbers, I'll disinherit you. Aint I the skipper of the "Jemima" —

Sam. Oh, uncle, you said that before.

Capt. Blast my eyes, I'll say it again. *(Enter Steve, L.)* Look here, messmate, I'm a sailor; not one of your fresh-water sailors, but a regular-built old sea-dog.

Sam (aside). Eight days old; hasn't got his eyes open yet.

Capt. I've climbed the rigging in the darkest night.

Sam (aside). So dark nobody could see him.

Capt. I've seen the waves roll mountains high.

Sam (aside). That's a great idea.

Capt. I've been alone in the middle of the ocean in a jolly-boat.

Sam (aside). That's a jolly lie.

Steve. Well, captain, what can I do for you?

Capt. I say, messmate, did you ever hear of the escape of the "Jemima Matilda" on her trip from Dismaltown to Puddock?

Steve. Never did.

Capt. Then, blast my eyes, but you shall now, messmate.

Sam. I say, uncle, don't tell that horrid fiction again.

Capt. Fiction! You young dog, I'll have you court-martialed. *(Steve takes out tobacco-box and takes a chew.)* Well, you must know, messmate — What you got there?

Steve. Tobacco; will you have a chew?

Capt. No, I thank you; I don't chew.

Steve. You don't? Well you are the first sailor I ever saw who didn't chew.

Capt. I say, messmate, give us a chew. *(Aside.)* If sailors chew this, I can.

Sam. Don't, uncle, don't chew that horrid stuff; it'll make you as sick as a horse.

Capt. Shiver my timbers, nevy, what's the use in being a sailor, if you don't do as sailors do? Give us another chew, messmate. Thank ye. You must know, messmate, that the "Jemima Matilda," of which I am the skipper, left the harbor of Dismaltown on the second of July for a trip to Puddock.

Sam. With a cargo of onions.

Capt. We hauled off from the wharf wing and wing.

Sam (aside). It takes a pretty good sailor to put a sloop wing and wing.

Capt. As the wind freshened, we put more sail on the mizzenmast, and took a reef in the capstan, and set a hen-coop on top of the caboose, as a look-out. Then came on a perfect hurricane. We were within the latitude of forty-two degrees below zero, when I went below to take an observation. I hadn't been gone long before there was a cry from the look-out of "There she blows!" I rushed on deck, and sure enough it did blow strong from the nor-nor-east, nor-east-by-nor, and the ship was nearly on her bulkheads. The crew clung around me and entreated me to save the ship. I alone was calm. I had all the heavy furniture of my cabin, consisting of a pine table, a musquito netting, and a looking-glass, brought up and consigned to the waves; but all in vain. Desperation nerved my arm, and seizing a hatchet, I rushed abaft the hen-coop, and with one terrific blow cut away —

Steve. The mast!

Capt. No, three feet of the cook's stove-pipe. But she righted, and we were saved. Then a new danger arose on our weather bow. Three fathoms to windward arose a rock with a shelving surface nearest us even with the water, but the farthest part rising four feet. We were in danger of striking, when I rushed to the helm, bore hard on the compass, doused the binnacle lights, and steered straight for the rock. Fortune favored the bold manœuvre, for a sudden squall from the sou-sou-west raised the ship upon the rock. She slid swiftly over, and came down into the water with such a shock that, blast my eyes, if all the salt junk in the caboose didn't turn of its own accord. Give us another chew, messmate.

Sam (aside). If my uncle aint a sailor, it isn't for want of ability to lie.

Steve. Captain, is there anything I can do for you?

Capt. Ay, ay, messmate; show me a room, and give me something comfortable.

Steve. Ay, ay, sir! A warm room and a good pipe.

Capt. Pipe! Blast my eyes, I don't smoke!

Steve. You are the first sailor that ever I saw who didn't smoke.

Capt. Oh, shiver my timbers, let's have the pipe!

Sam.' I say, uncle, don't smoke a horrid pipe; you'll be awful sick.

Capt. Blast my eyes, nevy, do you take me for a land-lubber? You just keep a sharp look-out here on the quarter-deck, while I turn in and take a shot in the locker. Heave ahead, my hearty *(to Steve)*, or, shiver my timbers, I'll rake you fore and aft. *(Exit Steve and Captain, L.)*

Sam. My uncle knows a thing or two, but I'm afraid that, with smoking and chewing, he'll get awful sick of this sailor business. Ah, here comes my goose. *(Enter Steve and Pete, L., with table-cloth, dishes, and a roast goose. They spread the cloth on table, c., and arrange dishes.)* What an elegant spread!

Pete. Anything else, massa?

Sam. Let me see: there's no ale; bring me some ale; and — why, there's no spoons!

Steve. Spoons?

Pete. Spo-spo-spo-spoons?

Sam. Yes, spoons. How do you suppose an individual is to eat without spoons?

Steve. I'll bring them, sir. *(Exit, L.)*

Sam. Well, African, what are you grinning at?

Pete. At de goose, massa, — at de goose. *(Enter Steve, L., with spoons.)*

Sam. Now leave. Get out. *(Steve and Pete come down.)*

Steve. Keep your eye on the spoons.

Pete. By golly, Steve, if he take de spoons, he must take African too. *(Exit Pete, R., Steve, L.)*

Sam. It seems to me that those individuals have a great deal of anxiety on my account. Well, now to business. Where's my "Art of Carving"? *(Pulls small book from his pocket.)* Now let me see. No. 1 is the head, this must be it. *(Points to tail.)* No, this is the head. Now for it. *(Reads.)* "Grasp the knife firmly in the right hand," — that's so, — "take the fork in the left;" but what shall I do with the "Art of Carving"? It doesn't say anything about that: I'll fix it. *(Places book on the table.)* Now *(reads)*, "stick the fork in No. 8." That must be No. 8. "Draw your knife across No. 11" — *(Enter Pete, R.)*

Pete. Did you ring, sar?

Sam. No, I didn't ring, you outrageous ignorant —

Pete. Beg pardon, sar. Must have been 84. *(Aside.)* Spoons are dar. *(Exit, R.)*

Sam. Blast 84! What does he ring for just as I've

got my knife across No. 11 ? I must go all over it again.
(Reads.) Put your fork in No. 4, draw your knife across
No. 11 — *(Enter Steve, L.)*

Steve. Did you ring, sir ?

Sam. Ring, you blasted upstart ? *(Aside.)* With my
fork in No. 4 and my knife across No. 11 ! How was I
to ring ? *(Aloud.)* Ring ? — no.

Steve. Beg pardon, sir; it must have been 82.
(Aside.) Spoons all right. *(Exit, L.)*

Sam. 82 be blowed ! This is a queer proceeding.
I'll try it again. "Put your fork in No. 4, draw your
knife across No. 11, force yourself, and off comes the
(pulls the goose on to the floor) blasted animal. *(Enter
Pete, R., and Steve, L.)*

Pete. ⎱ Did you ring, sir? *(Sam stands by the table
Steve. ⎰ trying to hide the goose with the table-cloth,
looking first at Pete then at Steve.)*

Sam. Ring? Blast your ignorance, no ! Where's
your bell ?

Steve. *(Pointing, R.)* There it is, sir.

Sam. When I want you, I'll ring it loud, and open
the door, — so get out. *(Exit Pete, R., Steve, L.)* After
all my trouble, I must go back to No. 4. *(Places goose
on platter.)* No, I wont; I'll push ahead and trust to
luck. *(During the remainder of this speech tries in various places to carve the goose.)* This is the toughest
old gander that ever I saw. I can do nothing with it.
O Annastasia ! that leg wont come off. O Annastasia !
if you could only see me now, — I can't start that wing.
Why did you not ask me to get a horn of the moon, or
extinguish the Etna volcano. O Annastasia ! — there's a
piece of the breast; what a horrid looking object ! What

shall I do with him?   I can't eat him, and I should get
laughed at if it should be seen.   I'll give him away to
some poor individual.   (*Looks out of door*, L.)   Nobody
about — yes, there's an urchin.   Sh! look here.

Bobby Small (outside, L.)   Shine your boots?   (*Enter, with box and brush*, L.)   Yes, sir, all right; put
yer foot there, and I'll give yer true Union polish in
about forty-five seconds.

Sam.   I don't want my boots polished.

Bobby.   Oh, can't stand the press?   Look ahere, gent,
stand on my head, play yer a tune on my chin, and give
yer the Union polish, all for five cents.

Sam.   I don't want your Union polish.   I'm an Englishman.

Bobby.   Oh, yer an Englishman!   Say, don't yer want
to go over to Bunker Hill?   Stand on my head, play yer
a tune, and carry yer over to Bunker Hill, for five cents.

Sam.   I don't want to go to Bunker Hill.

Bobby.   Well, say what do you want?

Sam.   Sh!   Do you want a goose?

Bobby.   Do I want — Say that again, gent.

Sam.   Do you want a goose?   This one?

Bobby.   What's the matter with the poor old gobbler?
somebody's been mauling on him.

Sam.   Yes, all right, just cooked; here, take him and
leave.   (*Ties up goose in a napkin, accidentally slip-
ping in a gravy spoon.*)

Bobby.   Thank yer.   I'll take him right down among
the Union Polishers, and if we don't polish his bones,
my name is not Bobby Small.

Sam (giving goose).   Well, Bobby, here you are.

Bobby.   Thank yer, sir; may yer live forever!   But

I say, can't I do something for yer? Stand on my head? No! Play yer a tune on my chin? No! Union polish yer? Oh! yer don't like that. Well, when yer do want a shine, just drop down into Brattle Square. You'll find me there in business hours, ready to stand on my head, give yer a tune on my chin, or give yer the Union polish. *(Sings "Jordan:")*

> "Take off yer coat, boys, roll up yer sleeves,
> Spread well de blacking on de boots,
> De people bound to shine, and no make believes,
> And de Union am de polish dat suits."

(Exit, L.)

Sam. Well, I've got rid of that unfortunate animal, and now let's see if I can find my uncle, the captain. *(Enter Pete, L.)* Here, African, clear away this truck. *(Exit, L.)*

Pete. Clear away de truck? By golly! I t'ink it pretty well cleared itself, bones and all. *(Enter Steve, L.)* I say, Steve, de old gobbler am clean gone.

Steve. Is it possible? Look under the table.

Pete. By golly! dere am no goose dar. Dat are feller is a what yer call him, he is.

Steve. What do you mean by a what yer call him?

Pete. Why, one of dem fellers, connubial, connubial.

Steve. Connubial? You mean a cannibal.

Pete. Dat's what I said, a connubial.

Steve. Well, cannibal or connubial, our gravy spoon is missing.

Pete. By golly! Steve, it's Smiff,—John Smiff. Cotch him wid de axe! cotch him wid de axe!

Steve. Here, take these things right down, and tell Mr. Hanscomb. Be quick, for the gong will sound for dinner in three minutes. (*Enter Sam*, L.) More spoons, monsieur. (*Exit*, L.)

Pete. More spoons, spoons, monster! (*Exit*, R.)

Sam. What does this mean? Oh, horror! a light dawns upon me. Spoons, spoons! I must have given away one of the spoons with the goose. I remember there was one in the dish. Oh, heavens! what's to be done? They'll have me arrested. Where can my uncle, the captain, be? I can't find him anywhere, and he's got all the money. Oh, Annastasia, why did you ask me to learn the horrid art of carving? Oh, what will become of me? Oh, agony, agony! I'll ring the bell and disclose all. (*Rings the bell*, R. *As the gong sounds outside, Sam stumbles back over the carpet-bag, then over a chair, falls behind table, and crawls out in front as the gong ceases.*) Oh, what have I done, what have I done? Hear the crockery go! I've pulled down a whole crockery shop. (*Enter Steve;* L.)

Steve (fiercely). Did you ring?

Sam. No, I didn't touch anything, — I say, much broke?

Steve. Much broke! you'll find out what's broke. (*Exit*, L.)

Sam. What's to be done? That upstart's gone for an officer. It wont do for me to stop here. I'll make a run of it. (*Starts for door*, L. *Enter Steve, with a broom.*)

Steve. You can't pass here.

Sam. Oh, excuse me; I'll go the other way. (*Enter Pete*, R., *with a paper.*) This port blockaded?

Pete. Yes, massa, by Burnside. (*Touches him in side with poker.*)

2

Sam. Oh, oh, you ignoramus! do you want to torture me?

Pete. Only a little game of poker, massa.

Sam (fiercely). This is insulting! What do you mean by stopping an Englishman in this way?

Steve. Want to overhaul you, to see if there is anything contraband aboard.

Pete. 'Taint de fust time a British *mail* has been stopped.

Sam. I must submit. What would Annastasia say? It must be that unfortunate goose. I can't pay my bill till I find my uncle, the captain. *(Enter Bobby, stealthily, L., with the goose. Makes frantic efforts to attract Sam's attention.)* There's that urchin again. What is he making such awful faces for?

Bobby (aside). The gent gave me a spoon with the goose. It must have been by mistake, so I brought it back. Perhaps the gent will stand a dime. *(To Sam.)* Sh, sh! I've got it.

Sam (seizing him). Got it! so have I. Audacious! *(Seizes goose.)* Here's the goose *(takes out spoon)*, and here's the spoon. Hurrah! I'm saved. *(Enter Mr. Hanscomb, L.)*

Hanscomb. Are you? That's a very ingenious dodge, Mr. John Smith, but it wont do. Steve, seize that man; and you, Pete, look after the boy. *(Steve seizes Sam; Pete takes Bobby by the collar.)* You're a handsome couple, you are! What have you to say for yourselves?

Bobby. Look here, contraband, don't soil my linen. I say, gent, what kind of a scrape have you got me into?

Sam. I am innocent, I am innocent, I am innocent!

Pete. Dat's a lie, dat's a lie, dat's a lie! Jest look at dat poor old gobbler; somebody's massacred him.

Hanscomb. Take them to the station-house at once.

Sam. Oh, dear! is there no escape? Oh, Annastasia, if thou couldst only see the agony of thy unfortunate Samuel! Will nobody save me?

Capt. (outside, L.) O Sammy, Sammy! where are you, Sammy?

Sam. My uncle, the captain, at last. *(Enter captain, L., his face very pale, wrapped in a blanket, and shivering.)*

Capt. Oh, Sammy, oh, Sammy, I'm so sick! I want to go home, I want to go home. I went down-stairs, and a chap there as was a sailor wanted me to go over to Chelsea, and the horrid ferry-boat made me sick, and the awful pipe made me sick, and I want to go home. *(Falls into Sam's arms.)*

Sam. In the " Jemima " ?

Capt. No, never; don't let me see the water again, or a ship, or a sailor. I hate the sea, and I want to go home. *(Falls into Sam's arms again.)*

Sam. But I can't go; I'm arrested for stealing.

Capt. Arrested for stealing! Who accuses the nephew of Capt. Nat Skillings of stealing?

Hanscomb. Capt. Nat Skillings, of Dismaltown, Nova Scotia?

Capt. Just so.

Hanscomb. I used to know a Capt. Skillings, of Dismaltown, but he was not a sea captain.

Capt. Well, I guess it's the same man. I sha'n't be one after to-day.

Hanscomb. Captain, don't you remember your old friend, Sol Hanscomb?

Capt. To be sure I do.

Hanscomb. Well, I'm his son.

Capt. Be you, though? Why, how you have grown! But what have you been doing to my nephew?

Hanscomb. That your nephew! I thought it was John Smith.

Capt. Not a bit of it. That's Sam Skillings.

Hanscomb. Not John Smith! I'm confounded.

Steve. Not Smith? I'm dumb.

Pete. Not Smiff? I'm (*Bobby touches him with the poker, which he has rescued*) scorched.

Sam. Yes, Sam Skillings, who would scorn to do a mean action, but who accidentally purloined one of this gentleman's spoons, for which he is willing to make all possible reparation.

Capt. Oh, I see how it is; Sam has been practising the art of carving.

Hanscomb. The art of carving? Why, I'll teach him that in twenty minutes.

Sam. Will you, though? I'll be greatly obliged to you; so will Annastasia, and my uncle, the captain, skipper of the "Jemima" —

Capt. Sammy, sink the ship. I've concluded that the sea don't agree with my constitution. I'll sell her. (*To audience.*) Is there anybody here wants her? She's A1¾, stanch and well-built, copper-bottomed, and tarred throughout, especially the cabin; Morgan stock, sound and kind in harness; will stand all winds, especially nor-nor-east, nor-east by nor, shiver my timbers —

Steve (offering tabacco-box). Have a chew, captain?

Capt. (falls into Sam's arms.) Oh, Sam, Sam, take me home!

Hanscomb. Ladies and Gentlemen, "The Fatted Calf" has been opened under rather unfavorable circumstances, but if you will give us another call, you shall find a hospitable landlord —

Steve. Accommodating waiters —

Pete. Who — who — who will gib you ebery detention, wid — wid —

Bobby. De Union polish.

Sam. And if a word from me would not be out of place, I would recommend this house, as I expect to stop here with my Annastasia on our bridal tour, on which occasion we expect to be accompanied by that extraordinary seaman —

Capt. Oh, Sammy, don't.

Sam. My uncle, the captain.

DISPOSITION OF CHARACTERS.

L. Steve, Hanscomb, Capt., Sam, Bobby, and Pete. R.

NOTE. — The characters of Sam and Capt. Skillings were originally performed as "Cockney Englishmen." The performers can use their own discretion, — make them Cockneys by placing "h's" before the vowels and dropping the "h's" where they belong, or they can be performed as Yankees from down East. As Artemus Ward says, "You pay your money, and you has your choice."

NO CURE, NO PAY:

A FARCE.

FOR FEMALE CHARACTERS ONLY.

CHARACTERS.

Mrs. Languish, a Lady who has lately acquired Wealth.
Alice, her Daughter.
Lucy Aiken,
Jenny Carter, } Friends of Alice.
Susan Dean,
Bridget, the Queen of the Kitchen.
Aunt Maria Midget, a little hard of hearing.

Scene. — *Parlor in* Mrs. Languish's *house. Small table and chair,* L. ; *arm-chair,* C. ; *rocking-chair,* R.

Enter Bridget, L., *showing in* Lucy Aiken.

Bridget. Tak' a sate, Miss Lucy, if ye plaze, while I spake to the young misthress. It's glad she'll be to see yer, for it's a hape of throuble we have here ony how.

Lucy. Trouble, Bridget! Why, what's the matter?

Bridget. Shure, mam, it's all along of the misthress; she's too sick intirely, and is failin', and failin', and failin.'

Lucy. Mrs. Languish sick? I am sorry to hear that.

Bridget. Oh! indade, and indade she is. Ivery breath she draws is nearer and nearer her last.

Lucy. What seems to be the matter?

Bridget. An' shure, ma'm, I dont know, except that she's failin', and failin', and failin'; an' its sorry the day whin she fell ill; she's the kindest and bist misthress in the world. (*Crying.*) Oh, musha, musha! Oh, dear! Oh, dear!

Lucy. Well, well, Bridget, be calm, and hope for the best.

Bridget. Faith, and that's what I'm doin'. Oh, here comes Miss Alice, the poor disconsilite orphan. *Exit,* L.

Enter ALICE, R.

Alice. (*Running to* LUCY *and kissing her.*) Why, Lucy Aiken! You dear, good-for-nothing thing! Where have you been all this while?

Lucy. It *is* an age since we met. I must congratulate you, and I assure you I do, with all my heart, on your altered position. So, the rich and crusty old uncle, who forgot his relations while living, has remembered you in his will?

Alice. Yes, Lucy; thanks to uncle Caleb, we are rich. And, I assure you, we were glad to be remembered.

Lucy. But, dear me, Alice, what a careless creature I am! How is your mother? Bridget tells me she is very sick.

Alice. Poor mother! this sudden turn in the wheel of fortune has been too much for her; she is a confirmed invalid. I don't know what to make of her. Dr. Tincture can find no symptoms of disease. He says she is in sound bodily health; her suddenly drop-

No Cure, No Pay.

ping her usual employments has occasioned her seeming illness.

Lucy. Seeming! Why, Alice, you treat lightly what your Bridget seems to consider a very serious illness.

Alice. Well, I do; for I am convinced nothing ails mother. Her head is turned with the idea that she is an invalid, because she thinks it fashionable for rich ladies to be ailing, and she has the queerest notions. I suppose you will laugh, but I am going to tell you her last freak. She is highly incensed at Dr. Tincture, refuses to see him, and declares her illness can only be cured by some mysterious agency. Yesterday she bade me prepare this note to be inserted in the evening papers. (*Reads.*) "No Cure, no Pay. — A lady who is suffering from a disease which baffles the skill of the medical profession, and who is desirous of testifying her appreciation of the efforts now being made to institute a school of female practitioners, offers the sum of five hundred dollars to any female who will cure her. Address, with real name, 'Bedridden,' Station A, Boston Post Office; and remember, No cure, no pay." Did you ever hear of such a nonsensical whim?

Lucy. What an odd idea! And do you propose to send it?

Alice. No, indeed; that is, if I can possibly prevent it. But she believes it has already gone. Dear me! I wish I could find a way to frighten her into health again.

Lucy. That's just what you must do. If you will be guided by me, her cure can be effected. You remember our "Private Theatricals" last winter, and what

fun we had. Let us turn our practice then to profit now.
There's Jenny Carter and Susie Dean all ready for any
harmless sport, I know. You leave this to me, and I'll
send your mother a few samples of the new school she
so much admires.

Alice. Oh, capital! capital! But are you quite sure
you can carry out this scheme?

Lucy. Sure. Remember what Richelieu says about
" the bright lexicon of youth," and leave all to me. Good-
by; I must run and see the girls. Set your heart at rest;
we'll have your mother well before she knows it herself.
Good-by. *Exit,* L.

Alice. Good-by. I have great faith in Lucy. And
I do hope this scheme of hers will be a success. Perhaps it is wrong to deceive poor mother; but that advertisement once inserted in the papers, we should have
no peace day or night. Here she comes. Poor mother;
she works very hard to keep up her sickness. I can
hardly refrain from laughing to see her bright, rosy face,
and the utter lassitude of her body.

Enter Mrs. Languish, R., *supported by* Aunt Midget,
very slowly.

Aunt M. Keerful, Angelina; keerful, my child.
Remember you're a dreffal sick woman; dreffal sick.

Mrs. L. (*Sinking into easy chair,* C.) Oh, dear!
Oh, dear! I know — I am. I know — I am weaker —
and weaker — every — day. My camphor-bottle — aunt
Midget — fan me — my child. (Aunt M. *applies* camphor, *and* Alice *fans* Mrs. L.)

Alice. Don't you feel any better, mother?

Mrs. L. No, child; your — poor — mother — is failing rapidly; a few short days— and then —

Aunt M. (*Sneezes.*) Massy sakes, child! who left that door open? Do you want your marm to catch her death? (ALICE *shuts door*, L.)

Alice. Have you had your breakfast, mother?

Mrs. L. Yes, child — all I wanted — but I have no appetite.

Aunt M. Well, Angelina, how do you feel now?

Mrs. L. Very feeble.

Aunt M. What does she say?

Alice. Very feeble.

Aunt M. Hay?

Mrs. L. Dear — dear! Aunt Midget, don't speak so loud.

Aunt M. Loud? Why, Angelina! you know how feeble my voice is. I couldn't speak loud. (*Sits in rocking-chair*, R., *and knits.*)

Mrs. L. Alice, do you — hear any thing from the advertisement?

Alice. Oh, yes, mother; I hear from it. Several people are anxious to see you.

Mrs. L. I knew it — I knew it. My cure can only come from such a source. Look in the paper — child — there may be some new discovery advertised.

Alice. (*Sits*, L., *and takes up paper.*) Yes, there are a number. (*Reads.*) "Dr. Kresote's Extract of Lignumvitæ for the cure of Lumbago " —

Mrs. L. Oh, dear! I must try that. I know I've got the lunbago.

Aunt M. Who's that? Tom Bago! Is that a new doctor?

13

Alice. (*Reads.*) " Elias's Great Cure-all " —

Aunt M. Who's that's got a new carry-all?

Mrs. L. Aunt Midget — please, don't.

Aunt M. Law, Angelina, what's the use of living, if you don't know what's goin' on?

Alice. " The most Wonderful Discovery of the Age ! A Speedy Cure for all Diseases of the Spine " —

Mrs. L. Oh, dear ! I know my spine is diseased —

Alice. " Heart Disease " —

Mrs. L. O — O — O — I know I've got that ! I've got such a pain here and here — and here.

Alice. " General Debility " —

Aunt M. General who? What new military man is that?

Alice. " Consumption " —

Mrs. L. Oh, dear ! that's my case ! I feel it ! I'm sure I'm a victim to that —

Aunt M. Yes, Angelina, I told you this morning at the breakfast-table, when you ate four hard-boiled eggs, six pertaters, a big piece of steak, and so many flapjacks ! sartin' sure it was a forerunner of consumption.

Alice. " And all diseases which flesh is heir to " —

Aunt M. Diseases of the hair ! Do tell ! have they got something new for that? I'm glad on it, for my hair is all a comin' out.

Mrs. L. We must try that. (*Bell rings,* L.) Dear me, child ! you must have that bell muffled ; and I think we had better have the street strewn with tan, it's so soothing.

Bridget. (*Outside,* L.) Doctor, is it? Away wid yer. We want no doctors in petticoats here at all at all.

Alice. (*Runs to door*, L.) Bridget, show the lady up here.

Bridget. (*Outside*, L.) Will I? Oh, come in, Mrs. Doctor, come in.

Alice. This must be one of the ladies whom I expected.

Enter BRIDGET, *showing in* JENNY CARTER, *who is disguised. Calico dress without crinoline; short-waisted, if possible; a small, red shawl on her shoulders, a large, old-fashioned bonnet, cap, and glasses; under her arm an umbrella.*

Bridget. Here's the she-doctor, mam. *Exit*, L.

Jenny. Ahem — ahem! Who's sick? Who wants the doctor? I am Dr. Higgins, M.D., just graduated from the Female College. Would you like to see my diploma!

Alice. It's not necessary.

Jenny. Where is the patient? Stop! don't speak! The eye of science is quick to distinguish suffering. I see her! — that form.tottering on the verge of the grave.

Mrs. L. Oh, dear! what did I tell you! (*Jenny passes* Mrs. L., *rushes up to* AUNT MIDGET, *seizes her hand.*)

Jenny. My poor woman, how are you?

Aunt M. (*Shakes* JENNY's *hand.*) Why, how do you do? My eyesight's kinder failiu'. It's Jerusha Hoppin — aiu't it? What a handsome bunnet you've got!

Jenny. My dear woman, time is precious. Let me see your tongue.

Aunt M. Well, I flatter myself I do look young for one who's seen so much triberlation.

Alice.   Miss — Mrs. Doctor, you've made a mistake. This is the patient.

Jenny.   Dear me, dear me! what a blunder! (*Comes back to table,* L., *takes off her bonnet, then places chair,* L. *of* Mrs. L., *and sits.*)   What's the trouble?

Mrs. L.   Oh, dear! — doctor — I don't know. I'm failing rapidly.

Jenny.   Let me see your tongue (Mrs. L. *shows it.*) Ahem! Bad, bad!

Mrs. L.   Oh, dear, doctor, do tell me the worst!

Jenny.   Have you a cough?

Mrs. L.   (*Forcing a very slight cough.*)   Dreadful!

Aunt M.   Why, that must be a female woman doctor.

Jenny.   Sleep well nights?

Mrs. L.   Not a wink.

Jenny.   Not a wink? Bad, bad! Any appetite?

Mrs. L.   Not a bit.

Jenny.   Not a bit? Bad, bad! Madam, yours is a very bad case.

Mrs. L.   Oh, do, doctor, tell me the worst!

Jenny.   Madam, you are suffering from a terrible disease, — a disease of which the profession know but little. Hum-bug; a disease caused by a depression of the eliminating vesticubia of the scarcophagus. Had you fallen into the hands of the masculine butchers of the medical profession, your fate would have been terrible; but we of the new school are destined to lay bare new fountains of health. I propose to treat your case by an entirely new method; one that is destined to make a great revolution in medicine. The Lionian Method. — I will briefly explain. You, madam, are suffering from prostration, — a superabundance of weakness. In your case, madam, it is necessary to throw off this superabundance of weakness; but how to supply the vacuum? What is needed? You see at once: strength. But where shall we find strength? — in the mineral world? No. In the vegetable world? No. Where shall we turn? To the animal world, and there we find strength; and where greater strength than in the lion, the king of beasts? There is our remedy. Madam, I prescribe for you a lion diet. Lion steaks for breakfast, roast lion for dinner, cold lion for supper; and lion broth, lion soup, and lion fricassees promiscuously. Obey me, and you are saved; hesitate, and you are lost.

Mrs. L. Dear me! but where shall I get the lions?

Jenny. That's none of my business. I prescribe the mode; you must find the means. You are rich; send and catch them. I would recommend your keeping a few live lions in your back garden, that you may have them fresh at all times.

Mrs. L. Lions in our back garden? Mercy! we should be eaten alive!

Aunt M. Lions? What! turn our back garden into a howling wilderness?

Mrs. L. Dear me, dear me! I can never find the means of cure.

Jenny. Then I cannot help you. So, if you will just hand me a check for five hundred dollars, I'll go. (*Puts on bonnet.*)

Mrs. L. (*Starting up.*) A check for what?

Jenny. A check for five hundred dollars.

Mrs. L. But you haven't cured me. You forget, " No cure, no pay."

Jenny. Ah, but I've prescribed a method that will be sure to cure. If you don't choose to try it, that's not my fault.

Mrs. L. You just start yourself out of this house. Quick, or I'll find a way to send you. Quick, I say.

Jenny. Very well, madam; very well. Remember the law. You'll find you must pay. Good-morning.

[*Exit,* L.

Mrs. L. Who ever heard of such impudence?

Aunt M. Why, Angelina, what are you doing? You'll kill yourself standing so long.

Mrs. L. (*Sinks back into chair.*) Oh, dear! Oh, dear! My camphor, — quick! Fan me, child, fan me!

Alice. Well, mother, your first attempt with the new school is a failure. You'd better give it up, and send for Dr. Tincture.

Mrs. L. Child, don't mention that horrid name again. (*Bell rings.*) Who can that be? Another one of those humbugs.

Alice. We will not have any more come in here, if you say so.

Mrs. L. Yes, let them come. Every means must be tried.

Enter BRIDGET, L.

Bridget. If you plase, mam, there's another old woman. Says she's a doctor.

Alice. Show her in, Bridget.

Exit BRIDGET, L.

Aunt M. Seems to me, Angelina, you're having lots of callers to-day.

Enter SUSAN DEAN, L., *disguised. An old-fashioned
"pumpkin" hood upon her head, an old, faded cloak
upon her shoulders, a bundle of "roots and herbs" in
one hand, a heavy cane in the other.*

Susan. How do you do, folks? Somebody sick here?
I'm Dr. Hannah Stebbins, a regular graduated physician.

Alice. So we understand.

Susan. Yes, my medical edication begun with doc-
terin' with roots and yarbs. But, dear me! which is the
sick woman?

Alice. My mother.

Susan. Oh, yes! the old lady in the specs. Well, she
does look kinder feeble. (*Crosses to* AUNT MIDGET.)
Heow do you do, mam? Kinder croning, hay?

Aunt M. Hay?

Susan. They tell me you're kinder complainin'.

Aunt M. Rainin', is it? Why, du tell! What lots
of rain we do have!

Alice. You've made a mistake. This is my mother.

Susan. Why, yeou don't say so. There's nothing
the matter with her — is there? What's the matter?
Got the rheumatics?

Mrs. L. Oh, dear! I don't know what's the matter.

Susan. Kinder stericky — ain't yer? Let's see your
tongue. It's awful red! Let me feel your pulse. Dear
me! Why, what can be the matter?

Mrs. L. I am very weak.

Susan. Got a crick in your back?

Mrs. L. I don't know, but I think I have.

Susan. Headache?

Mrs. L. (*Putting her hand to her head.*) Oh, terrible!

Susan. Purty bad way, yeou are. Let me see. There's catuip, — that ain't powerful enough; then there's penny-*rial* and wormwood, thoroughwort and hy-sup; them won't do yeou any good; we must try the new grassalogical treatment.

Mrs. L. The grassalogical treatment! What is that?

Aunt M. Hay?

Susan. A new discovery of our larned sister, Dr. Sally Wiggins. The Scripters tell us, "All flesh is grass." Therefore, when the flesh is weak, what more nat'ral than that we should fly to its great counterpart in nature, the grass?

Aunt M. (*Aside.*) Talking about counterpanes, — I'd like to show her my new patch-work quilt.

Susan. On this theory Dr. Sally has founded her new treatment; and I think it will be the best thing yeou can try. Take for breakfast every day grass tea; grass greens biled for dinner, with a leetle pork or bacon; grass tea for supper — nothing else, and sleep on the grass nights. If natur' won't work a cure in your case, then I'm much mistaken.

Mrs. L. Sleep on the grass? Why, you're crazy!

Aunt M. Why, I do believe that woman wants to turn our Angelina out to paster, jest like a cow.

Mrs. L. I confess I do not see the logic of your new treatment.

Susan. Yeou don't? Well, it does look kinder strange, but it's the new school; and if woman is ever to find her *speare,* her speare must be in some new school.

Mrs. L. I shall decline following any such nonsensical prescription.

Susan. Very well, mam. If you won't, you wont; and that's all there is about it. So, when you're ready to settle, I'm ready to start.

Mrs. L. (*Starting up.*) Ready to settle! What do you mean?

Susan. Five hundred dollars. That was your offer.

Mrs. L. No cure, no pay. What have you done?

Susan. Given you an original mode of treatment. If you do not choose to follow it, that's not my fault.

Mrs. L. You just take your roots and herbs and your new treatment, and start out of this house, or you'll get worse treatment.

Susan. Well, well, if this isn't an ungrateful world! You're a pretty sick woman, you are.

Mrs. L. Alice, call Bridget.

ALICE *exit*, L.

Susan. Yeou needn't call any of your hired folks; I'm going; but if there is any law in the land, you shall hear from me. You're a pretty sick woman, you are.

Exit, L.

Aunt M. Why, Angelina, there you are standin' ag'in! You'll ruin your constitution jest as sure as can be.

Mrs L. (*Sinks back.*) Oh, dear, what a trial!

Enter BRIDGET, L.

Bridget. Did you ax for me, mam?

Mrs L. Bridget, don't you let any more of these people into the house; they'll be the death of me. Do you hear?

Bridget.   Faith, I do, mam; and sorry a one will I
let in at all at all.   *Exit,* L.

Aunt M.   Trial and triberlation, child! that's the lot
of us weak mortals.

Enter ALICE, L., *disguised as an old lady; shawl, large
bonnet, spectacles, &c.*

Massy sakes! who's that?

Alice.   Somebody's sick here — hain't there?

Mrs. L.   Where did *you* come from?

Alice.   Hay?

Mrs. L.   Where did you come from?

Alice.   I'm a leetle hard of hearing. You'll have to
speak louder.

Mrs. L.   Dear me! who sent you here?

Alice.   Thank you; I don't care if I do take a cheer.
(*Sits,* L.)

Mrs. L.   Dear, dear! where can Alice be! Who
sent you here?

Alice.   Oh, yes, I hear now, when yer speak loud.

Mrs. L.   Aunt Midget —

Aunt M.   Well, child.

Mrs. L.   Do try and talk to this woman; she's deaf
as a post, I'm sure.

Aunt M.   Poor, is she? Wants cold victuals. I s'pose.

Mrs. L.   No, no; she's a doctor.

Aunt M.   (*Pulling her chair close to* MRS. L., *and
speaking across her to* ALICE.) What's the matter?

Alice.   (*Moving her chair close to* MRS. L., *they both
speak very loud.*) Hey?

Aunt M.   What's — the — matter?

Alice. I'm deaf. (*Pronounce* deef.)

Aunt M. Dear me! she want's some beef. Well, if poor folks ain't gitting proud! I guess you'll have to content yourself with good cold bread.

Alice. Yes; it is caused by colds in the head.

Mrs. L. Dear me! set the blind to lead the blind. Aunt Midget, this old lady is very deaf.

Aunt M. You don't say so. (*Very loud.*) What do you want?

Alice. To treat the lady.

Aunt M. Hay?

Mrs. L. Gracious! what a confusion! My good woman, aunt Midget, this lady, is also very deaf.

Alice. I want to know. (*Very loud to* AUNT M.) I want to treat this lady.

Aunt M. Want to treat her? (*Very loud*). What with?

Alice. (*Louder.*) I'm a doctor.

Aunt M. Doctor, hey! Medical or dedical?

Alice. I'm a female physician.

Aunt M. Musician too! What do you play on?

Mrs. L. Stop, stop, stop! Do you want to craze me, you two? Bridget, Bridget! My good woman, I do not require your services.

Enter BRIDGET, L.

Here, show this woman out of the house, quick!

Alice. I'm a regular —

Bridget. Oh, no more of yer blarney! Start yourself quick!

Alice. But, my dear lady, you advertised —

Bridget. (*Pushing her off,* L.) Ah, away wid yer! Away wid yer!

Mrs. L. (*Sinks into her chair.*) Oh, dear! was ever a poor sick woman so abused! My camphor, aunt Midget; my camphor! Where can Alice be?

Enter ALICE, L.

Alice. Here I am, mother; I was called down stairs to see a lady, a healing medium. She is very desirous of seeing you.

Mrs. L. I will not see her. Those we have had have nearly killed me.

Alice. But, mother, this is an entirely different sort of person. You must see her, for she is coming up stairs now.

Mrs. L. Oh, dear, dear! Am I never to have any peace?

Enter LUCY, *disguised. A bloomer costume (a bathing-dress will answer the purpose), an old-fashioned "front" of hair with side curls, a straw hat and parasol.*

Lucy. My dear child, which is your afflicted parent!
Alice. This is her.
Lucy. (*Seats herself,* L. *of* MRS. L.) She does, indeed, seem afflicted! That care-worn face, those weak and feeble limbs, are sure signs of the presence of disease.

Mrs. L. Here is one who understands me at last.

Lucy. The power has been given me to heal the sick. (*Twitches her right arm.*)

Mrs. L. Mercy! what's the matter?

Aunt M. That girl's going into a fit.

Lucy. It's nothing; be as quiet as you can. (*Left arm twitches.*)

Aunt M. Gracious goodness! I tell you, Angelina, that gal's in a fit! (LUCY's *head jerks, and she stares fixedly at* AUNT M.) See her glare at me! I tell you she's crazy. Angelina, if you don't have that woman taken away, I'll holler right eout!

Lucy. Sh—! I behold a vision! I see a woman before a wash-tub—a stout, rosy, healthy woman. She looks like you; and she rubs and sings, rubs and sings. (*With imitation of rubbing.*)

Mrs. L. That's me—that's just like me!

Lucy. I see her again! She's ironing now; and she irons and sings, irons and sings. (*Imitates.*)

Mrs. L. Just like me—just like me!

Lucy. And now she sweeps (*imitates*), and now scrubs (*imitates*), singing all the while. Hark! what is it she sings?

Mrs. L. (*Singing.*)

"Let us sing merrily, lightly, and cheerily,
    Let us be gay,
    Let us be gay;
Throw away sorrow; why should we borrow
    Tears from to-morrow
    To darken to-day?"

(*To be found in the "Excelsior Song-Book."*)

Lucy. Yes, yes! That's it! But now it changes. I see her again: she appears feeble and weak, and complains. Oh, how she complains! (*Imitates.*)—"Oh,

dear! Oh, dear! I'm so weak — I'm so weak! My
camphor, aunt Midget! Fan me, my child!"

Mrs. L. Oh, dear! that's me.

Lucy. (*Gesticulating, as though shaking somebody.*)
What is this that now urges me to seize this woman and
shake her?

Aunt M. Angelina, that gal's going to fight somebody. Don't yer come a-near me.

Lucy. (*Slowly approaching* Mrs. L.) All this woman
needs is exercise, and I must give her exercise. (*Imitating shaking.*)

Aunt M. (*Jumping into chair.*) Massy sakes! this
is a raving lunatic.

Mrs. L. (*Starts up.*) Come, come, young woman,
this is quite enough.

Alice. You musn't touch my mother.

Aunt M. That gal's a Shaker; I know she is.

Lucy. (*Still approaching her.*) To shake this woman
— to shake this woman!

Mrs. L. This woman declines being shaken. I'll do
all the shaking myself. (*Seizes* Lucy *and shakes her.*)
What do you mean by such conduct? Who are you?
(*Shakes her again, which shakes off her "front" and hat.*)
Lucy Aiken! Why, what does this mean?

Lucy. That I have turned physician, owing to the
extraordinary inducements held out in an advertisement
entitled "No Cure, no Pay."

Mrs. L. What?

Alice. Yes, mother, I thought it a pity to waste
money in advertising when we had three such good female
physicians in the neighborhood.

Enter JENNY CARTER *and* SUSAN DEAN, L., *disguised as*
before.

Here are the other two.

Mrs. L. And pray, who are they? (JENNY *and*
SUSAN *throw off their bonnets.*)

Jenny. A disciple of the lionian school!

Mrs. L. Jenny Carter!

Susan. And a student of the grassalogical treatment.

Mrs. L. Susan Dean! Well, I am amazed.

Aunt M. (*Getting down from chair.*) If that gal's
got through her tantrums, I'd like to get down!

Mrs. L. But there was another — a deaf old lady.

Alice. (*Imitating.*) Hay?

Mrs. L. Why, Alice! have you been concerned in
this too? Do you know it was very wrong to deceive
your mother in this way?

Alice. Perhaps it was, mother; but I think you are
better for the very singular treatment you have met
with.

Aunt M. Law, child, what are you thinking of?
You have been standing nearly five minutes.

Mrs. L. And I propose to stand five minutes more,
for the purpose of thanking these young ladies for the
very excellent manner in which they have treated my
complaint. Ah, Lucy, that little touch of the old life
you gave me has awakened my slumbering energies. I
think I shall be able to go about and do a portion of
that duty which is given the 'rich to perform — succor
the needy and relieve the distressed. In such employ-
ment I need fear no return of my complaint. But how
can I reward you?

Alice.   Remember your promise; five hundred dollars —

Lucy.   Which we gladly renounce, looking for reward in the approval of our friends here.

Mrs. L.   But will they grant it? If, like me, in your practice they have found a cure for idle complainings, they certainly will; if not, you must all remember the conditions — No Cure, No Pay.

DISPOSITION OF CHARACTERS AT END:

L.   Susan, Jenny, Lucy, Mrs. Languish, Alice, Aunt Midget.   R.

HUMORS OF THE STRIKE.

A FARCE.

FOR MALE CHARACTERS ONLY.

CHARACTERS.

GREENBAX, President of the Broadaxe Horse Railroad.
HARTSHORN, a Director.
TRUMPS, Superintendent.
KNOCKDOWN, Conductor.
WHIPSTOCK, Driver.
HARDHEAD (a little deaf).
FINNEGAN, a Fenian.
DAN, a New-York Butcher's Boy.

COSTUMES, MODERN.

· ———

SCENE. — *President's Room.   Chair*, L.   *Table*, C.

Enter KNOCKDOWN, L.   WHIPSTOCK, R.

Knock.   Whipstock, my boy, how goes the strike?

Whip.   As well as could be expected.   It's evident we shall have to give in.   Old Greenbax is still determined not to pay the advance asked for.

Knock.   Won't he?   We'll see about that.   The strike has continued but eight days, and they have used up all means in their power to get conductors and drivers. I saw the seven o'clock car standing before the station, waiting for somebody to put it through. We have taken good care nobody shall be found; and I rather think this predicament will bring our worthy president to terms. There's nothing like a little pluck, my boy.

Whip. Oh, yes; it's all very well for you to talk, who have a chance at the pickings; but as for me, I'm pretty well played out; and if old Greenbax don't come down soon, I shall, with a rush.

Knock. Nonsense! Never say die, my boy.

Whip. I don't mean to; but if this thing continues much longer, Mrs. Whipstock will say it for me, emphasized with a broomstick. Halloo! here's old Greenbax. Now for a breeze.

Enter GREENBAX, R.

Green. (*As he enters.*) Trumps! Trumps! I say, where can that fellow be? Trumps! (*Sees* KNOCK-DOWN *and* WHIPSTOCK.) Halloo! what are you doing here? Ready to go to work, hey!

Knock. Yes, sir, ready to go to work — at the advance prices.

Green. Hum! (*To* WHIPSTOCK.) And are you ready to drive?

Whip. Certainly — at the advance prices.

Green. (c.) Hum! Will you both serve us faithfully?

Whip and Knock. (*Advancing eagerly on each side of him, and speaking quickly.*) Oh, yes, sir; yes, indeed!

Green. At the advance prices? I'll see you farther, first, and then I won't. No, sir; we pay you too much now. Clear out, both of you. I don't want you around here. Quit! Exit! Vamose!

Whip. Did you ever! The old curmudgeon! *Exit* R.

Knock. No, I never! The skinflint! *Exit,* R.

Green. (*Seating himself at desk.*) Here's a pretty condition for the Broadaxe Horse Railroad to find itself placed in. A parcel of whipsnappers dictating to Horatio Greenbax, president of the corporation. Strike away, you scoundrels! You'll find those who have the longest pockets can strike the hardest and stick the closest. (*Enter* TRUMPS, R.) Well, Trumps, what's up now?

Trumps. We are, I should say. Here's the seven o'clock car waiting for both driver and conductor, and none to be had.

Green. Then get new ones.

Trumps. It's very well to say get new ones; but where to get them, is the question. Our discharged men have induced everybody in the neighborhood to refuse.

Green. They have, have they? (*Voices heard outside shouting,* "*Halloo!*" "*Conductor!*" "*Time's up!*" "*Halloo!*" "*Hurry up!*" "*Hurry up!*")

Trumps. There, you hear that; the passengers are impatient.

Green. Well, well; drive it yourself.

Trumps. I can't do that; somebody must look after the company's property. (*Voices heard again impatiently shouting.*)

Enter HARTSHORN, L.

Harts. Mr. Pwesident, what is the meaning of this wow, and wiot, and wumpus? 'Pon my word, this is decidedly wulgaw; we shall be disgwaced with such an outwageous disturbauce in fwout of our door — we shall, indeed.

Green. The fact is, Mr. Hartshorn, the company finds itself destitute of both drivers and conductors, in consequence of the strike.

Harts. Stwike! what a wevolution! You alawm me — you do, indeed.

Green. Well, don't get frightened; you won't be struck.

Harts. What's to be done?

Green. Don't know; unless you volunteer to drive that car down.

Harts. I volunteaw to dwive a paiw of vulgaw howses down Bwoadway, and one of these filthy caws too! I nevaw! The effluviaw fwom those cadavewous cweatures is howible! 'pon my word, howible! (*Voices again.*) There's the wow agaiu!

Enter HARDHEAD, R.

Hard. Where's the president of this confounded road?

Green. I believe I have the honor to be its presiding officer.

Hard. Hey?

Green. I am he.

Hard. Hey? Speak louder; what are you mumbling about?

Green. (*Very loud.*) I am the presiding officer.

Hard. Coffee, sir? I didn't say any thing about coffee. I've had my breakfast, and, if it hadn't been for that infernal car, should have been down town before this.

Green. This old gent is a little hard of hearing.

Trumps. It hasn't affected his vocal organs, anyhow.

Harts. Yaas; he's got an impediment in his eaw.

Hard. What do you all stand there growling for? Why don't you answer me?

Green. I am the person you want.

Hard. Hey?

Green. (*Very loud.*) I — am — the — President. (*Lower.*) Confound your picture!

Hard. Oh, you are; then you ought to be ashamed of yourself. What's that car waiting for?

Green. Somebody to drive.

Hard. Hey?

Green. (*Very loud and angrily.*) Want somebody to drive.

Hard. Somebody's wife? What business have you to keep a car waiting for somebody's wife? I don't ask you to wait for my wife — do I? Where's your conductor?

Green. He's on a strike.

Hard. Hey?

Green. (*Very loud and excitedly, and flourishing his arms.*) I tell you he's indulging in a strike.

Hard. (*Raising his cane.*) Oh, that's your little game, is it? You want to indulge in a strike! Well, indulge, then. Come on, you scoundrel; I'll strike!

Green. No, no! (*Dodging behind* HARTSHORN.) I don't mean any thing of that kind. Keep off!

Harts. Good gwacious! what a tewible monstaw!

Hard. (*To* HARTSHORN,) — Oh, you'll have it — will you, Whiskers? You want a crusher — do you?

Harts. No, no; I don't want a cwusher! (*Dodges behind* GREENBAX.) I won't have a cwusher!

Trumps. (*Stepping before* HARDHEAD, *and speaking very loud.*) Beg pardon, sir; but you misunderstand. Our drivers have struck for higher wages.

Hard. Oh, that's it. Why didn't he say so? (*To* GREENBAX.) Well, what are you going to do about it? I must go down town at once.

Green. (*Loud.*) If you will be patient a few minutes, we will try to accommodate you.

Hard. Look here, Mr. —— (*to* TRUMPS), what is that individual's name?

Trumps. GREENBAX.

Hard. Look here, Mr. Beeswax; if you don't hurry up that car, I'll have you arrested as a swindler. (*Voices outside again.*)

Trumps. Come, Mr. Greenbax, something must be done at once.

Green. What can I do?

Trumps. Hire the men at the new prices.

Green. Never! I said I wouldn't, and I won't, if no cars run to-day.

Trumps. Very well, sir; I have done all I can do. (*Exit.*)

Hard. Are we going down to-day or not?

Green. I wish you was down where you belong, with all my heart. (*Louder.*) Very warm to-day, sir.

Hard. Hey?

Green. It's very warm to-day.

Hard. Pay? I'll pay you if you don't start that car soon. (*Goes up to table and sits.*)

Green. O, pshaw! it's no use talking to him. Well, Hartshorn, what's to be done?

Harts. · 'Pon my word, I don't know. S'pose you dwive down yourself.

Green. Me? When I do, just inform me—will you? (*Noise again outside.*) Halloo! Who's this?

Enter FINNEGAN, R.

Fin. Is the prisidint widin, I dunno?

Green. Well, I do. He is; and I am he.

Fin. Yer are — are yez? O, yer spalpeen! and it's there ye are, thaif!

Green. Come, come; be a little more respectful.

Fin. Respictful, is it? By my sowl, and ain't you the sarvant of the public? and ain't I the public, bedad? What do yer mean by kaping me standing outside there squatting in a car, and waiting to be took to the arms of Biddy and the childers, afther I've fit, bled, and died for ould Ireland up in Can-a-dy, shure I'd like to know?

Hart. Good gwacious! what a fewocious fowcigner!

Fin. And who the deuce are you, onyhow? You chatter like a monkey, and you look like a baboon! By my sowl, I believe you're Barnum's What Is It!

Green. Come, come; this won't do.

Fin. Won't it? and who's to hinder, I'd like to know? Faith, do ye mind who I am? I'm a full-blooded Fenian; ready to sthrike for ould Ireland; and if that car don't start soon, I'll strike you, ye black-guard. (*Flourishing his shillalah.*)

Green. Come, come; be quiet. (*Dodging behind* HARTSHORN.) Pacify him, Hartshorn.

Harts. Pacify him? Good gwacious! here's another

stwiker! Don't flouwish that club in that mannaw.
Gweenbax will talk to you. (*Dodges behind* GREEN-
BAX.)

Green. Put up that stick. You shall have a conveyance in five minutes.

Fin. Conveyance, is it? I want no conveyance. I
want a car, and that quick.

Hard. (*Starting up and shouting.*) Is that car going
or not?

Fin. Faith, here's another belated gint. (*To* GREEN-
BAX.) Don't yer hear the gintleman?

Green. Confound the gintleman, and the car too.
Was ever a president in such a fix? Here's another!
Well, come on all at once.

(*Enter* DAN, R.)

Dan. Say! where's the president of this here road?
Say!

Hard. Is that car going?

Fin. Fetch on your conveyance, ould chap.

Green. One at a time, if you please. (*To* DAN.) I
am the president. What do you want?

Dan. Well, say, old cove, what do yer mean by
keepin' folks waitin' in this style, say?

Fin. Faith, ould, gint, if yer don't spake up, there'll
be " say " enough to dhrown ye.

Green. There's a little delay on account of the strike.

Fin. Sthrike, is it? A sthrike, bedad! I'm on hand
like a picked-up dinner. I sthruck a blow for ould Ireland
in Can-a-dy, and then I sthruck for home; and, bedad,
I'll sthrike for any thing at all, at all.

Dan. I say, Pat, hush yer jaw ; we'll jest clean out this institution.

Fin. Faith, that we will. It's a dirthy place onyhow.

Hart. Good gwacious! there's going to be more stwiking!

Dan. Look here, Smellin' Bottle! (*Seizes* HARTSHORN *by the collar, and brings him to the centre.*)

Hart. Good gwacious! Welease my coat! You awe too polite — you awe indeed!

Dan. Am I? Jest look a here, Smellin' Bottle! and you too, prez — look sharp! fur I'm a goin' to talk to yer like a first-class sermon! I drives fur old Swizel, I does ; and I kills fur Swizel too ; and I'm goin down town in that car in five minutes! You understand?

Hard. (*Shouting.*) Is that car going, or is that car not going?

Dan. Say, old gent, you jest subside.

Hard. Hey?

Fin. Faith, the ould gint's as dafe as a haddock. (*Goes up to table and talks to* HARDHEAD *in dumb show.*)

Dan. Now, prez, I want yer to understand I'm a goin' down town ; and I want a driver and a conductor.

Green. But I tell you there is a strike.

Dan. Yes ; and there'll be another very soon. Here, Smellin' Bottle, I guess you can drive pretty well.

Harts. Good gwacious! Me? O, nevaw. I should be exhausted at once! I should indeed!

Dan. Then we'll exhaust you. Come, heave ahead, and take the ribbons.

Harts. But, good gwacious! considaw ; I should soil my dwess ; I should indeed!

Dan. Well, we'll fix that. Here, Pat.

Fin. (*Coming down.*) Here yer are, my darlint.

Dan. Bring some old clo's in here from that next room — the dirtiest yer can find.

Harts. Good gwacious!

Fin. Faith, that I will. (*Exit, R.*)

Green. I protest against this proceeding. You are trespassing upon the premises of the Broadaxe Railroad.

Dan. Oh, simmer down, now; your turn will come soon.

Enter FINNEGAN, R., *with a couple of dirty old overcoats and a couple of shocking bad hats.*

Fin. Here you are.

Dan. Now, Smellin' Bottle, jump into this. (*Holding up the dirtiest overcoat.*)

Harts. Good gwacious! what a howible coat! No, nevaw; twy the pwesident. (*Dodges behind* GREEN-BAX.)

Dan. All right. (*Seizes* GREENBAX.) Prez, jump in.

Green. No; I will submit to no such outrage. I am the president of this corporation.

Fin. Thin we'll invist you wid this robe of office. (*Dan and* FINNEGAN *seize* GREENBAX, *and thrust him into the coat.*)

Green. Oh, you shall suffer for this!

Fin. We do, my darlint; now for your crown. (*Claps hat on his head.*) Ivery inch a king!

Dan. Now, then, for Smelliu' Bottle. (*Seizes* HARTS-HORN.)

Harts. Good gwacious! I'm innocent; I am indeed! I'm only a poor diwector.

Fin. Thin come here directly. (*Seizes him, puts on coat and hat, he all the time protesting.*)

Green. Oh, if there is any law, you shall suffer for this!

Hard. Is that car going?

Dan. Directly. We've procured a driver and conductor, and now we're off. Come, Pat, lead off with the prez — I mean driver.

Fin. Faith, that I will.

Dan. And I'll take Smellin' Bottle. (*They take* GREENBAX *and* HARTSHORN *by the arm, who struggle and protest.*)

Green. (*To* HARDHEAD, *who comes down.*) This is an outrage. I call upon you to protect me.

Hard. Hey?

Harts. Yes, yes; pwotect me, pwotect me!

Hard. Hey?

Fin. Bedad! that ould gint is like a horse; he's full of hay!

Dan. Now we'll be down town in a jiffy. Come on.

Enter TRUMPS, R.

Trumps. What's the meaning of this?

Dan. We've procured a conductor and a driver for the seven o'clock car.

Trumps. We don't want them.

Dan. Yes; but *we* do.

Trumps. No; for the conductor and driver have come to terms; and if you'll jump aboard, we'll be off in a jiffy.

Green. Strike over?

Trumps. Entirely.

Harts. Good gwacious! that's lucky!

Dan. You can bless your lucky stars, prez.

Green. I do; and if ever there's another strike on this road, I'll resign at once.

Fin. (*To* HARDHEAD.) Strike's over!

Hard. Hey?

Fin. (*Loud.*) The strike's over.

Hard. Anybody knocked down?

Dan. The conductors will attend to that part of the business.

Trumps. Come, gentlemen, jump on; can't wait any longer.

Green. Jump on, gentlemen; the strike has concluded to our satisfaction; let us hope it has to the satisfaction of all who have taken this little trip with us on the Broadaxe Horse Railroad.

DISPOSITION OF CHARACTERS.

R. Trumps, Finnegan, Greenbax, Hartshorn, Dan, Hardhead. L.

BREAD ON THE WATERS.

A DRAMA IN TWO ACTS.

CHARACTERS.

DR. HARLEM, Principal of Greenlake Seminary.
HARRY HARLEM, his son.
FRED HASTINGS, } Pupils.
BOB WINDERS, }
JONATHAN WILD BUTTS, the Town Constable.
LUCY HARLEM, the Doctor's Daughter.
MRS. LORING, Housekeeper.
DILLY (picked from the streets).

COSTUMES.

DR. HARLEM. Act 1, Black suit, white cravat, long white hair. Act 2, Dressing-gown, &c.
HARRY. Act 1, Lad of eighteen. Roundabout jacket, rolling collar, &c. Act 2 (disguised). Gray wig and beard, sailor's blue shirt, white trousers.
FRED. Act 1, Lad of eighteen. Roundabout jacket, rolling collar, &c. Act 2, Stylish modern costume.
BOB. Act 1 (Very fat), Costume same as Harry and Fred. Act 2 (genteel figure), Very fashionable.
BUTTS. Act 1, Blue coat, brass buttons, short pants, iron-gray wig, shabby hat. Act 2, same as in Act 1.
MRS. LORING. Act 1, Old lady's suit. Act 2, Same as in Act 1, with the addition of cap and spectacles.
DILLY (aged 13). Act 1, Short dress, curls, &c. Act 2, Young lady's modern dress.
LUCY (aged 16). Act 1, Dress neat and pretty. Act 2, Young lady's modern dress.

Act 1. Scene. — *Parlor in the house of* Dr. Harlem. *Table*, l., *with chair* r. *of it; armchair*, l. c. ; *small table with chair*, r. ; Lucy, r., *sewing;* Mrs. Loring *seated in armchair, reading.*

Mrs. L. Lucy, my child, how very quiet you are!

Lucy. Indeed, Aunt Loring, I cannot help it. You know to-day is the very last of the term. School closed; all the pupils gone except Fred Hastings and Bob Winders, and they leave us to-day : the thought of the quiet humdrum life we are to lead for the next two months makes me feel very sad.

Mrs. L. The change will be a relief to all of us. Think of your father : he needs the rest which the close of the term will bring.

Lucy. I do think of him ; and for his sake I am glad. But still we lose many friends in the young gentlemen who have left us. I'm sure we shall miss them.

Mrs. L. Especially your particular friend, Fred Hastings ; hey, Lucy?

Lucy. Oh! of course. You know he is very agreeable, Aunt Loring, and has been very kind to us.

Mrs. L. He is no favorite of mine. He has been very agreeable, especially to you ; while to your brother Harry he has been altogether too kind.

Lucy. Why, Aunt Loring! Harry thinks there never was such a friend.

Mrs. L. Harry is young; he has seen little of the world : and the gay, dashing style of Fred Hastings has won his admiration. But Master Fred Hastings has already led him into mischief Their pranks in the village have reached my ears, and, I fear, those of your father. Fred Hastings is not a fit companion for our Harry; and it will be a relief to me when he quits this place never to return.

Lucy. Don't talk so, Aunt Loring. You are mistaken in him.

Mrs. L. I hope I am. But, during the ten years I have been housekeeper for your father, I have seen a great many young men, and learned to read their characters; and I say that Master Fred Hasting has too much money, too much assurance, and too much love for what is called sport, ever to make a good man.

Lucy. I do hope you are mistaken. I'm sure you must be.

Mrs. L. Well, well, child, we shall see.

Butts. (*Outside*, c.) Don't tell me. How do you know? None of your lying. I'll find out for myself. (*Enter* BUTTS, C.) How do you do, marm? Hope you're well, Miss Lucy. Where's the doctor?

Mrs. L. He's out, Mr. Butts. What is the matter?

Butts. Matter! What should be the matter, when a set of jackanapes are allowed to roam through the village, pillaging, burning, and insulting? I won't have it: the law shall be respected.

Mrs. L. Burning and pillaging! Why, Mr. Butts, have any of our young gentlemen been engaged in such disreputable proceedings?

Butts. Worse than that, marm. Worse than that. I'm disgusted with seminaries. If I could have my way, there shouldn't be any thing like a school in the land.

Mrs. L. Then I'm very glad you do not have your way. What is the cause of complaint now?

Butts. The majesty of the law has been outraged; and I, as the representative of the law, have been insulted. Those rascals of yours have been at their pranks. Going to my office this morning, I found a crowd of the rag, tag, and bobtail of the village gathered about it, hooting and yelling at some object in the window. Madam, imagine my indignation when I found that object to be a stuffed figure wrapped in my dressing-gown, with a foolscap on its head, and labelled "Jonathan Wild Butts, Thief-taker," — seated in my armchair too, at the open window. Think of that, marm! — an outrage, a diabolical outrage, upon justice!

Mrs L. Who could have done it?

Butts. You ask that, marm? — you who have lived for ten years in this den of iniquity, this nursery of roguery, this incubating machine of vice? Who did it? — why, Dr. Harlem's pupils, of course.

Lucy. Why, Mr. Butts! They're all gone except Fred Hastings and Bob Winders.

Butts. Except — Add your brother Harry, and you have the ringleaders in every assault upon the peace and quiet of the place. I know them. I've winked at many of their misdeeds; but, when they assault justice, I tell you Jonathan Wild Butts has his eye on 'em. I say, respect the law, respect the law.

Mrs. L. I assure you, Mr. Butts, I have a great respect for the law and its officers. Take a seat. The doctor will soon return.

Butts. No, I thank you, marm. I'll call again. It's

my duty to keep an eye on rogues; and I flatter myself
I know my duty. Let the wicked tremble; for justice is
on their track. (*About to exit,* C., *runs against* DILLY,
who enters, C.)

Dilly. Dear me, Mr. Butts. Don't knock a body
down.

Butts. (*Taking her by the ear, and bringing her down
stage.*) Ah, ha, you little baggage! I've got you at
last.

Dilly. Don't, Mr. Butts: you hurt. I ain't done nothing.

Butts. Look me in the eye.

Dilly. Which one, Mr. Butts?

Butts. Silence!

Dilly. Well, you needn't holler so: I ain't deaf.

Butts. Silence! You took my horse and chaise yesterday while I was in Mr. Bates's house, drove through the
town like mad; and, when I found them, they were
locked up in the pound, the horse in a perspiration, and
the chaise nearly stove to pieces. What have you to say
to that?

Dilly. Let my ear alone. I won't tell you a word
until you do.

Butts. Speak out, quick! What did you take my
chaise for?

Dilly. La, Mr. Butts! I didn't mean to hurt it. You
posted a notice on the church-door, warning people to
beware of leaving horses in the street over twenty minutes; for, if they did, their horses should be put in the
pound, and their owners fined.

Butts. What's that got to do with my horse?

15

Dilly. Respect the law, Mr. Butts. I saw your horse stand at Mr. Bates's door over half an hour; and you know what's sauce for the goose is sauce for the gander: and so I drove him to the pound. Ain't you much obliged?

Butts. Much obliged, you young jackanapes? If ever I find you meddling with my horse again, I'll have you locked up in a pound where you won't get out in a hurry.

Dilly. La, Mr. Butts, don't get angry! What's the use of making laws, if you break them yourself.

Butts. Oh, bother! Precious little you know about law. Good-morning, Mrs. Loring; good-morning, Miss Lucy (*going,* c.).

Dilly. Good-morning, Mr. Butts: going to have a ride?

Butts. Oh, bother!

Dilly. I say, Mr. Butts —

Butts. Well, what now?

Dilly. Respect the law.

Butts. Oh, pshaw! (*Runs off,* c.)

Dilly. Ha, ha, ha! What a queer old customer!

Lucy. Why, Dilly!

Mrs. L. Dilly, child, you mustn't talk so.

Dilly. That's what Harry calls him.

Mrs. L. That's no reason why you should speak so. Mr. Butts is a very worthy man, and tries to do his duty.

D'lly. He's a constable, and I do hate constables: they're always round poking their noses into every thing, and spoiling all the fun.

Mrs. L. It is his duty, child, to look after mischief-makers.

Dilly. But he makes such a fuss about it, and he always manages to catch the wrong ones.

Lucy. He didn't catch the wrong one to-day. Why, Dilly, how could you do such a thing?

Dilly. Pooh! It is easy enough if you only know how to drive.

Mrs. L. That poor horse!

Dilly. Well, it's Mr. Butts's fault that he is poor. He ought to feed him : I'm sure he's rich enough! Harry says he's an old —

Mrs. L. Stop, child! never mind what Harry says.

Dilly. But I do mind what Harry says. Harry's my father and mother and brother all in one. I'm sure I shouldn't know what to do without Harry.

Mrs. L. You have great cause to love him, for to Harry you owe all you have.

Dilly. Yes : he found me a little bit of a girl in the streets, and brought me home. Don't I love him for it, though? He calls me such queer names! Don't you think, auntie, this morning, he called me " Little Bread upon the Waters." What a queer name! I'm sure I don't know what it means.

Mrs. L. I'll tell you, Dilly. Nine years ago, the night before you were brought here, Dr. Harlem, Harry, and myself were sitting in this very room. The doctor, as-usual, was reading from the Scriptures before retiring for the night. During the reading, this sentence attracted Harry's attention, " Cast thy bread upon the waters, for thou shalt find it after many days." Harry looked up with his bright eyes. "That's a queer sentence, father," said he. "Ah, my boy!" said the doctor,

" there's many sentences in this book to puzzle young heads like yours, and many to puzzle older ones than mine. ' Cast thy bread upon the waters' means, do all the good you can in this world, never looking for reward ; for it will always come, sooner or later. Do a good deed, be it to benefit rich or poor, high or low ; for your reward will surely come. The next morning, Harry drove his father to the village at a very early hour, as the doctor was going a journey, and wanted to catch a train. On his return, he saw a little bundle of rags by the wayside. He alighted, and was surprised to find a little girl four or five years old, almost dead, — a poor little sick, suffering thing, evidently left to die by some inhuman mother.

Dilly. That was me, wasn't it, auntie?

Mrs. L. That was you. Harry looked at you, and was about to turn away, when he remembered the lesson of the previous night. " Father says, ' Cast thy bread upon the waters,' " said he ; " so this little one shall go home with me." The doctor was very much surprised on his return, and very much inclined to send you to the poorhouse ; but Harry begged so hard to keep you, that he relented, and here you have been ever since.

Dilly. That's why Harry called me, " Bread upon the Waters." I wonder if such a little crumb as I am can ever repay him.

Mrs. L. No doubt, Dilly.

Dilly. Perhaps I shall turn out to be some rich heiress, that some cruel uncle wanted to get out of the way. If I do, won't I make Harry rich !

Mrs. L. There's not much chance of that. No clew could be found to your parentage.

Dilly. And I hope there never will be. I don't want to leave Harry and you, auntie, and Lucy, and the dear good doctor. If I'm a nobody, I mean to be happy ; and, if ever I can do any thing for Harry to repay him for — for — for — (*Bursts into tears.*)

Mrs. L. There, there, Dilly, don't cry. We all love you dearly ; and, while you live, there is a warm home for you in Greenlake. Come with me. I've got a new canary in my room. (*Exit,* R.)

Dilly. A canary? Oh, my! ain't that splendid? (*Exit,* R.)

Lucy. Harry in danger! I do not believe it. Fred Hastings is a dear, delightful fellow, and I am sure would lead nobody into danger.

Bob. (*Without,* C.) O Lord! O murder! oh, bring somebody here quick! (*Enter,* C., *dragging a trap, in which his foot is caught.*)

Lucy. Why, Bob, what have you been doing?

Bob. Practising your favorite song, " I've been roaming, I've been roaming ; " and this is the consequence.

Lucy. Ah! too many sharps in that tune for you.

Bob. Altogether. I don't like the measure. Won't you be kind enough to release me?

Lucy. Certainly. (*Releases his foot.*)

Bob. Thank you. Ah, Lucy, if I only had you to release me from all the traps I get into !

Lucy. Oh, pshaw ! you should keep out of them. Now, I'll warrant you've been in somebody's melon-patch.

Bob. Lucy, you wrong me. But it's just my luck. I never shall be understood. I'm born to be unappreciated in this world. I haven't been in any melon-patch at all.

I climbed Farmer Butts's wall to gather a bouquet for you, when I stuck my foot in it. It's just my luck. I never tried to gather a rose but what I stuck my hands full of thorns.

Lucy. Ah, Bob, you went too near Farmer Butts's melon-patch.

Bob. Well, now you mention it, I did take a look at them there bouncers, and they seemed to say, "Come and take us melons;" but this trap said, "*Can't elope,*" and fastened its cruel teeth in my tender ankles. Just my luck.

Lucy. O Bob! I'm ashamed of you.

Bob. Now, don't, Lucy! I'm an unfortunate chap. I was born to be unlucky. I tell you, you should have had the most beautiful melon, — I mean bouquet, — if it hadn't been for this trap. Just my luck! Here I've been sent to this school by my fond but mistaken parent to be fitted for the bar or the pulpit. Fit subject I am for either. The only bar I hanker for is a horizontal bar. I'd like to be a gymnast, join a circus, or something of that kind; but there, you see, I'm too fat. It's just my luck. If I go out with the boys on a frolic, I'm sure to get caught. If I race on the water, my weight either capsizes the boat, or leaves me a mile behind. I tell you, Lucy, I'm born to ill luck.

Lucy. Oh, no, Bob! Have more confidence in yourself.

Bob. Confidence! Well, I like that. Confidence in what? I'm always at the foot of the class, always the last one up in the morning, and always the last in every thing. Oh, dear! I wonder what will become of me. If it wasn't for Harry, I should drown myself. No, I couldn't do that. I'm too fat : I couldn't sink. Just my luck.

Harry. (*Outside,* c.) Halloo ! halloo ! house ! house ! house !

Fred. (*Outside,* c.) Fish ! fish ! fish !

Lucy. There's Fred and Harry.

Dilly. (*Runs in,* R.) Oh, here's Harry ! Harry, here we are. (*Enter* FRED *and* HARRY, c., *with poles and fish-baskets.*)

Harry. Halloo, Dilly ! such a mess of trout for dinner !

Fred. Such capital sport ! Halloo, Bob ! where have you been ? We are looking for you !

Bob. Oh, I've been fishing too.

Harry. No ! Have you? What luck?

Bob. Oh ! I caught some.

Lucy. Yes : brought them home in a trap too.

Harry. Oh, ho !

Fred. Ha, ha !

Harry. Been in that melon-patch again ?

Fred. O you rascal !

Harry. You promised to wait till dark.

Bob. Sh— Confound it !

Fred. Selfish chap ! Wanted them all for himself.

Bob. Oh, bother ! I was only reconnoitering.

Harry. And got snatched by the sharpshooters.

Bob. Sharpshooters ! you may well say that. Such sharp, shooting pains as I've had in my ankles !

Harry. Served you right.

Bob. Just my luck !

Harry. Never go into anybody's melon-patch without your friends.

Fred.   No, sir!   Greedy boys always get punished.

Dilly.   O Harry! what splendid trout! what bouncers!

Harry.   Well, you bounce into the kitchen with them, quick; we must have them for dinner.

Dilly.   That I will.   (*Singing.*)

> " Fishy, fishy, come bite my hook;
>   You may go captain, and I'll go cook."

Exit, r.

Fred.   Well, Lucy, our happy school-days are drawing to a close.   To-night I must leave for home.

Bob.   And so must I. Ah, Lucy,

> "Those happy days are over;
>   There's naught but grief and pain " —

Harry.

> " When in a trap you set your foot:
>   So, don't do it again."

Oh, pshaw!   Boys, don't be sentimental: let's end the term with a frolic.

Fred.   I'm agreed.   What shall it be?

Harry.   What say you to a race on the lake?   Our wherries are at the landing.   We sha'n't have another chance.

Fred.   I think we owe some attention to the ladies, as this is our last day.

Lucy.   If I may speak for the *ladies,* I think nothing would please them better than a race.

Harry.   There's a jolly little sister for you.   Come, boys, I challenge you to a race across the lake and back; the prize to be — what?

Fred.   What do you say, Bob?

Lucy. If Bob says *what*, it will be *water-melons.*

Fred.
Harry. } Ha, ha! Caught again, Bob.

Bob. Now, Lucy, that was too bad.

Lucy. So it was Bob; and, to show my repentance, you shall be my champion in the race. Here, sir! you shall wear my colors. Kneel, and receive from the hands of your sovereign this white ribbon. (*Pins white ribbon on his breast.*) Keep it pure and unsullied, and bring it back to me as a trophy of victory.

Bob. Lucy, I'll do my best; but you know what it will be: I shall be last. Just my luck!

Harry. Oh, pshaw! Bob. Remember the fable of the hare and the turtle.

Bob. Confound it! do you mean to call me a turtle?

Fred. Well, well, whose champion am I? (*Aside.*) That Bob Winders has got ahead of me already. (*Enter* Mrs. Loring *and* Dilly, R.) Ah! here's Mrs. Loring. Madam, we are to have a race on the lake. Miss Lucy has accepted Bob here as her champion: he is already decorated with her ribbon. May I not hope that you may be induced to look with favor on your humble servant?

Mrs. L. Well, I'm sure, Master Fred, if my favor can help you to victory, here is my ribbon. (*He kneels, she pins red ribbon on his coat.*)

Lucy. All hail the champion of the Red!

Dilly. Going to have a race? Oh! ain't that jolly? Whose champion are you, Harry?

Harry. They've left me out in the cold. No, Dilly! Whose champion? Yours, little lady, if you will accept me.

Dilly. Oh, my! Will you, though? Oh, that is real jolly; but you want a ribbon: wait a minute till I let down my hair. There, now! wear that (*pins blue ribbon on him*); and, if you don't bring it as a trophy of victory, I'll never speak to you again.

Fred. All hail the champion of the Blue!

Dilly. Red, White, and Blue, — hurrah for the race of the Red, White, and Blue!

Mrs. L. The victor should be rewarded with an ensign. Suppose, Lucy, we go and make one while the young men are preparing for the race. (*Exit*, L.)

Lucy. That's a capital idea! (*Exit*, L.)

Dilly. Oh, let me help!

Harry. What can you do, little girl?

Dilly. Little girl? — I want you to understand, Mr. Harry, that I'm a young lady. I can cut out the stars if I can't do any thing else. (*Exit*, R.)

Bob. If I'm not much mistaken, you'll cut out a great many stars when you grow older.

Harry. Good for you, Bob. Well, lads, when shall we start?

Fred. It's just ten o'clock. Let's start in half an hour: 'twill give the ladies a chance to make their flag.

Harry.
Bob. } *Agreed.* (*Enter* BUTTS, C.)

Butts. I've caught you, have I? — you rascals, you rapscallions!

Harry. Come, come, Mr. Butts, hard words!

Fred What in the world is the matter now?

Bob. Old Hookey looks wrathy.

Butts. Old Hookey! — young man, respect the law.

Harry. What's the matter, Mr. Butts? Whose eggs are missing now?

Bob. Whose chimney stopped up?

Fred. Whose water-melons sloped?

Butts. Eggs, chimneys, water-melons, — Oh! I shall choke.

Bob. Do: 'twill save the sheriff a job.

Harry. Come, come, speak out man. What burglary has been committed?

Fred. Whose cow stolen?

Bob. Whose cat drowned?

Butts. Stop, stop, stop! In the name of- the law, I command you! I've been outraged, my office broken into; and I charge you three with the perpetration of this foul outrage.

Bob. Oh, ho! a hen-coop plundered?

Harry. Hold on, Mr. Butts: this is a serious charge. We acknowledge we have sometimes overstepped the strict boundaries of the law; but to break into a man's office is something not even the mischief-loving pupils of Greenlake Seminary would be guilty of. Explain yourself!

Butts. My office was broken into between the hours of seven, P.M., last night and seven, A.M., this morning; my window thrown open; a stuffed figure placed in my armchair with a scurrilous label attached to it: now who did it?

Harry. Not I, Mr. Butts, I assure you!

Fred. I never thought of doing such a thing.

Bob. Nor I.

Butts. 'Tis false: all three were concerned in it.

Harry.   Do you charge us with falsehood?

Fred.   Mind what you're about : I won't be called a liar.

Bob.   No, sir ! If you say we lie, you'll find yourself lying on the floor.

Butts.   There's a lie somewhere.

Harry.   Oh, come ! I can't stand that.   Let's throw him into the lake !

Fred.   Good ! I'm with you.

Bob.   Yes : let's cool him off.

Butts.   Would you offer violence?   Young men, respect the law.

Harry.   Here, boys, grab his legs.   I'll take his head.

Bob.   No : let me have the lightest part.

Butts.   Keep off, — I say, keep off !

Harry.   It's no use, Butts ; in you go.

Fred.   The lake is waiting to receive you.

Bob.   We'll make a water-butt of you, Butts.

Butts.   Help, help, murder ! (*They seize him in their arms, and carry him to the door. Enter* DR. HARLEM. *They drop* BUTTS, *and go,* R. *and* L.. *Enter* DILLY, L.)

Doctor.   Well, well, young gentlemen, you seem to be amusing yourselves in an unwonted manner.   May I inquire the cause of this assault?

Butts.   That's it, doctor, — assault with intent to drown.   It's a diabolical conspiracy against the law.

Doctor.   Harry, Master Hastings, Master Winders, I am waiting for an explanation.

Harry.   Father, that man charged three of your pupils with falsehood : we couldn't stand that.   He was hot and angry.

Bob. And so we thought we'd just cool him off, that's all.

Butts. But they're a pack of jackanapes, violating the law, and then denying it.

Doctor. Gently, Mr. Butts. My boys, however mischievous they may be, are ready to own their faults without resorting to falsehood. What is your complaint?

Butts. They broke into my office, insulted me by placing a stuffed figure in my window, with my name upon it, and this confounded ridiculous thing on its head (*pulls foolscap from his pocket, and places it on his head*). Behold the insulted majesty of the law!

Doctor. Allow me to look at that cap, Mr. Butts. This is made of one of my papers ; and, as it bears my name upon it, it certainly came from this place. Now, who is the culprit? Harry, I have heard of your pranks in town, though you fancied I was ignorant of them. You will answer me truly. Is this your work?

Harry. No, sir. I have not been near Mr. Butts's office for three days.

Doctor. Master Hastings?

Fred. I assure you, doctor, I had nothing to do with it.

Doctor. Master Winders, can you throw any light on this proceeding?

Bob. What! I dress old Butts in a foolscap? No, sir. I couldn't see any joke in that ; that's what I call twitting on facts.

Doctor. Then who is the culprit?

Dilly. If you please, doctor, it was me.

All. You, Dilly!

Dilly Yes : it was me.

Butts. Why, you little scarecrow, do you mean to say that you did this? I don't believe it.

Dilly. La, Mr. Butts, you're never satisfied. You've been growling because nobody would confess; and now, when I'm ready to own it, you won't believe me.

Doctor. Dilly, if this was your doings, you will please explain it.

Dilly. Well, then, I went to Mr. Butts's office this morning to let him know his horse was in the pound.

Doctor. His horse in the pound?

Dilly. Yes: I'll tell you about it.

Butts. There, there! no matter about that.

Dilly. Well, I thought you wouldn't care to hear about it. Well, I went to Mr. Butts's office, and Mr. Butts wasn't there: the door was locked; so I tried the window. It was unfastened. I jumped in, saw Mr. Butts's dressing-gown and boots, dressed up something to look like him, and opened the window.

Butts. What did you do it for?

Dilly. To scare the rogues, Mr. Butts. They would think it was you. It was just as good as though you were there.

Butts. You little, confounded, saucy! — I'll dress you! I'll make an example of you, now I've caught you!

Dilly. La, Mr. Butts, didn't you never catch a rogue before?

Butts. Silence!

Doctor. Leave her to me, Mr. Butts. Dilly, I'm astonished that a young lady of your age should be guilty of such a proceeding.

Dilly. Dear me, doctor, I didn't mean any harm : I only wanted a frolic, and it was such a good chance !

Butts. Frolic? — an insult to an officer of the law, you call a frolic? I've been insulted. You let me catch you in my office again, that's all ! Frolic ! — shades of the chief justices, ghosts of departed judges ! Oh, I shall choke ! (*Exit*, c.)

Doctor. If I hear of such a frolic again, Dilly, I shall be very angry with you. Don't do it again. (*Exit*, R.)

Dilly. There, now ! the doctor's angry. I didn't mean any harm. It's such fun to plague Mr. Butts !

Bob. Served him right, the old scamp !

Harry. Stop, Bob ! don't encourage her : she's wild enough already. Dilly, come here.

Dilly. What for, Harry? You going to scold me?

Harry. Yes, Dilly. This frolic of yours has grieved me very much. You are too old now to indulge in such pranks.

Dilly. Why, Harry, you and Fred and Bob hoisted Mr. Butts's horse up into the steeple ; and I'm sure you are all older than I.

Harry. That's a different matter altogether. We are young men, and you are a young lady.

Dilly. Well, don't you think young men ought to behave themselves, Harry?

Harry. Yes, of course ; that is — sometimes. Oh, pshaw ! What I mean is, Dilly, I don't want you to do such a thing again. It will grieve me very much.

Dilly. Then I'll never do it again. I'm sure, Harry, if you want me to be a good girl, I shall try ever so hard ;

for I love you dearly, Harry : and if ever I should grieve you, I — I — I — (*Weeps.*)

Harry. There, there! Run off, and finish cutting out your stars : that's much better than cutting up pranks.

Dilly. Oh, the stars! I forgot all about them.

Harry. Confound it! I must turn over a new leaf.

Bob. Yes, practice before you preach. Well, Dilly, how comes on the flag?

Dilly. Nearly ready. Will you come and hold a skein of silk for Lucy? (*Exit*, L.)

Bob. For-Lucy? Will I? Won't I? (*Exit*, L.)

Fred. It strikes me that Bob Winders is mighty attentive to Lucy.

Harry. Of course, he is. Why, Fred, you're not jealous?

Fred. That sister of yours is an angel, Harry.

Harry. That she is, Fred.

Fred. Do you know, Harry, that the saddest of our parting is the thought that I shall meet her no more? You and I are such good friends, Harry, that you will not laugh when I tell you I love her dearly, truly.

Harry. Ah! a boy's love, Fred. We know how that will end. New scenes and new faces will blot out all remembrance of her.

Fred. I tell you, no, Harry. If I am a boy, I have lived a man's life for the last five years. Hers is not the first fair face which has attracted me ; but all fade before hers. Harry, I tell you I shall leave this place with the firm resolve to one day return, and ask her to be my wife.

Harry. Your wife, Fred?

Fred. Yes, my wife. You would not object to that?

Harry. I should, most decidedly.

Fred. How?

Harry. Yes, Fred Hastings: I'd rather see my sister laid in her grave than marry you.

Fred. Harry, you're crazy!

Harry. Not a bit of it. Look you, Fred. You're a gay fellow, and with you time flies lightly and merrily. But you're a rich man's son. Your purse is always full. You know too much of life. Boy as you are, you can drink as deep as the oldest; you can shake a dice-box as glibly as the most expert, shuffle a pack of cards with the boldest, and bet your money with the fastest. I can very easily tell your future life, — a gay life and a merry one; and, with such a companion, a pure, loving girl like Lucy would be miserable. I know all this; for you have led me into it. So, Fred, say no more about it. Lucy is too good for you ever to dream of.

Fred. Why, Harry, what's the matter? You have engaged with me in all these sports that you speak of. Do you turn upon me now? Harry, you are not yourself.

Harry. No, I am not. When you came to this school, I was a happy lad who had never heard of this gay life; content to stay at home with my dear sister and Dilly, with but one desire, — to please a father who was very proud of me. You came. New life, new enjoyments, were before me; and, like a thoughtless boy, I plunged into them. Well, I suppose it is one of the phases of life which tempt all; but I wish I had never, never, seen it.

16

Fred.   But, Harry, what has caused this sudden change?

Harry.   I'll tell you, Fred.   You introduced me to Capt. Pitman's house, to look on at the game.   I was content, at first, to look on ; but one night you tempted me to play.   I lost seventy-five dollars to Capt. Pitman, and I had not the means to pay it.   The captain was very kind :   he said the money was of no consequence :   I should give him my I. O. U. for the amount, and, when convenient, pay it.   I gave him a note.

Fred.   That was all right.   He doesn't want the money.

Harry.   Ah! but he does.   He met me this morning ; said he was very sorry, but he must have it at once.   I declared my inability to pay it.   He persisted, and warned me, that, if the money was not in his hands to-day, he should be compelled to call upon my father for an explanation.

Fred.   He cannot collect it.   You are a minor.

Harry.   Collect it !   Do you suppose my father would hesitate to pay, when he knows, that, on his refusal, the whole story would be made public?   Fred Hastings, rather than look upon my father's face — his honest face — when he should feel his son was a gambler, I'd throw myself into the lake.

Fred.   Oh, come, Harry ! he shall not know it.   I got you into the scrape, and I'll see you out.   The doctor holds money belonging to me, from which I draw for my convenience.   I'll go to him, get the money : you shall pay Capt. Pitman, and nobody be the wiser.

Harry. Will you, though? That's kind of you, Fred; and I'll repay you with the first money I have.

Fred. I'll go at once.

Harry. And I'll look after the boats. But don't think any more of Lucy, Fred; for I tell you, you can't have her. She's too good for you. (*Exit,* c.)

Fred. Too good for me! A saint at last! What a rascal I must be! Too good for me! Ah, Harry Harlem, you don't know me yet with all your keenness. Too good for me! — we'll see. Oh! I'll help you out of the scrape, I'll help you out. I can shake a dice-box, can I? I can bet my money, can I? You've seen all this? But there's one little sleight-of-hand trick that you haven't seen yet, Master Harry Harlem. I'll help you out of this scrape with a vengeance. (*Exit,* R. *Enter* Bob.)

Bob. Just my luck! I've tangled all their silk, cut their cloth in the wrong place, and upset every thing in the room. Just my luck! The idea of a chap of my temperament sitting down before Lucy Harlem to hold a skein of silk, while her bright eyes were burning holes in my susceptible bosom! Oh, it's horrible! I'm over head and ears in love with her. When she touches me, the blood rushes to my head, and I rush off. I think she likes me. I'd like to go down on my knees before her, and say, "Lucy, I am yours." But there, I'm too fat. She might say, "There's too much of you." Here she comes. I've a great mind to say something. (*Enter* Lucy, R.)

Lucy. Why, Bob! what did you run away for? You tangled my silk all up, and left me to unravel it.

Bob. O Lucy! you've tangled me all up, and I don't believe I shall ever be unravelled.

Lucy. Why, what's the matter?

Bob. Lucy, I'm going away to-day.

Lucy. I'm so sorry you're going just at this time!

Bob. You are? You don't know how happy you make me. Why at this time?

Lucy. Because the water-melons are just ripe.

Bob. Oh, pshaw! What's water-melons to me?

Lucy. A great deal, I should think. Don't you like them?

Bob. Yes; but I like you just as well.

Lucy. Why, Bob!

Bob. No, no! I mean— (*Aside.*) I've a great mind to speak. (*Pops down on his knees.*) Lucy— (*Enter* FRED, R., *with a portfolio in his hand.*)

Lucy. Oh! there's Fred.

Bob. Just my luck! (*Jumps up.*)

Fred. Why, Bob, what's the matter? Have you hurt you?

Bob. No, I ain't hurt me. (*Exit,* C. *Enter* DILLY, L.)

Fred. I'm glad you are here, Lucy. I leave you to-day, and, that you may not entirely forget me, may I beg your acceptance of this. (*Presenting a watch.*)

Lucy. Oh, what a splendid little watch! Thank you a thousand thousand times for your kindness.

Dilly. Oh, what a beauty! Dear me, Fred, ain't you going to give me something to remember you by?

Lucy. Hush, Dilly.

Dilly. I'm sure I shall forget you if you don't.

Fred. Oh! I haven't forgotten you, Dilly. Here,

take this. I've often heard you say you wanted a portfolio. You shall have this. Should I ever become a great man, you can boast that you own something which no one but I have ever used.

Dilly. Oh, thank you, Fred! That's just what I wanted! Isn't it nice? I'll go show it to auntie at once. (*Exit*, L.)

Fred. Lucy, may I not hope that the many happy hours we have spent together here may sometimes recall me to your remembrance?

Lucy. Don't talk so, Fred! I hope we shall meet again often. There is no one whom I shall miss more than you.

Fred. Do you mean that, Lucy? May I hope sometime to return, and— (*Enter* HARRY, C., *in boating costume, blue. Aside.*) Pshaw! he back again?

Harry. Well, Lucy, are you all ready for the race?

Lucy. When you are, Harry. Look at my beautiful present. From Fred too: isn't he kind?

Harry. Very.

Lucy. Well, I declare: is that all you can say?

Harry. I'm busy now: don't talk. Get Aunt Loring and Dilly. We must be off.

Lucy. We'll all be ready in a minute. (*Exit*, L.)

Fred. Here, Harry, here's your father's check for seventy-five dollars: settle with Capt. Pitman at once.

Harry. Thank you, Fred! I'll run down and pay him.

Fred. And I'll get ready for the race. Look out for yourself; for I shall beat you. (*Exit*, R.)

Harry. Don't be too sure of that. I'll get this debt off my mind. (*Turns to door, meets* BUTTS.)

Butts. Oh, here you are, here you are! I've been looking for you.

Harry. You're always looking for somebody. What's to pay now? Who do you want?

Butts. You, Harry Harlem: I've got a little business with you. The law has its eye on you.

Harry. Well, I've no objection, as long as it's the eye, and not the hand.

Butts. But the hand follows the eye.

Harry. O pshaw! I'm in a hurry: if you have any business with me, speak out.

Butts. I've a little note against you, placed in my hands for collection by Capt. Pitman.

Harry. Capt. Pitman! In your hands?

Butts. Which, of course, you can't pay; so my next business is with your father.

Harry. Not just yet. Where is the note?

Butts. Here it is; seventy-five dollars, — a large sum for a son of Dr. Harlem to lose by gambling.

Harry. Sh! — Don't speak so loud.

Butts. Here it is; seventy-five dollars.

Harry. And here is a check for the amount.

Butts. A check!

Harry. My father's check: it's good, I believe.

Butts. Good as gold. Here's your note. (*Aside.*) There's another job slipped through my hands.

Harry. So you see, old Butts, it isn't necessary to see my father. There's your money. Good-day!

Butts. Will you take a little bit of advice from me?

Harry. No, sir. I won't take any thing from you. You'd like to catch me tripping; but you haven't got me yet, Mr. Butts.

Butts. No, not just yet; but, if your acquaintance with Capt. Pitman continues, it won't be long. Goodday! (*Exit,* c.)

Harry. I'll take good care to cut the acquaintance of Capt. Pitman. I've had a narrow escape; and I'll keep out of his den. (*Enter* LUCY, MRS. LORING, *and* DILLY, *with flag,* L.)

Dilly. Here's the flag, Harry : isn't it a beauty?

Harry. It is, indeed; and I'll do my best to win it for you, Dilly. Where's Fred? (*Enter* FRED, R., *in boating costume, red.*)

Fred. Here's Fred, ready and " eager for the fray."

Harry. Good! Run for Bob, and we'll be off.

Dilly. Oh! he's always last. (*Enter,* BOB, R., *in boating costume, white.*)

Bob. Of course, I am; just my luck! I tell you its no joke to robe myself in these uncomfortable clothes. I've ripped two shirts and three pairs of —

Harry. Hold on, Bob.

Bob. What's the use in my attempting to race? Anyhow, I shall be the last in. It's just my luck!

Harry. Don't growl, Bob. It's just your luck to be the best fellow in the world. What could we do without you? All the small boys swear by you. If they're in trouble, who so quick to help as Bob Winders? If there's an old lady within ten miles wants an armful of firewood, who so quick to bring it as Bob Winders? If I was in trouble, and wanted the help of a friend, a real friend, there's no one I would call on sooner than Bob Winders.

Bob. Bully for you, Harry. I'd go through fire and

water for you; for you've helped me through many tight places: but it's no use: I shall lose the race. It's just my luck!

Harry. Do your best, Bob. Come, lads, let's be off.

Dilly. Yes: the race, the race, — hurrah for the race of the Red, White, and Blue!

(*Exit* DILLY *and* HARRY, LUCY *and* BOB; MRS. LORING *and* FRED *about to follow. Enter* DR. HARLEM, R.)

Doctor. Mrs. Loring, one moment; that is, if you have no important business.

Mrs. L. Will you excuse me, Mr. Hastings, one moment? (FRED *bows and exits,* C.) I was merely going to see the race on the lake. The young people desired it; and, really, I felt myself almost a girl again.

Doctor. I will detain you but a moment. I have just received an anonymous epistle, which annoys me very much. It is not the first I have received. It refers to Harry.

Mrs. L. To Harry, doctor?

Doctor. Yes. I am advised by an unknown friend to keep my eye on him, as he is in the habit of keeping bad company. Mrs. Loring, have you seen any thing wild about him for the last two months?

Mrs. L. No, nothing more than usual. Since school commenced, he has taken part in many of the frolics to which boys are accustomed. I think he will behave more soberly when they are all gone.

Doctor. I am exceedingly anxious. I have heard of his pranks in the village: I have also heard he is somewhat in debt.

Mrs. L. I think very likely.

Doctor. You take it very coolly, Mrs. Loring.

Mrs. L. Because I have full faith in Harry. Certain friendships he has formed must, of necessity, be broken to-day ; and when he is once more with us, believe me doctor, he will be our own Harry again.

Doctor. I hope you are right, Mrs. Loring. Should harm come to that boy, it would kill me. I have set my heart on making a noble man of him ; and, should he fail me — (*Enter* DILLY, C.)

Dilly. O auntie, quick ! they're just going to start. Come, doctor, come and see the race. Why, how slow you are ! Come, auntie, come right along. (*Pulls* MRS. LOR- ING *off*, C.)

Doctor. Mrs. Loring must be right. She has had my children under her eye so long, that she is better able to judge their characters than I with my numerous duties constantly occupying my attention. Some meddling person has sent these notes to annoy me. (*Enter* BUTTS, C., *hurriedly.*)

Butts. O doctor, doctor ! such a crime ! such a high-handed outrage, a diabolical crime ! Oh the villain, the villain !

Doctor. What's the matter now, Mr. Butts?

Butts. Keep cool, doctor, keep cool ! It's a terrible blow, but keep cool : take example from me. Oh the reprobate, the villain !

Doctor. Well, well ! what is it?

Butts. Are we alone ? I would have no ear listen to the tale of horror ; no voice but mine break the silence ! (DILLY *dances in*, C., *flapping the flag in* BUTTS's *face.*)

Dilly. They're off, they're off ! Such a splendid

start! Come quick, you'll lose all the fun. (*Dashes out*, c.)

Butts. Confound that little imp! she's always in the way.

Doctor. Never mind her! what is this crime?

Butts. O Dr. Harlem, Dr. Harlem!

Doctor. Mr. Butts, will you be kind enough to explain yourself in as few words as possible? These ejaculations of yours may be pleasing to you, but I do not enjoy them.

Butts. Dr. Harlem, I am an officer of the law. It is my proud boast, that I am one of the supporters of the scale of justice, — that scale which —

Doctor. Stop, Mr. Butts. If you have come here to deliver an oration on justice, you'll excuse me, as I have far more important matters to occupy my attention.

Butts. Dr. Harlem, I have a tender heart, and the sight of misery is terrible to me.

Doctor. What's that to do with me?

Butts. Doctor, compose yourself, imitate my stoicalness. You are a father — (DILLY *rushes in*, c.)

Dilly. Oh, such a race! they're half-way across the lake, and Harry's ahead, Harry's ahead! (*Rushes out*, c.)

Butts. Plague take that girl!

Doctor. Never mind her, but speak.

Butts. Dr. Harlem, I have had occasion to call upon you in regard to the conduct of your pupils many times. To-day, I called upon one of your young men to collect a note placed in my hands by Capt. Pitman. The note was paid by giving me this check.

Doctor. My check! How is this?

Butts. Is it your check?

Doctor. No, it is not: it is a forgery.

Butts. Yes, I knew it. Ha, ha, ha! You cannot blind the eyes of justice. Good, good: I've got him!

Doctor. Who — who did this? (*Enter* DILLY, C.)

Dilly. They've reached the other side. Harry turned first: he's ahead, he's ahead! (*Exit*, C.)

Butts. Drat that girl! she's a nuisance.

Doctor. Mr. Butts, who was the author of this forgery?

Butts. One of your pupils.

Doctor. His name.

Butts. Well, well, don't be in a hurry.

Doctor His name, I say. (*Enter* DILLY, C.)

Dilly. They're coming back. Bob Winders has upset, and Harry's ahead.

Doctor. Dilly!

Dilly. Oh, come and see the race! You'll lose the best of it.

Doctor. Dilly, you see I am very much engaged. Don't enter this room again, or I shall be very angry.

Dilly. La! I thought you wanted to know about the race. (*Exit*, C.)

Doctor. Now, Mr. Butts, the name of this offender.

Butts. His name is — Harry Harlem.

Doctor. Harry Harlem! Butts, you lie!

Butts. What! this to me, an officer of the law? Dr. Harlem, recollect yourself. Respect the law.

Doctor. Pardon me, Butts. I was hasty. But you are mistaken. My son Harry —

3

Butts.   Gave me that check in this very room.

Doctor.   This is terrible!   My son Harry forge the name of his father?   I tell you you are mistaken.

(*Outside:* "*Hurrah, hurrah, hurrah for* HARRY HAR-
LEM!")

Butts.   Here he is: ask him.   (*Enter* HARRY, FRED, LUCY, MRS. LORING, *and* DILLY, C.)

Dilly.   Harry's won the race!   Harry's won the race!

Harry.   'Tis true: I've won the colors.

Fred.   I've been handsomely defeated.   (*Enter* BOB, C.)

Bob.   And I've got gloriously ducked.   Just my luck!

Harry.   Congratulate me, father!   I've beaten the best sculler in the school.

Doctor.   Stop!   Before you secure my congratulations look me in the face, Harry Harlem, and answer me this: Have you seen Mr. Butts before to-day?

Harry.   Oh, several times.

Doctor.   Have you paid him any money?

Harry.   Why — I — yes, I have.   (*Aside.*)   Butts has turned traitor.

Butts.   Didn't I tell you so?   Didn't I tell you so? He gave me the check.   I'll swear it.

Doctor.   Harry, you hear.   What have you to say?

Harry.   I did give him that check.

Doctor.   So, sir, not content with making yourself the terror of the village, not content with disturbing the quiet of our once happy home with your wild courses, to crown your evil life you commit a forgery.

All.   A forgery?

Doctor. Yes, a forgery. This son of mine — hear it, all of you — this son, of whom I was so proud, has forged the name of his father to pay a gambling debt.

Harry. 'Tis false!

Doctor. False, boy! Can you deny this? — this check, which you confess you gave to Butts?

Harry. I did give him the check; but it was given me by another, one who can explain every thing. You could not think me so base as to forge the name of the kindest and best of fathers? That check was given me by Fred. Hastings.

All. Fred Hastings?

Fred. Let me see it. 'Tis false! That check has never been in my possession.

Harry. Fred Hastings, do you deny it?

Fred. Most certainly. Harry, I would willingly lend you my name to help you out of a scrape; but this is a crime I look upon with abhorrence. You must bear the blame yourself: I cannot help you.

Harry. Am I awake?

Doctor. A lie to cover a crime! O Harry, Harry! Is this the reward for all my love, my pride in you?

Harry. Father, what can I say? One whom I thought a friend has bitterly betrayed me. I do not know, I cannot imagine, a reason for this; but, as true as there is a heaven above, I am innocent of crime.

Doctor. Have you not frequented the gambling-house of Capt. Pitman?

Harry. I have. To my shame, I confess it.

Doctor. Then you are no longer son of mine. You have bitterly betrayed the trust reposed in you, and you

cannot hold up your head in honesty. Go! The world
is wide: find where you can a resting-place. My house
shall no longer harbor a gambler and a forger.

Mrs. L. Doctor, doctor, calm yourself!

Lucy. O father! don't speak so! (*They lead him
to chair,* R.)

Doctor. The cool, heartless villain!

Harry. Dr. Harlem (I will no longer call you father,
since you yourself cut me off), I have indeed deceived
and disgraced you by thoughtless folly; but of this crime
I am innocent. You are right. Your house is no longer
a fit place for a gambler. I can claim no friends here
now.

Mrs. L. Oh, don't say that, Harry!

Doctor. Silence! Who bandies words with that villain is no longer an inmate of my home.

Dilly. Then you can set my bandbox outside the
door at once. Dr. Harlem, you're a mean old doctor,
so you are! O Harry, Harry! I don't know what it's
all about; but I know there isn't a better Harry in this
world than you. (*Rushes into his arms.*)

Harry. Hush, hush, Dilly! 'Twill all come right
some day.

Bob. Harry, there's my hand. The case looks hard
against you, and I suppose I should be on the other side;
but I believe in you, and I stand by you. If you're a
villain, as they say you are, I can't see it. It's just
my luck!

Harry. Bob, you're a trump!

Dilly. You won't go, will you, Harry?

Harry. Dilly, I must. You cannot understand it. I

am accused of a crime, with no power to prove myself innocent. The time will come when I can prove it. Till then, I shall go from here.

Dilly. Oh, take me with you, Harry! take me with you! You are the one I love best in the world. I should die without you!

Harry. No, Dilly: you must stay here. Be good and gentle with father, and watch, Dilly, watch; for the time will come when even a little maid like you can serve me.

Doctor. Oh the villain, the villain! to seek to plunder his old father! The villain, the villain! Has he gone?

Harry. In one moment, doctor: my presence is hateful to you. I have disobeyed you, and must bide the consequences. Farewell! Where'er I go, I shall always remember you as the kindest and best of fathers. Farewell!

Butts. Stop! You are my prisoner.

All. Prisoner?

Doctor. No, no, Butts! Let him go. I make no charge.

Butts. But the bank does. I have a warrant for his arrest.

Dilly. You mean old Butts! You're always sticking your nose into other people's business.

Doctor. But, Butts, listen to me. (*Takes* BUTTS, R., *and they talk together earnestly.*)

Harry. (L.) Oh, this is too much! Must I be arraigned as a criminal?

Dilly. Why don't you run away? I would.

Harry. Thank you for the hint, Dilly.

Dilly. Your boat's down at the foot of the garden.

Harry. And, if I strike across, I can reach the road. Ah, Dilly! yours is a wise little head. Bob, here. (Bob *crosses* R.) Can I depend upon you? Will you stick by me?

Bob. Like a poor man's plaster. It's just my luck!

Harry. Then meet me in half an hour at the big oak by Jones's lot.

Bob. I'll be there.

Harry. Now keep old Butts here, and I'll be off. Dilly, good-by. Heaven bless you! Be a good girl, and have faith in Harry.

Dilly. That I will! (Harry *kisses her, and creeps out,* C.; *the* Doctor *is with* Butts, R.; Fred *and* Lucy, *with* Mrs. Loring, *back* R., *talking together.*) Oh, if he can only get away! (*Follows him to door,* C., *and stumbles over the trap, which was placed by* Bob, L. C.) Dear me! I've nearly broke my ankle! Why, what an ugly-looking trap! I must take care of that.

Butts. I tell you it's no use, doctor. Law is law, and your son must go to jail.

Doctor. But, Butts, I am the only loser by this. The bank has lost nothing.

Dilly. (*Coming down* R. *of* Butts.) Mr. Butts, what will you do with Harry?

Butts. Lock him up in jail, where you ought to be.

Bob. (*Coming down* L. *of* Butts) But look here, Mr. Butts, I'm ready to bail him, or my father is. Don't take him away, that's a good fellow. I'll help you to take all the rogues there are in the village, only let him off.

Dilly. (*At door*, c.) He's reached the boat, and he's off. (*Drags trap down behind* BUTTS, *and sets it.*)

Butts. Look here, young man! I know my business. Harry Harlem must go to jail.

Dilly. Oh! don't take him to jail, that's a good Mr. Butts! I won't dress up any more figures, and I won't steal your horse and chaise again, if you'll only let him go.

Bob. Now, do, old Butts! You're a kind-hearted old fellow, I know you are!

Butts. Silence! The law must be respected. (DILLY *and* BOB *pull him* R. *and* L. *to attract his attention during the previous lines. At this part, they have him in front of the trap.*)

Fred. (*Back*, c.) Gracious! there's Harry half-way across the lake! There's innocence for you!

Doctor. Escaped? Thank heavens!

Dilly. (*Dancing, and clapping her hands.*) Good, good, good!

Butts. The prisoner escaped! (BOB *pushes him back into the trap.*) O murder, murder! What have I done?

Bob. Put your foot in it, old Butts.

Dilly. Good, good, good!

Butts. (*Rushing round and dragging the trap.*) Lost my prisoner! Murder, help! O Bob Winders, you've ruined me.

Bob. Have I? That's just my luck!

(*Quick curtain.*)

ACT II.

FIVE YEARS SUPPOSED TO ELAPSE.

SCENE *same as Act.* 1. — *Table,* R. C.; *arm-chair,* L. C.; *small table,* R. C.; *with chair* R., *in which is seated* MRS. LORING, *knitting.*

Mrs. L. Dear me, how time does fly. It's five years this very day since our Harry disappeared. Five long years, and no word, no sign, from him. Perhaps he's dead. Poor boy, innocent or guilty, his loss has been a sad blow to his father. Since that day, he has never been the same man. Prostrated by a long illness, the result of that terrible excitement, feeble in body, wandering in mind, he is but the wreck of the grand old doctor of former days. The school has been given up, the house mortgaged, and what the end will be, Heaven alone can tell. But for Dilly, this would be a sad house. Dear child, she is the ruling spirit. When the blow fell, forsaking all her roguish pranks, she proved herself a woman. The doctor cannot stir without her, and we have all come to depend upon her quick and ready judgment. To-morrow the interest on the mortgage is due. I know we have no money to meet it, no friends to assist. Ah, me, I fear the house must go, and that I am convinced would kill the doctor. (*Enter* LUCY, R.)

Lucy. Aunt Loring, I have come to you for advice. Mr. Hastings sent me a note this morning, in which he declares his love for me, and asks me to become his wife.

Mrs. L. I have long suspected this would be the result of his stay here. Does it surprise you, Lucy?

Lucy. You know how persistently he has visited us for the last three months, and how attentive he has been to me. He is very agreeable, and — and —

Mrs. L. You love him. Is that it, Lucy?

Lucy. No, no! I do not, and I sometimes wonder at myself: I like to be with him, he is so gay and so attentive; but, when he begins to speak of love, I don't know why — but a face comes between his and mine, the face of my dear brother Harry, and then I almost detest him.

Mrs. L You do not believe him guilty of the charge made by Harry?

Lucy. I do not know what to believe : I only know I wish he would never speak of love to me; but still —

Mrs. L. Well, Lucy?

Lucy. We are poor, very poor: this life we now lead cannot last much longer. Some day this place must be given up; then what will become of father, you — all of us? Dilly works hard to keep the wolf from our door, and I am but a poor drone in the hive. Mr. Hastings is rich : were I his wife, this place might be secured, father made comfortable, and you and Dilly happy.

Mrs. L. And yet you do not love him?

Lucy. No, no : I cannot while this uncertainty exists about Harry.

Mrs. L. Then do not marry him. A marriage without love is a blasphemy; and a marriage with Fred

Hastings could not be a happy one. Give him his answer, plainly and fairly, and leave our fate to be adjusted by a higher and wiser power. Hark! here's Dilly: do not speak of this before her; it would make her unhappy.

Dilly. (*Outside,* c.) Ha! Ha! Ha! what a queer old doctor! you make me laugh so, my sides ache, you're so funny. (*Enter* c., *supporting* DOCTOR. LUCY *runs and places arm-chair* c., *in which they seat him.*) There, I've given you a good long walk; now be a good boy, be quiet, and entertain me. (*Sits on stool at* L. *of* DOCTOR. LUCY *kneels,* R.)

Doctor. Ah, Dilly, you're a funny girl — a little rogue — you want to keep me all to yourself.

Dilly. Of course I do: ain't you my cavalier, my true and faithful knight, ready to break lances and fight for me?

Doctor. Yes, yes! ah, dear me, dear me! —

Lucy. What's the matter, father?

Doctor. Ah, Lucy, my child, your father's getting old. I can't tramp so far as I could once. Mrs. Loring?

Mrs. L. Well, doctor.

Doctor. Isn't it most school-time?

Dilly. (*Aside.*) Dear me, the school again!

Doctor. You know we must be very prompt, or we shall set a bad example.

Mrs. L. You know it's vacation now, doctor.

Doctor. Dear me! so it is, so it is! strange I should forget it. But isn't it a very long vacation, Mrs. Loring?

Mrs. L. About the usual time.

Doctor. The pupils will be coming back soon, won't

they? We must have every thing neat and tidy. Green-lake Seminary must keep up its reputation. I shall be glad to see the lads, — Hastings, Winders, and all the rest of them. What rogues they are: I hope they'll behave better this term, and keep our Harry — no, Harry's dead.

Dilly. O doctor! don't talk about the school: let that take care of itself. Talk to me.

Doctor. Harry's dead. What day is this, Dilly?

Dilly. The 1st of August.

Doctor. Harry's dead. Five years ago; it was a beautiful day when we buried him. Don't you recollect it Dilly: we placed a marble slab over him — we took it from the village bank. I don't understand why we did that. Do you, Dilly?

Dilly. No matter, doctor. Let's talk of something else: you know you promised me a sail on the lake this afternoon.

Doctor. (*Looking at his watch.*) Nine o'clock: come, boys, to your places, — to your places. Master Root, you were very imperfect in your history yesterday: be careful sir — be careful. Master Hastings, why must I speak to you so often about your grammar. Master Winders, you were in Farmer Bates's orchard last night. Harry, Harry, — dear, dear, I forgot! Harry's dead.

Lucy. Dear father, don't talk any more about Harry.

Doctor. Why, Lucy, child, where have you been all day? Where have you been?

Lucy. I've been here, father, waiting for you.

Doctor. Waiting for me? Why, I haven't been away. Yes, yes, I have: Harry drove me to the cars early this

morning.   I found something by the way, — this little girl
(*patting Dilly's head*): her name's "Bread on the
Waters."   That's what Harry calls her.   She's going to
live with us, — ain't you, little girl?

Dilly.   Indeed, indeed, I am, doctor.

Doctor.   Harry says, " Keep her, father, keep her ;"
and Harry's a good boy, — a good boy.   Where is he
this morning?   Why don't you speak?   Somebody run
and call him.

Dilly.   Why, doctor, you know he's gone a long
journey.

Doctor.   Dear me ! so he has, so he has, — a long journey to the bank.   He's a good boy — a good boy — he'll
be back soon.

Dilly.   Oh ! why don't he come? why don't he come?

Mrs. L.   Dilly, Dilly, be calm.

Doctor.   Don't be in a hurry, little girl.   Don't be in
a hurry (FRED *appears*, C.) : all in good time — all in
good time.

Fred.   May I come in?

Lucy.   Mr. Hastings?

Dilly.   He here again.

Mrs. L.   Certainly, walk in.

Fred.   Ah ! thank you, delightful morning, ain't it.
You grow young, Mrs. Loring.   Ah, Lucy ! I hope I find
you well, and Dilly too.   How's my old friend the
doctor, this morning?

Doctor.   Ah, Butts, how are you?

Lucy.   You are mistaken father: it's Mr. Hastings.

Doctor.   Ah ! Master Fred, I'm glad to see you.   Back
to school again, hey?   Well, well, lad, be more careful
of your grammar this time.   Study, boy, study.

Fred. Of course I will. With so renowned a master, as Dr. Harlem, I mean to study hard, and then I shall be sure to succeed.

Doctor. Come, Mrs. Loring, you see the boys are coming back : let's go and see if every thing is in order. (MRS. LORING *takes his arm.*) Greenlake Seminary has a reputation to sustain. Come : good-by, Dilly.

Dilly. Good-by, doctor. Now, don't tire yourself, for you must take me out for a sail this afternoon.

Doctor. Yes, yes, when Harry gets back : you know we can't do any thing without Harry. (*Exit* DOCTOR *and* MRS. L., R.)

Fred. The doctor appears feeble this morning, Lucy.

Lucy. Yes : poor father fails very fast. At times his reason wanders, and for whole days he is as you have seen him to-day.

Fred. Poor doctor : is there no help for him?

Lucy. None, I fear.

Dilly. You are mistaken, Lucy. There is one thing that would set him right.

Fred. And pray what is that?

Dilly. The return of Harry, with his innocence clearly established.

Fred. Ah, indeed ! you know that can never be.

Dilly. You think so?

Fred. I know it. It's no use now to mince matters. Harry forged that check to get himself out of a scrape. He will never return.

Dilly. I think he will.

Fred. You have great faith, Dilly.

Dilly. In Harry? Yes. I believe him innocent;

and I am sure the day will come when he will stand beneath his father's roof in the calm, proud consciousness of vindicated innocence.

Fred. You are a brave girl thus to stand by him, — a convicted felon.

Dilly. 'Tis false. He is no felon.

Fred. His flight —

Dilly. Was my act. Would I had never counselled him to it! Had he remained, all would have been made clear.

Fred. Ah, you suspect —

Dilly. Yes; but I do not accuse.

Fred. Dilly, you are an enigma. Do you know that doubting Harry's guilt places me under suspicion?

Dilly. Does it?

Fred. Dilly, you surely do not suspect me?

Dilly. Mr. Hastings, we will speak no more of this.

Fred. But, Dilly —

Dlly. I repeat, I accuse no one. The time will come when all this will be made clear. We must wait.

Fred. (*Aside.*) That girl *does* suspect me. (*Aloud.*) You're quite right, Dilly. It's a disagreeable subject, and unworthy our attention this bright, beautiful morning. Come, Lucy, it's too pleasant to be cooped up indoors. What say you to a sail?

Lucy. I shall be delighted to go. Dilly, will you go with us?

Dilly. Thank you; but I have something very particular to attend to this morning. You must entertain Mr. Hastings.

Lucy. I'll do my best, Dilly; and I won't be gone long.

Fred. There's a beautiful breeze on the lake.

Lucy. I'm all ready. Good-by, Dilly.

Dilly. Lucy, one moment.

Lucy. Certainly. (*To* FRED.) Will you excuse me?

Fred. Oh, don't mind me! I'll stroll down the path and wait. (*Exit, c.*)

Dilly. Lucy, that man loves you.

Lucy. I know it.

Dilly. You know it? He has spoken then.

Lucy. No. He has written, and now awaits my answer.

Dilly. And you, Lucy; do you love him?

Lucy. Why do you ask, Dilly?

Dilly. Because it would break my heart to know you did. O Lucy! think of Harry, your dear brother, falsely accused. Think of his words five years ago regarding this man.

Lucy. I do think of them, Dilly, often, very often; and, remembering them, I can say to you, No, I do not love him.

Dilly. Oh! bless you for those words: they lift a weary load from my heart. While Harry is away —

Lucy. I am heart whole. I know your suspicions, Dilly; and, till they are proven true or false, Fred Hastings can have no claim upon me. Good-by! he's waiting.

Dilly. Good-by, Lucy! (*Exit* LUCY, c.) The time will surely come, but when — when that old man tottering on the brink of madness shall be in his grave, when this loved home shall have passed from us, when old age and gray hairs shall be upon us. Faith, — yes, I have faith; but this watching and waiting is weary and wearing. No clew by which to work, nothing but bare suspicion; and yet I have faith. This man Hastings, after nearly five years' absence, appears again among us. He knows I suspect him; and yet he dares to woo the sister of his betrayed friend. Oh! why *don't* Harry come? If he would only write; but no, no word, no sign. Pride keeps him silent; but I know he will one day return. Heaven grant it be not too late to save his father! (*Enter* BUTTS, C.)

Butts. O Dilly, Dilly! such a crime! such an outrage, a high-handed, diabolical assault on law and justice!

Dilly. Why, Mr. Butts, what's the matter now?

Butts. Sh—! don't speak so loud. We must be cautious: my reputation depends upon it. I haven't breathed a word of this to a single person; but you know since the time you managed to help Harry give me the slip, I've had a great respect for you, and always come to you for advice.

Dilly. What is this new outrage?

Butts. A forgery, a stupendous forgery.

Dilly. Here in our village?

Butts. No: in California.

Dilly. California! What's that to do with us?

Butts A great deal to do with *me*, Dilly; for I am the humble individual destined to bring the perpetrator to justice.

Dilly. You, Mr. Butts?

Butts. Listen, Dilly. Three months ago, the Malone Bank of Sacramento lost twelve thousand dollars by the payment of a check purporting to be signed by the firm of Dunshaw & Co., wine-merchants, presented by one John Robinson a noted gambler and stock-speculator. Three days after, the check was found to be a forgery. In the mean time, the said John Robinson had embarked in a steamer bound for New York. The firm of Dunshaw & Co. immediately offered a reward of five thousand dollars for the arrest of the said John Robinson. I have just received a note from some unknown party, giving me the intelligence of the forgery, and acquainting me with the fact that the said John Robinson is in this vicinity. Five thousand dollars! Why, Dilly, I shall be a rich man.

Dilly. When you get the forger.

Butts. Precisely. That won't be long. I've got my eye on him.

Dilly. You suspect.

Butts. Do I! I tell you, Dilly, when Butts gets his eye on a culprit, there's no escape.

Dilly. Mr. Butts, didn't Mr. Hastings come here from California?

Butts. He did. By the by, he might give me information, — valuable information.

Dilly. Suppose he should be John Robinson?

Butts. Oh, pooh, pooh, Dilly. It isn't possible. Suspect him? why you're not so sharp as I gave you credit for. He's here openly. Do you suppose John Robinson would travel about in his original hair and whiskers? No, John Robinson is disguised. I've got my eye on him. There's been a very suspicious character prowling about the village for the last two days. It's him, John Robinson. But he won't prowl much longer. Oh, no!

4

Butts has his eye on him, Butts has his eye on him. Good-by, Dilly! Don't speak of this, — not a word, not a syllable. Five thousand dollars! He's trapped, he's trapped. (*Exit* c.)

Dilly. This is very strange. Why should this John Robinson come here? I wish this matter was in any other hands than those of Mr. Butts. Zealous as he appears, he was never known to ferret out any crime of more importance than that of robbing an orchard. He'll be sure to make some mistake. (*Enter* Mrs. Loring, r.)

Mrs. L. I have persuaded the doctor to lie down, Dilly. Can I be of any assistance to you?

Dilly. No, thank you.

Mrs. L. The interest on the mortgage is due to-morrow.

Dilly. O auntie, I know it is; and we have not the money to pay it. I know not where to go to procure it. We must ask Mr. Hartshorn for further time.

Mrs. L. I fear that will be useless. Mr. Hartshorn is the principal of a rival seminary : he has long desired to possess this place ; and, I fear, will not let the opportunity pass when he can procure it at a very low price.

Dilly. Oh, do not say that, auntie ! If he refuses, who will aid us?

Bob. (*Outside* c.) Just my luck ! (*Enter,* c. *with carpet-bag.*) Halloo, here you are, here you are !

Dilly. (*Rushing up, and seizing his hand.*) Why, Bob Winders, you dear old fellow ! where *did* you come from? I declare I must hug you. (*Throws her arms round his neck.*)

Bob. That's right, Dilly. Hug away. I like it : it's

just my luck. (*Gives his hand to Mrs. L.*) Mrs. Loring, I'm glad to see you looking so well.

Mrs. L. Robert, welcome, a thousand times welcome.

Bob. Well, now, that's hearty. Dilly, how you've grown! My eyes, what a bouncer!

Dilly. Why, Bob, how *you* have altered!

Bob. Altered. I suppose you refer to my weight. "How are the mighty fallen!" Well, I flatter myself I have altered. and for the better. It's a deused sight more comfortable; and there's no end to the money saved. Provisions have sensibly lowered in price, and the tailors look decidedly gloomy, since I've donned this slender habit. I'll tell you how it came about. When I presented myself to my respected parent on my return from school, his first exclamation was, "Good gracious! how fat that boy grows!" followed by a lengthy survey of my by no means diminutive person. "This will never do, boy : you must travel." Being of an obedient disposition, and being plentifully supplied with funds, I did travel. I first attempted to 'cross the ocean, was shipwrecked, and for twenty days skimmed the cold ocean in an open boat, my daily food being one biscuit. It would naturally be supposed that a loss of superabundant flesh would follow. It didn't. I increased in weight. Finally, after much tribulation, I reached England. I was blown up on the Thames : not an ounce of my flesh forsook me. I was smashed up on a railroad. Flesh still immovable. Paraded Paris, rushed into Russia, sighed in Siberia, pecked into Pekin, leaned against the Leaning Tower at Pisa, roamed in Rome, swam in Greece, picked a bone in Turkey, and finally brought up in California, weighing twenty pounds more than when I left home. Just my luck! But here Providence befriended me. I started for the mines. Domesticated myself in a little place called Leankin, was persuaded to run for office, and, by the time the campaign was over, I was run with a vengeance, — run out of pocket, run off the track by my opponent, and run down to my present slender proportions.

Dilly. O Bob! you've been unfortunate. I'm so sorry!

Bob. Unfortunate! — not a bit of it. When I'd lost all my money, I fell in with my partner, — a glorious fellow my partner. We worked in the mines together till we had amassed a snug little capital, then started business in San Francisco; and to-day there is no more successful firm in California than that of Winders & Co.

Dilly. I'm so glad! But, Bob, have you no tidings of our Harry?

Bob. Harry! Why, Harry's here, isn't he?

Dilly. Have you forgotten the events of five years ago?

Bob. Oh, I remember! Harry ran away to escape being jugged by old Butts.

Dilly. And you know nothing of him

Bob. Me! Why, bless you! how should I know any thing about him? Hasn't he been heard of?

Dilly. Since that day we have never heard of or from him. His poor father has been very ill, and now is almost bereft of reason.

Bob. You don't mean it! This will be news for Har— I mean my partner.

Dilly. Your partner? What is this to him?

Bob. Oh, nothing! only he is naturally interested in any thing that interests me ; that's all.

Mrs. L. Yes, Robert, your old master has seen sad times since you left. This house is mortgaged, and must now pass from him.

Bob. No! You don't mean it?

Dilly. The interest is due to-morrow, and we've no money to pay it. Oh, if Harry were only here !

Bob. As he isn't, let me be your banker. Here's my wallet: it's in the condition in which I was five years ago, — it's overburdened, and wants tapping.

Dilly. No, no, Bob! You are very kind; but we have no claim upon you, and I could not think of taking your money.

Bob. Claim! confound it! Isn't this the home of my old master? and do you suppose I am going to stand by and see it pass from his hands when I have plenty? No, Dilly. Harry and I were brothers here at school ; and, when his father is in trouble, I'm bound to aid him for the good he has done me, lickings and all.

Dilly. Oh, no, no, Bob! do not ask me to take it.

Bob. Well, then, I won't. Mrs. Loring, who holds this mortgage?

Mrs. L. Mr. Hartshorn.

Bob. Then I shall do myself the honor to call upon Mr. Hartshorn, and put him in good spirits by paying the interest.

Mrs. L. O Robert! you have a kind heart.

Bob. Have I? Well, I've got a full purse too, and it's pretty heavy ; and, as I've got rid of heavy weights, if this doesn't lighten soon, I shall throw it into the lake.

Mrs. L.   Well, well, have your own way.

Bob.   I always did. It's just my luck. I'm very dusty. Shall I go to the old room?

Mrs. L.   Yes; and I'll show you the way.   O Robert, Heaven will surely bless you. (*Exit*, R.)

Bob.   Bless her dear old face!   Dilly, it does seem good to be in this house once more.

Dilly.   O Bob, we're so glad to see you!   You have comforted sorrowing hearts to-day.

Bob.   Have I? Well, that's pleasant. But, Dilly, where's Lucy?

Dilly.   She's on the lake with Fred Hastings.

Bob.   Fred Hastings!   He here? Just my luck!

Dilly.   Lucy will be glad to see you, Bob.

Bob.   I hope she will, Dilly; for I've come a great ways to see her.   Good-by! (*Exit*, R.)

Dilly.   Good-by!   Dear old fellow! how fond Harry was of him! Ah, me! if Harry would only come now! (*Turns, and meets* HARRY, *who has entered. c., disguised as an old man, gray wig, beard, red shirt, and sailor trousers.*)

Harry.   A morsel of food, I beg. I have travelled far, and I am very hungry.

Dilly.   Hungry! Poor old man, sit down. I will bring you some food. No one is ever refused in this house. (*Exit*, R.)

Harry.   Thanks, thanks! Heaven bless you! Home again at last, after five long years; once more I stand within the dear old house. How familiar every thing looks! There's the arm-chair in which father sat, the

little stool on which I nestled at his side, there's Aunt
Loring's knitting-work, and Lucy's book, — every thing
just as it was in the old times ; and that was Dilly, my
little Dilly, grown to woman's estate. Oh ! how I long
to clasp her in my arms ! They told me I must not
come in here ; but I could not help it. I *must* know if
I am remembered here, or if the bitter accusation
made against me has driven me from these hearts.
(*Enter* DILLY, *with meat and bread, which she places on
table,* R. C.)

Dilly. There, that's the best I can do. You are
heartily welcome. Sit down, and make yourself comfortable.

Harry. Thanks, thanks ! (*Sits* R. *of table.*) I'm so
hungry ! You have a kind heart, a kind heart, young
lady ! Heaven will surely bless you for your kindness
to a poor old wanderer.

Dilly. Now, don't stop to be complimentary.

Harry. (*Pretending to eat, but watching* DILLY *attentively.*) May I ask whose house this is?

Dilly. This is Dr. Harlem's house.

Harry. Dr. Harlem, Dr. Harlem? Oh ! I remember, — the master of the seminary.

Dilly. Are you acquainted here?

Harry. Long ago, long ago ! In better days I knew
this place.

Dilly. But you don't eat.

Harry. Oh, yes ! I do. I'm very hungry. Dr. Harlem, — he was a kind, good gentleman.

Dilly. Ay, that he was and is. But times have
sadly changed. Illness has almost unsettled his reason.

18

Harry. (*Starting up.*) Gracious heavens!

Dilly. How you startle me! What ails you?

Harry. (*Recovering himself.*) Nothing, nothing.
I'm very old, and the fear of losing *my* reason haunts
me. When you spoke of that old man, you startled
me. I beg your pardon.

Dilly. Well, sit down. If you don't eat, I shall fear
you are not pleased with what I have prepared.

Harry. But I do eat (*eating ravenously*); don't
you see I do? I'm very hungry. (*After a pause.*) Dr.
Harlem, — are you his daughter?

Dilly. Oh, no! His daughter Lucy is on the lake.

Harry. But didn't he have a son?

Dilly. Yes, he has a son.

Harry. Yes, yes, I remember! — a wild, reckless lad.
He was sent to prison. He was a forger.

Dilly. 'Tis false! He was noble, generous, and
good; and those who dare accuse him of crime are base
slanderers.

Harry. (*Aside.*) She's true, she's true! (*Aloud.*) I
beg your pardon; I was told —

Dilly. Told? — how dare you, beneath his father's
roof, partaking of his charity, repeat this falsehood?
Oh, shame, shame, upon you!

Harry. I beg your pardon once more. It was ungrateful in me, I spoke without thought. Forgive me,
I will go.

Dilly. No, no, sit down! Forgive *me;* for it was
wrong in me to speak thus to one who never knew
Harry.

Harry. Ah! Harry has a warm friend in you.

Dilly. I hope he has; for his kindness to me can never be repaid. For five years, every thought of mine has been to find some way to clear him, some way to prove his innocence. But, alas! his father's illness has required all my attention; has kept me at his side: and I have found no way to serve him.

Harry. If he is innocent, wait: the time will come when the truth will triumph. Have faith, my child, have faith.

Dilly. I have, I have! But you're not eating.

Harry. Oh, yes, I am; for I am very hungry. Heaven bless you for your kindness to an old man (*placing his hand on her head*), and bless you for your trust in one who wanders through the earth with a blasted name.

Doctor. (*Outside,* R.) Dilly, Dilly, here, quick!

Dilly. The doctor calls me; I must go Now make yourself comfortable; I'll soon return. (*Exit,* R.)

Harry. My father's voice! — sick, almost bereft of reason; and I cannot go to him. The sight of me might kill him. O false friend! the time will come, the time will come! Heaven send it soon, or my heart will break. (*Sinks into chair* R. *of table, and buries his face in his hands. Enter* BUTTS, C., *very stealthily.*)

Butts. Five thousand dollars! Now, who would imagine that mass of hair and old clothes was worth five thousand dollars? And yet it is. Once within the clutches of this limb of the law, I'm a rich man. Oh, ho, Butts, you're a sharp one, you are! (*Strikes his hand on table.*) Wake up, you're wanted. (HARRY *raises his head.*) At last we meet.

Harry. Meet! Who are you?

Butts. Oh, you don't know me! Well, that's not singular; but I know you; I've had my eye on you: you're a deep one, you are! But I've got you! California too hot, hey? Well, we'll give you a warm corner here, John Robinson. Oh! I know you: you can't humbug Butts. Suppose I should tell you just when you left California, John Robinson? how much money you took, John Robinson? — suppose I should lay my hand on your shoulder, John Robinson, and say you are my prisoner, John Robinson, — what would you say, John Robinson?

Harry. That, if you lay a finger on me (*producing a pistol, and presenting it*), I'll blow what little brains you have into yonder lake.

Butts. (*Dropping under the table.*) Murder! put up that infernal machine. Help, murder!

Harry. Shut up! If you speak again you're a dead man. Come out here! (BUTTS *obeys*). Now take a seat, and make yourself comfortable.

Butts. (*Sitting* L.) Comfortable?

Harry. The tables are turned, hey, Butts?

Butts. Oh, you villain, you villain! But you can't escape me; I'm an officer of the law; never known to take a bribe. I believe in justice, and justice will surely overtake you, John Robinson.

Harry. I sincerely hope I shall some day have justice.

Butts. The hemp has grown, the rope twisted, that will twist your little neck, John Robinson.

Harry. So you are Butts the thief-taker, are you? Well, I'm glad to meet you. I've a little business with you. Butts, an officer of the law, who believes in justice, and yet turned his only son out of doors.

Butts. How! What do you know about my son?

Harry. I know that he is dead.

Butts. Dead! My Bill dead!

Harry. Yes; it was my hand that closed his eyes, away off in the mines of California.

Butts. My boy dead!

Harry. He told me the story of his life. He loved a poor girl, and his father turned him out of doors.

Butts. She was a vile —

Harry. Stop, Butts! She was a pure, noble woman: her only fault was loving your scamp of a son. He married her. I have his word for it and the marriage-certificate. He married her nineteen years ago; took her to the little town of Elmer, fifteen miles from here. They had a child.

Butts. A child! I never heard of that.

Harry. Oh! you was too busy looking after rogues. You forgot your own scamp of a son. When the child was four years old, the mother died, broken-hearted; for your son was a villain. Bill determined to try his luck in California. But the child was an encumbrance that must be got rid of. So one dark night, Bill took her in his arms, and started for his father's house, to leave her on the doorsteps. But Bill, not having led a virtuous life, was wanted by certain officers of the law. They tracked him. Bill found they were after him, and, with fatherly care, flung his offspring by the roadside, and fled. He died three months ago in California.

Butts. And the child?

Harry. Ah! the child is safe.

Butts. Thank Heaven for that! Where is she, my grandchild?

Harry. Safe, I tell you. I, and I alone, know where to find her.

Butts. John Robinson, you're a noble — no — I mean you're a — Oh! lead me to her. I'm an old man. This child — I long to clasp her in my arms.

Harry. Lead you? Well, Butts, under the circumstances, that is a very cool proposition. You forget: by your own admission, I am your prisoner.

Butts. You are free, only give me the child.

Harry. Five thousand dollars for John Robinson, hey, Butts?

Butts. If it were fifty thousand dollars, give me the child, and you are free.

Harry. I'm astonished, Butts! you an officer of the law, never known to take a bribe!

Butts. Oh, curse the law! John Robinson, if you are a man, lead me to that child.

Harry. On one condition, Butts.

Butts. Name it.

Harry. There's a man named Belmer stopping at the village inn: bring him here in half an hour.

Butts. And the child?

Harry. Bring Belmer here in half an hour, and the child shall be placed in your arms.

Butts. Bless you, John Robinson, you're a trump! I'll be here in half an hour. Robinson, you're a brick! (*Exit,* c.)

Harry. So the train is laid. I'll take myself off, lest the sight of that dear girl's face unman me. If all works well, when next I enter here none shall have cause to blush for Harry Harlem. (*As he is about to exit, c., he meets* LUCY, *who enters,* C. *He stands aside, bows, and hurries out,* C.)

Lucy. A strange old man! Who can he be?

(*Enter* FRED, C., LUCY *sits,* R.)

Fred. Lucy, I entreat you unsay those words. Give me at least the power to hope.

Lucy. No, Fred: I am convinced a union between us would be unhappy.

Fred. But give me some reason, Lucy. You love another?

Lucy. No.

Fred. Then why reject *me?* I love you truly, devotedly. Become my wife; and, if you do not love me now, I will find some way to make you.

Lucy. No, Fred: I repeat it is impossible. My father needs my care. Were he well, I think he would not sanction it, and — and —

Fred. Lucy, you are not just to me or your father. He needs your care: he needs something more than that. I know how his small fortune has gradually dwindled away, that his house is mortgaged, that he has not a penny in the world. Become my wife, Lucy. I am rich. Give me the power to aid him?

Lucy. No, no, Fred: better as it is. Dilly, Aunt Loring, I, will work night and day to gain for him every comfort.

Fred. But think, Lucy. The best you can do will only make him comfortable for a little while. With a pressing creditor like Hartshorn, this house must at last be given up.

Lucy. I know it must, I know it must. Heaven help my poor father!

Fred. I offer you my hand: accept, and to-morrow the mortgage shall be paid, principal and interest. See, Lucy, I'm at your feet. I love you truly, sincerely.

Lucy. My poor father! What shall I do? oh, who will aid us now? (*Enter* BOB, R., *with fishing-pole, stumbles against* FRED, *who is kneeling.*)

Bob. Just my luck! I beg your pardon. Why, Lucy!

Lucy. (*Rushing to him.*) Bob Winders, dear Bob, how glad I am to see you! (*Throws her arm round his neck.*)

Bob. Just my luck! Why, Lucy, I hardly knew you.

Fred. (*Aside.*) What sent him here at this time? (*Aloud.*) Bob, old boy, where did you drop from? (*Gives his hand.*)

Bob. Why, Fred, is it you, still fluttering round the old flame, hey? Where did I drop from? From the four quarters of the globe. I've been in England, France, Russia, everywhere, including California.

Fred. California!

Bob. Yes, California. It's a fine place, California, the Golden State. Lots of gold to be got by digging; and, if you object to that, money can be easily got by signing your name to a slip of paper. Just before I left, a chap raised twelve thousand dollars by putting a name to a blank check. But it wasn't his name; 'twas the

name of Dunshaw & Co.: his was John Robinson.
" O Robinson, how could you do so?"

Fred. It was discovered.

Bob. Of course it was. Robinson sloped; but he'll
be caught, he'll be caught! Lucy, I see you are engaged.
I'm going out to try the trout. I used to like the sport ;
and I rather think the trout liked me, for I never managed to hook many of them. Just my luck! Good-by!

Lucy. Oh, don't go, Bob! I want to talk to you. I've
scarcely seen you.

Bob. Well, there isn't so much of me to see as there
was. But I'll be back soon. (*Aside.*) There's popping
going on here, so I'd best pop off. (*Exit*, c.)

Lucy. The dear old fellow, Harry was so fond of
him! Don't you think he has altered, Fred?

Fred. Very much, Lucy. But, he is still the same
blundering fellow he always was. But for him, just now,
I should have had your answer, I think your favorable
answer.

Lucy. I have told you, Fred, I do not love you. Do
not, I entreat you, urge me to a course I know I should
regret. I would do any thing for father —

Fred. Then marry me, Lucy. Give me your hand.
I will wait for your love.

Lucy. To save my father, Fred — (*Enter* DILLY,
R.)

Dilly. Lucy, our old friend Bob Winders has arrived.
Have you seen him?

Fred. (*Aside.*) Confound that girl! she's always in
the way.

Lucy. Yes, he passed through here just now: I never

saw such a change. (*Enter Doctor*, R., *with the portfolio used in Act 1.*)

Doctor. Dilly, Dilly, don't scold! I wandered into your room in search of you. I picked up your portfolio ; and I want you to write to Harry.

Dilly. Write to Harry?

Doctor. Yes : write to Harry. Tell him to come home : we want him. Don't you understand, child? Write, write, write!

Dilly. (*Takes the portfolio. The* DOCTOR *sits in an arm-chair*, L. C.) What can I say to him, doctor?

Doctor. Say — say? What can you say to Harry? I believe the child is mad. Say that we want him here ; that his old father's heart is breaking, breaking. breaking. You want him, don't you, Dilly?

Dilly. Heaven knows I do!

Doctor. Then write : quick, quick! (DILLY *sits behind table*, R.C., *and opens the portfolio.*)

Fred. Ah, Dilly, I see you still preserve my present of five years ago.

Dilly. Preserve it? Yes ; but I have never opened it. The memory of that day is not pleasant to recall. Now, doctor, you shall tell me what to write.

Doctor. Commence " Dear, dear Harry."

Dilly. Oh, of course! " Dear, dear Harry "—(*drops her pen, starts, and remains with her hands clasped, her eyes fixed upon the portfolio. Aside.*) What do I see? am I dreaming?

Doctor. Yes, " Dear, dear Harry." He is dear. — my own dear son. Who says he's dead? It's false : he stood by my bed last night. Who says he's a forger?

'Tis false. He's a good boy, a good boy — first in his class — the largest number of credits — no checks for Harry Harlem! Checks! they said he forged my name, — the name of his old father; and they took him, put him in prison, and hanged him by the neck till he was dead, dead, dead. A forger! 'tis false, false, false.

Lucy. Why, Dilly, what's the matter?

Fred. (*Approaching table.*) Dilly, child, what ails you?

Dilly. (*Starting up, and closing the portfolio.*) Away, away! — you, of all men! I beg your pardon: I know not what ails me. (*Takes portfolio, and comes down,* L.) (*Aside.*) The proof, the proof at last! What shall I do? who trust? I dare not leave Fred Hastings here with Lucy: I fear his influence. Oh, if I could but make the doctor understand!

Doctor. Have you written, Dilly?

Dilly. Not yet, doctor (*sits on stool at his side,* L.). I want to talk with you first; I want to tell you a story.

Doctor. But I don't want to hear a story; I want you to write to Harry.

Dilly. Listen to me a moment, doctor. You'll like this story: it's about a boy very much like Harry.

Doctor. Then he was a good boy, a good boy!

Dilly. Yes, he was a good boy until he gained a friend, a false friend, who led him into temptation.

Fred. (*Aside.*) What is the girl up to now?

Dilly. This false friend taught him to gamble.

Doctor. That wasn't like Harry: he never gambled.

Dilly. He lost a large sum he could not pay. The false friend proffered assistance; gave him a check purporting to be signed by the boy's father, with a very plausible story to account for its being in his possession.

Fred. (*Aside.*) What is she driving at?

Dilly. The fraud was discovered; the boy punished.

Doctor. The boy! It should have been the friend.

Dilly. You're right, doctor; it should. But the proof was strong against the boy, and he suffered. Even his own father believed him guilty.

Doctor. False friend! false father!

Dilly. But the boy had another friend, weak but true: five years after, among the papers of this false friend, she found the proof to clear the boy.

Doctor. Proof! What was it?

Dilly. (*Opening portfolio.*) It was like this, doctor.

Doctor. Like this?—like this?— Why, I see nothing. A portfolio blotting-paper!

Dilly. But on the paper?

Doctor. Marks, nothing but marks. Yes, yes, they assume shape,— Aug. 1, Aug. 1. Gracious heavens! what is this? what is this?

Fred. I see it all. (*Rushes up, and seizes the portfolio.*) Girl, girl, would you kill the old man? You must not so excite him: no more of this. I'll fling this accursed thing into the lake. (*Runs up,* C., *and throws the portfolio off.*)

Dilly. What have you done? what have you done?

Fred. Saved the old man from a fever. No more of your confounded stories, Dilly.

Dilly. Fred Hastings, you are a villain! In that portfolio is the proof of your guilt: it shall not be destroyed. (*Runs up,* C.; *Hastings seizes her by the wrist.*)

Fred. Hold, mad girl! Hard words; but, for the sake of the old man, I forgive you. If that portfolio contains proof of my guilt, it's too late now: it's at the bottom of the lake. Who can bring it thence? (*Enter* BOB, C.)

Bob. Just my luck! I knew that lake contained bouncing trout; but I never knew before that it produced any thing so nearly resembling a flounder. (*Holds up portfolio.*)

Dilly. It's mine, mine, Bob.

Fred. Curse that fellow! He's always in the way.

Dilly. Listen all. I charge that man Hastings with the perpetration of the forgery of which Harry Harlem was accused five years ago. The proof is here. On the blotting-leaves of this portfolio once owned and used by him are indelibly impressed the written lines of the check, — "Aug. 1, 1858. Seventy-five — Andrew Harlem," — left there when he blotted the check. (*Enter* MRS. LORING, R.)

Lucy. Gracious heavens!

Mrs. L. Is it possible?

Bob. By thunder!

Doctor. I don't understand, Dilly; I don't understand.

Fred. You're right, doctor: it is hard to understand, especially as Harry and I were such good friends. We used our writing materials in common. Of course, he wrote the check on that portfolio; that's plain.

Lucy. Mr. Hastings, I remember the words with which you presented that portfolio to Dilly, "Should I ever become a great man, you can boast you possess something which no one but I have ever used."

Dilly. His very words.

Fred. You, too, turn against me, Lucy?

Lucy. To clear a dear brother's name, against you and all the world.

Bob. (*Aside.*) Ah, ha! I shall have her yet: it's just my luck.

Fred. My friends, I pity your delusion. It is natural we should stand by those we love; but this is a clear case. Harry Harlem is now an outcast skulking from justice, while I — Who dare accuse me of any crime? (*Enter* HARRY, C., *disguised.*)

Harry. Be that task mine.

Dilly. That old man again!

Fred. Yours! Pray may I inquire who you are?

Harry. One who for five years has watched your course, knowing you to be a villain, waiting for the proof; one who has watched you first squander the rich inheritance of your father, then fall among the ruined and degraded, living as a speculator and gambler; one who has proof of your last crime, the forging of the name of Dunshaw & Co., — the hunted felon under the name of John Robinson. (*Enter* BUTTS, C.)

Butts. John Robinson here! then who the deuse are you?

Harry. Belmer — did you find him?

Butts. Mr. Belmer waits without.

Fred. Belmer — that name! He here? Then I am caught at last.

Harry. Yes: Belmer, the detective of Sacramento, waits for you. Shall I call him in?

Fred. No, no: I'll see him outside. So, so! run to earth like a fox! Well, I'll put a good face on it.

Friends, I have a pressing engagement; will you excuse me? I should not have come to this place; but — but —

Lucy. Fred, Mr. Hastings, you once professed a regard for me: if it was sincere, I beg you clear my brother's name.

Fred. For your sake, Lucy, yes. I did forge the name of Dr. Harlem to the check used by Harry.

Dilly, Lucy, Harry. (*Together.*) At last!

Fred. At last? (*To Harry.*) Who are you that to-day stand forth as my accuser?

Harry. One who, after five long years of absence, now stands beneath his father's roof cleared of every semblance of stain. (*Tears off his wig and beard.*)

Fred. Harry Harlem!

Dilly. (*Rushing into his arms.*) My Harry, my Harry! Oh, welcome, welcome! Here, doctor, doctor, Harry's come! Harry's come!

Doctor. (*Starts up.*) Harry's come! Where is he? where is my boy?

Harry. (*Kneeling.*) Here, at your feet, dear father.

Doctor. My boy, my dear boy, we've waited long for you; but I knew that you would come.

Lucy. Dear, dear brother! (*Embracing him.*)

Harry. Lucy, best of sisters!

Bob. Ladies and gentlemen, allow me to introduce to you the junior partner of the firm of Winders & Co.

Dilly. Your partner!

Harry. Yes, Dilly, my true and fast friend. From the day I left here, we've been inseparable. A true friend, a true friend!

Fred. If you will pardon me, I think I'll go.

Butts. I think you'd better. Mr. Belmer is very anxious to see you.

Fred. Butts, you're a stupid old fool. (*Exit*, c.)

Bob. He can't help that: it's just his luck.

Butts. I think I'd better follow him.

Harry. No: Belmer will secure him. Never fear.

Mrs. L. Harry, welcome home once more!

Harry. Ah, Aunt Loring, still as buxom as ever! thanks, thanks!

Doctor. Well, I declare I feel like a new man.

Dilly. Ah, I told you Harry would make all right.

Doctor. Ah, that he has. I'll open school again.

Butts. I say, Harry, you've no ill will against me?

Harry. Ah, Butts, I've no ill will against any one now, I'm so happy.

Butts. The child, Harry?

Harry. Dilly, how can I ever repay you for your kindness to my father, for your faith in me? To you I owe the good name I bear to-day: how can I repay you?

Dilly. O Harry, you ask me that?—you to whom I owe my happiness, this dear home, these kind friends?

Harry. Dilly, you have a relative living.

Dilly. A relative?

Harry. Yes, a grandfather. Your father died in California: I know his history. Your mother is also dead. Your father's name was William Butts.

Butts. And I'm your grandfather. O Dilly, Dilly! who'd have thought it?

Dilly. You my grandfather!

Harry. There is no mistake: you are his grandchild. I have the proofs.

Butts. Come right here and kiss me. Who would have thought it? Why, Dilly, this accounts for your being such a thief-taker: it runs in the blood.

Bob. (*Aside.*) Precious little inheritance in that line she received from you.

Dilly. You my grandfather! Is it possible? Then I am really somebody after all.

Butts. Somebody? Yes, indeed! Grandchild of Jonathan Wild Butts!

Dilly. But I don't want to be anybody's grandchild. Harry's my father: I don't want any other. And, if I am to go away from here, —

Harry. Don't be frightened, Dilly. It's a good thing to know you have relatives; but I do not propose to renounce my claim. You are my rightful property: I found you by the roadside when deserted by your father. I will still claim relationship; but, Dilly, it must now be as your husband.

Dilly. My husband!

Harry. Yes, Dilly, be my wife. I have had you in my thoughts night and day for the last five years. You have proved your love for me as a sister; now I shall claim a dearer title.

Dilly. O Harry, I do not deserve it!

Doctor. She does, Harry; and, if you don't marry her at once, I will.

Butts. What! rob me of my grandchild just when I have discovered my treasure? I don't like it.

Dilly. Oh, yes, you do, grandpa! for I shall love you dearly, I know; that is, if you let me have my own way.

Butts. And that way is into the arms of a husband, I suppose? 19

Dilly. (*Giving her hand to Harry.*) So Harry says; and I always do just what Harry tells me.

Harry. Dear, dear Dilly!

Bob. So, Harry, you're going to take a new partner into the concern?

Harry. Yes, Bob: remember the Scripture injunction, " Go, and do thou likewise."

Bob. Lucy, what say you? Will you take an interest in the concern? The senior partner is desperately in love with you.

Lucy. O Bob, you've been a kind friend to my brother Harry!

Bob. That's got nothing to do with it. I'm getting rid of all superfluous stock; and I find I've got too much heart. So I'll throw it into the market. If you want it, it's yours at your own price. Yes: I'll take yours, and call it an even trade.

Lucy. Well, I suppose I must say it's a bargain.

Bob. Thank you: we'll just put a revenue stamp on that contract (*kisses*). I've got the best of the bargain: just my luck!

Doctor. Ah, that's right, that's right! just as it should be! We're a happy family now, thanks to Dilly! Ah! we have much to thank her for.

Harry. Ay, that we have! Father, your words have come true at last, — " Cast thy bread upon the waters," —

Dilly. " For thou shalt find it after many days."

Doctor. Yes, yes: returning peace and happiness after many days, after many days.

DISPOSITION OF CHARACTERS.

R., BOB, LUCY, DOCTOR, HARRY, DILLY, BUTTS, MRS. LORINO, L.